A PLUME BOOK

THE PERFECT MOTHER

Lev Gorn

NINA DARNTON is a former staff writer for *Newsweek* and a former frequent contributor to the *New York Times*. As a freelancer, she has written for several news outlets, including the *Los Angeles Times*, the *Washington Post*, *Travel and Leisure*, *More*, and *Elle*. She has also contributed on-air essays for the *PBS NewsHour* and covered the Polish Solidarity movement for National Public Radio. She published *An African Affair* in 2011. This is her second novel. She lives with her husband in New York City.

Also by Nina Darnton

An African Affair

THE PERFECT MOTHER

a novel

NINA DARNTON

A PLUME BOOK

PLUME
Published by the Penguin Group
Penguin Group (USA) LLC
375 Hudson Street
New York, New York 10014

USA | Canada | UK | Ireland | Australia | New Zealand | India | South Africa | China
penguin.com
A Penguin Random House Company

First published by Plume, a member of Penguin Group (USA) LLC, 2014

P REGISTERED TRADEMARK—MARCA REGISTRADA

CIP data is available.
ISBN 978-0-14-219673-1

Printed in the United States of America
10 9 8 7 6 5 4 3 2 1

Set in Granjon
Designed by Eve L. Kirch

To my children, Kyra, Liza, and Jamie,
from their imperfect but loving mother

THE
PERFECT
MOTHER

CHAPTER 1

It was midnight and, lying next to her husband in their Philadelphia home, Jennifer Lewis was fast asleep. It had been a good day. Lily, their sixteen-year-old, had just found out she had made both the soccer team and the honor roll. Eight-year-old Eric was fast asleep after a day at the circus. And Emma, their twenty-year-old college girl, was having the time of her life in Spain for her junior year abroad. Life seemed so perfect that when the phone rang, Jennifer didn't even have the usual flare of panic engendered by an unexpected middle-of-the-night interruption. Her husband, Mark, woke first.

"Get it, will you, honey?" he mumbled, still half-asleep.

She reached over to pick up the phone.

"Hello?"

It was Emma's voice, shaken and vulnerable, through torrents of tears.

"Mom," she sobbed. "You told me not to do anything stupid, and I did."

Now Jennifer was wide-awake and very anxious. She was aware of a lot of background noise, a jumble of voices, some shouting.

"That's okay, sweetheart," she said, controlling her voice. "Tell me what happened.

"I went to a bar. I drank too much. I felt funny. There was cake and stuff. I think the brownies were laced with hash."

"What happened, Emma?"

"Someone was killed, Mama."

"Someone you knew?" She was horrified.

"They think I did it. They think I killed him. Tell Daddy. I need a lawyer. Please come."

"Why do they think you did it? Where are you?"

"I'm at the police station, Mom. I can't talk. Please just come."

There was another sound of people yelling, and then the call was cut off.

At first, Jennifer was so stunned she didn't even put down the telephone receiver.

Mark had turned on the light and was sitting up next to her. "Jennifer," he prodded. "Honey, what happened?"

She slowly hung up the phone and turned to him. Her voice was shaky, confused. "I don't understand what happened."

"Tell me what she said."

She repeated the conversation, and as she spoke, her confusion turned to panic. She reached for his hand and held it tight. "We have to go there right away, Mark. I'll check the plane schedules. Can you find a lawyer? I mean, not a corporate lawyer like you—a criminal lawyer and the best one in Spain. Can you do that?"

She left the bed before he could answer and headed for the bathroom. She tore through the crammed shelves of her medicine cabinet, wildly displacing bottles of aspirin and Advil and sweeping aside soaps and makeup until she found what she was looking for: a small bottle of Valium that had been prescribed more than a year ago for a back spasm—she hoped taking one would calm her down. Mark followed her and put his arm around her.

"Shh, honey. Hold on. She'll be okay. We'll take care of this. Please, Jen, you have to be calm if you're going to help her."

She turned to him and buried her head in his chest, fighting back tears. "We watched *Midnight Express* the night before she left. Remember? She just watched it to humor me, but I was trying to warn her about how dangerous it is to take drugs in a foreign country. But she said the brownies at some party were laced with hash. That's not her fault. They're accusing her of murder, for God's sake. It's totally crazy."

She wrapped her arms around him as he stroked her hair.

"I know it is, and that's why it's going to go away. And she's in Spain, not Turkey thirty-five years ago. This is Europe, not the third world. I'll line up a lawyer and find out what we need to do. And whatever it is, Jen, anything at all, we'll do it. But she needs you right away. There's probably a plane tonight. You'll have to fly to Madrid and then catch another plane to Seville. I'll join you as soon as I can."

"No, Mark—she needs us both. And I need you too. You have to come with me."

"I can't, honey. We have to make arrangements for Lily and Eric," he said.

"I'll call my parents."

"They have to get here. It all takes time. And I'm in the middle of a case. I have to work some things out at the office before I can leave."

He saw her frown and knew she was about to object. "We're going to need a lot of money for this, Jen," he said quickly. "We have to make some hard decisions. You go first. You'll get her out on bail right away. You can start talking to the lawyer and find out what our next step is. I'll come next weekend."

She nodded, accepting his logic. She knew she had a lot to do before she got on the plane, but she didn't seem able to get started. Not yet.

"She sounded so frightened, Mark," she said in a small voice.

"Of course she did," he answered. "She must be scared out of her mind. That's why we have to hurry up and get her out."

"She can't even really speak Spanish that well; she must seem like some rich, spoiled American to them. God knows what they'll do to her." She popped the Valium into her mouth and swallowed it with a gulp of water.

"I just don't understand how a mistake this big could happen. There must be something we can do even before I get there. Can't we call the State Department? Don't you have some friends in Washington?"

"I'm going to work on all of that, honey. Don't worry. You just get packed and get ready to go."

"What should we tell everyone?" she asked.

"Maybe we should tell them the truth. It's insane, but we're going over to straighten it out."

"Are you serious? We can't tell them our daughter has been accused of murder. We can't tell our kids that. We can't tell my parents that."

He sighed. "Okay, okay. You're right. We'll have to think of something."

She tried to organize her thoughts. She had to get the kids up for school in a few more hours and tell them some fiction as to why she was rushing off to Spain that night. She had to call her parents and get them to come and stay, using the same fiction. She had to examine the plane schedule, buy her ticket, figure out how to get to Seville from Madrid, and cancel everything she had planned for the next few weeks. And she had to pack. She dragged her traveling bag out of the closet and opened it, throwing some underwear, socks, panty hose, and her makeup kit inside. Then she paused, looked hard at the clothes hanging in her closet, and burst into tears. Just exactly what do you wear when your daughter has been accused of murder and you are bailing her out of jail?

She dried her eyes with the back of her hand. She threw pants, shirts, and a few dresses on the bed and took stock. A former actress who had picked up extra money in her college years as a model, Jennifer understood dressing for a part. She knew she would need to go to the jail, and if they couldn't get the case dismissed, she might even have to appear next to her daughter in court. She was also aware that she was a very attractive woman, a quality she had found helpful throughout her life. She took pride in her striking blue eyes and thick, lustrous brown hair and spent three mornings a week at the gym to maintain her toned, elegant body, still firm and youthful although she had celebrated her forty-sixth birthday a month earlier. She calculated that the dress code in Spain would be more formal than it was in the States. She needed something conservative and respectable—and so did Emma, she reasoned, but she could pick that up when she got there. At the last minute, she also threw in her favorite dress, a simple sleeveless black sheath that showed off her slim figure and long legs. Concentrating on her wardrobe occupied her mind as the Valium kicked in, so she began to feel a little calmer. She would tell everyone that Emma had suffered a minor injury in a car accident and she was going to make sure she got the proper treatment. Luckily Eric and Lily adored their grandparents and would be thrilled they were coming to stay.

Her mind drifted back to Emma's plight. Oh, dear God, don't let this scar her. Jennifer had spent all the years of her children's lives protecting them from potential wounds, consciously building positive self-images, and working tirelessly on their creative and intellectual development. She'd hung mobiles of the planets moving around the sun, covered the walls and ceiling with star stickers that twinkled in the dark, lain in bed with them telling them stories or reading books until they fell asleep. She'd ferried them to lessons and playdates and children's museums. As they grew older, she'd helped them with term papers and, with Mark, who joined her whenever he could, attended all their soccer games, concerts, and theater productions.

The girls treated her as their confidante, told her everything, and although of course she knew they weren't perfect, she trusted them implicitly. They worked hard, made honors grades each year, were active in school organizations and lauded by their teachers. She'd hear about friends whose kids took drugs or got involved with a bad crowd, or were rebellious and hateful to their parents, and she would discuss each case with her daughters. She never said so, not even to Mark, but she couldn't help believing that the secret of their apparent success was simply that she had been a stay-at-home mom who was always there for them, alert to potential minefields and keeping lines of communication open. She was proud of them and proud of herself.

Her eyes were growing heavy, and although she was sure she

couldn't sleep, she thought she might lie down and close her eyes for a few minutes. She awoke with a start when her alarm went off at 6:30, time to wake Eric and Lily. Lily, she discovered, was already up and in the shower, but Eric was sprawled on his back on top of his covers, Spider-Man staring up at her from his pajamas. She bent down to kiss him awake. He reached up his arms to hug her and she snuggled into him, inhaling the sweet scent of the shampoo he'd used last night. She made pancakes, and as they all ate breakfast, she calmly told them that Emma had been in a minor car accident and broken her leg and she needed to go to Spain to sort things out. Her cover story seemed to work. Neither the kids, nor her parents when she reached them, suspected anything terrible had happened. All that expensive acting training and hard-won experience had served some practical purpose in her life after all, she thought.

She made herself a cup of coffee and went into Mark's study to see what progress he had made. The time difference—it was six hours later in Spain—had worked in their favor, and he had already made her plane reservations, located the best criminal lawyer in Spain, and arranged for the lawyer to travel from his home in Madrid to Seville to meet Jennifer when she arrived the next afternoon. It was too early to reach any of Mark's contacts in the State Department, but he assured her he would at the start of business hours.

She stepped into the shower. For some reason she began to think about her pregnancy with Emma. It was to be her first child, and she had worried about the problems people discussed in those days: the specter of postpartum blues or not bonding with the baby. And then there were the big decisions: day care or nanny, full-time motherhood or continuing her promising acting career. She was also afraid of the pain of childbirth, which she had nonetheless insisted on doing naturally, without an epidural or any medication. And she did feel pain. She remembered squeezing Mark's hand as she pushed and pushed and finally gasping, "Give me some gas," and hearing the doctor say, "Too late," as, with what felt like an explosion, Emma burst into the world.

But her concerns disappeared as soon as the nurse placed her baby in her arms. She had looked at her, counted her fingers and toes, marveled at the miracle of perfection she had produced, felt that surge of fierce love and protectiveness, that rush of hormones, that tie of blood and pain, and she knew she would never leave this child. It took a little time for it to play out, but really that was the moment her old life ended and her new one began.

It was hard not excluding Mark, she recalled. Suddenly her only concern was for the baby. She wanted everything to be perfect, and she wanted to control every aspect of the baby's life. She was reluctant to let him do anything—she had to pick the clothes, soothe the crying, rock her to sleep, yet she knew that relegating Mark to this secondary role was bad for him, bad for their relationship, bad for his own bonding with the baby, and it also made it hard for him to give her the help and support she needed. She tried to include him, to share some of the care and the decisions, but in the end, he went back to work and she stayed home and became the center of their family life. It was the same when the other children arrived—even more so, because by then there was a pattern they all fit into. He was so busy trying to make partner in the law firm, traveling often and staying late at the office, someone needed to assume the central family role, and she thought he was grateful she chose to step in. He played with the children, consulted on decisions when asked, accompanied them on excursions that Jennifer planned, and attended the birthday parties she organized. They loved him, she thought with satisfaction. He provided a glow as comforting and dependable as the moon's. But in that small family universe, she, Jennifer, was the sun.

She dressed quickly and had just finished packing when the phone rang. She could see from the caller ID that the call came from Spain, and she answered it quickly.

"Hello," came a woman's distant voice that sounded American. "May I please speak to Mr. or Mrs. Lewis?"

"This is Mrs. Lewis." Her voice was tight and she felt short-winded.

"My name is Julia Zimmerman. I'm a friend of Emma's on the Princeton program in Spain." The voice stopped, as though hesitant to go on.

"Yes," Jennifer prodded.

"I don't know if Emma was able to get through to you, but she's in trouble and I wanted to be sure you knew."

Jennifer took a deep breath. "Yes, we know. She called early this morning from jail."

"Oh, good," Julia Zimmerman said. "The thing is, she really needs you to come right away and to get her a good lawyer. The police are interviewing everyone, and people are saying terrible things about her. I know she couldn't have done this. I just wish Paco hadn't disappeared."

"Paco?"

"Her boyfriend. She was with him earlier last night, before this all happened. I know he could clear her, but no one knows where he is."

"Her boyfriend?"

Julia paused, confused. "I'm sorry. I thought you knew. They lived together. Well, some of the time."

Jennifer bit her upper lip.

"I really have to go, Mrs. Lewis. I'm sorry, but the police told me not to talk to anyone and I could get in trouble."

"Wait—please, Julia. What terrible things are they saying about Emma? Who is saying these things? Who was killed? How is Emma connected to all this?"

"I'm sorry, I can't tell you on the phone. Maybe we can talk when you come."

"But how can I reach you—" Jennifer began, but Julia interrupted.

"I'll e-mail you," she said hurriedly, and hung up.

In the eight months that Emma had been in Spain, during which she and Emma had e-mailed back and forth every day, Jennifer had never heard that her daughter had a boyfriend named Paco.

She went back to her preparations, her mind racing. She decided not to tell Mark—why upset him more before she had the whole story? She went to the supermarket to stock up on supplies for Mark and the kids, got cash from the ATM, retrieved her passport, and finished her errands. Then she called a car to take her to the airport. Tomorrow, she would know more.

CHAPTER 2

Jennifer had two hours to kill after she checked in for her 9 P.M. flight, so she called home. Aricelli, their longtime housekeeper and babysitter, answered the phone. Mark must have known he'd be late and called Aricelli to fill in. Lily would be furious—she considered herself much too old to have someone in the house to look after things, even though she couldn't be counted on to get off the phone long enough to get Eric to sleep on time or make sure he ate his dinner. Jennifer felt a wave of disappointment and, as usual, she worked hard to suppress it. She listened to Mark's cell ring unanswered and left a message, her voice cold but controlled.

"Mark, I called home and was surprised you weren't there yet, especially today. I'm at the airport. I'll board in about an hour. Please call me, and please go home. Oh, and don't forget that Eric does soccer after school tomorrow. He'll need his ball and uniform, which are in the sports closet, top shelf. Please put them in his backpack so he doesn't forget them. If I don't talk to you before I leave, I'll call when I arrive."

Mark didn't call. Jennifer boarded the plane, and just as she settled into her seat, her cell phone rang. Mark. She didn't answer and turned it off. She thought again of Emma, alone and scared in jail, and felt the already familiar ache. Being a mother is like being held hostage, she thought, with no prospect of release—even when your children are grown, probably even when they have children of their own.

Her mind wandered to what only yesterday had seemed like pressing problems: helping Eric make an erupting volcano for his third-grade science fair; finishing *The Sun Also Rises* so she could help Lily write a paper on it for her junior English class. This business, this middle-of-the-night phone call, was absurd. Ridiculous. It would probably be cleared up by the time she arrived, she thought, but it was good she was going. Emma must be so upset. What a terrible thing for her to go through.

The drinks cart stopped in front of her and she asked for a Scotch, pushing away the memory of her daughter's shaking, frightened voice. It wasn't Jennifer's usual drink—wine was more her style—but she took a sip, grimacing at the strong taste and feeling a comforting warmth in her throat. She took another sip.

She thought about how proud she had been of Emma when she got accepted to Princeton and then last summer when she started interning for the International Rescue Committee. That was so lucky, she mused. She had met a woman at a dinner party who happened to be on the board, and Jennifer told her how bright and committed Emma was. Of course once Emma went for the interview, they hired her. How could they not?

When she told Mark about it, he had said, "If I come back in a second life, I want it to be as your child." Jennifer had answered that he had her as his wife, wasn't that good enough? But he just laughed.

She took another sip of the Scotch. It went down smoother this time.

Emma had always been passionate about social justice. She'd done volunteer work with the Innocence Project when she was in high school, and of course she believed that just about every prisoner was actually innocent. How bitterly ironic it was that she was herself now falsely accused.

After a restless night, rumpled and groggy, her breath stale, she disembarked in Madrid, went through customs, and set off for the domestic terminal for her connecting flight to Seville. After landing in Seville, she found her way to the baggage area, where she spotted a man bearing a sign with her name on it. He was probably in his early thirties, wearing a black leather jacket. But she soon noticed that he was accompanied by a dignified-looking man of about fifty whose dark brown hair was flecked with gray and who was dressed in an immaculate navy blue suit, sky blue shirt, and red and blue tie.

"Mrs. Lewis?"

She nodded.

"My name is José Sancho Gomez. I am a criminal lawyer and I've been asked to consult with you about your daughter's case," he said in perfect, unaccented English, which sounded slightly foreign only because of its formality.

"Thank you so much for coming. I was hoping I could see Emma before anything else. Can we arrange for her bail?"

"I think perhaps it will be better if we talk a bit first." He offered to carry her hand luggage and she gave it to him. The driver took her suitcase. "Spanish law is a bit different from yours," he said, steering her toward the exit. "Bail is rarely set for a murder case. But Emma is not arrested and has not been charged. The police have the right to hold her for seventy-two hours. If they don't find any evidence that she is guilty, they cannot hold her longer and they will release her. This could all be over in two more days."

"Oh, thank God. When can I see her? She needs to know I'm here."

"I understand. We will go to the police station in a little while and they will let you see her. I have already been there and she is coping well. They are questioning her again now, so we have a little time to talk before they will allow you in. Why don't we use that to explain the situation so far? Since I am from Madrid, I have no office here, but we can talk in a colleague's chambers."

They had reached the exit, and leaving her suitcase with her, the driver left to get the car.

"But shouldn't you be with her when she is questioned?" Jennifer asked.

"Yes, of course she must have a lawyer with her, but my colleague is accompanying her. He is from Sevilla; he knows the prosecutor and the investigating magistrate. It will be better for him to be there at this stage." A black Peugeot pulled up at the curb and José led her to it.

She didn't speak during the fifteen-minute ride to the center of the city, lost in her thoughts and concerns. José, however, emitted a steady stream of local trivia, as though she were a tourist. His patter irritated her and she tried to ignore it. As they reached the center, however, she glanced out the window. She'd never been to Seville and understood immediately why Emma loved it. The city was exquisite. The sun shining so brightly on the Gothic cathedral felt like a good omen. Still, she was determined to resist the city's charms. But the heat and humidity, unusual for this time of year, were inescapable. She took off her light cotton jacket, grateful she had remembered to dress in layers.

They crossed the river at the Puente de San Telmo, passed the Plaza de Cuba, and stopped in front of 66 Calle Sanchez del Aguila, a well-kept four-story building. As they entered, Jennifer noticed a brass plaque affixed to the door. José saw her looking at the engraving, which read ABOGADOS. "It means 'law office.' We are going to the second floor," he said, ringing for the elevator. "Actually, that would be your third floor. In Spain, we don't count the main floor as you do in the U.S."

The elevator was small; it had room for no more than three people and even two felt cramped, and the hallway on the third floor was dark with small leaded windows just below the ceiling. The office, however, was cozy, with a large mahogany desk dominating the room, two black leather client chairs, a small couch, and several antique maps of Seville on the walls. José sat at the desk and she sat facing him. He offered her a cup of tea, which she refused. He took a cigarette out of his pocket and asked her if she minded if he smoked. She did, but said she didn't.

"How much do you know about this case?" he asked.

"Nothing. My daughter called us in the middle of the night and said she was in trouble. She went to a party. She thinks she ate some brownies laced with hashish, and somehow she ended up being suspected of murder. We'll do anything to help her. We want to bring her home."

"Your husband is not here?"

"He will be."

José nodded. "Let me tell you what we know so far." He glanced down at some papers, seemingly to refresh his memory, then leaned back in his chair and looked up at the ceiling as he spoke.

"In the early hours of Tuesday, April twenty-fifth, the last night of our annual *feria* when there are many people celebrating in the streets, your daughter placed a call to zero-nine-one, the emergency police number. She was crying and apparently was difficult to understand, but she told the operator to send the police to her home address immediately. When asked the problem, she said someone had died."

He paused, leaning forward to consult the report on his desk.

"Go on, please," Jennifer urged.

"When the police arrived they found Emma sitting on a chair in the corner, her eyes glazed and seemingly in shock. A young man, a Spanish student from Almería, was lying on the floor in a puddle of blood. He had been stabbed multiple times in the arms, chest, and neck and was dead."

"Oh, God, my poor baby."

The lawyer looked at her. "Well, yes. But the first sympathy of course was for the dead boy."

"Of course, I'm so sorry. I'm just . . . I'm trying to understand how my daughter could have been in this situation."

"She said the boy tried to rape her and the police officers took her straight to the hospital for examination. The doctors didn't find any physical problems and she refused permission for a rape test. This was not wise because although it is her right, it doesn't look good and raises suspicion. She was then brought to the police station for questioning. In Spain, she cannot be held more than eight hours without a lawyer present, but remember she was picked up in the middle of the night. Just like in your country, she has the right to forgo having her lawyer present during questioning, and also like your country, I'm sure they put pressure on her to do that. They'd have asked her why wait for your lawyer—unless you have something to hide.

"You know after a night in the cell, people tend to talk. It's dirty, dingy, you're crammed in with others, the food is terrible, and if you want to use the bathroom a policeman must accompany you to the door. And some of these policemen can be frightening. I had a case where the officer was shouting at a young woman and banging his hand hard on the table to emphasize his words, leaning in very close to her face and terrifying her. It wasn't long before she was ready to *cantar La Traviata*, as we say here—sing like a canary, I think is the English expression. But I walked in at the right moment and told her to stop talking."

Obviously distressed, but refusing to be sidetracked, Jennifer pressed him for more information. "Please, what did Emma say happened?"

"She said she'd been at a bar where she had a few beers and ate some brownies that were apparently laced with hashish. She'd gone home alone. As she neared her apartment this man started following her. He pulled out a knife and forced her inside, where he threw her on the bed and tried to rape her. She fought him and screamed."

Jennifer gasped and put her hand over her mouth.

"I'm sorry," José said. "I know all this is difficult for a mother to hear. But there is much more and you will have to be strong." He opened a cabinet, poured a glass of sherry, and offered it to her, but she waved it away. He drank it himself in one gulp.

"Go on, please," Jennifer said. José returned to the desk and looked again at the file.

"She claims that a passerby heard her pleas and burst in the door of her ground-floor apartment, which had not been locked. He fought with the attacker and killed him in self-defense. Emma was a witness so he would probably not have been prosecuted, but the boy—the newspapers are already calling him *el buen samaritano*, the Good Samaritan—told her he is an Algerian and is here illegally. He said he could not be found by the police and he ran off, leaving Emma alone in the apartment with the dead boy. She immediately called the police."

"Then why is she in jail? She's a victim, not a criminal."

"I'm afraid the police believe that remains to be seen. At the very least she is a material witness, and she is an American, which makes her a flight risk. They are looking for the Algerian. By tomorrow the whole country will be looking for him."

"How is Emma? How could anyone question her if she was in shock?"

"I saw her briefly this morning before you arrived. She is handling herself well under the circumstances. I believe they did not interrogate her right away. A detective is supposed to simply ask her what happened and write down her answer. The questioning now will be more thorough."

"When can I see her? Is there any way to get her out before the full seventy-two hours?"

"We will see. It depends on what evidence they find. It is possible they will charge her with something. They have collected samples from the crime scene and the pathologist has examined the body."

"Does that mean a grand jury?"

"We do not have a grand jury system in Spain. That function is filled by a judge—in this case, Sr. Ramón Delgado, who acts as investigating magistrate. He meets with the defense, the prosecution, and the suspect and decides whether or not to take the case to trial."

"Just one person makes that decision? What does he base it on?"

The lawyer answered in the neutral tone of a law professor. "The judge is given reports of the crime scene, the pathologists' findings (there must be two separate pathologists examining the body under Spanish law), and the interrogation of the suspect. He also orders the police to do follow-up investigations where necessary: find witnesses, question friends and colleagues, and make reports based on which he makes his decision."

Jennifer wished Mark were with her. He would understand this better, but she struggled to follow and take notes so she could fill him in later.

"It is important that we work to absolve your daughter of guilt at this stage," José continued. "In our system, there is, as I said earlier, no right to bail in a homicide case. The time between the charge and the trial can be anywhere from two to four years. If they charge her, your daughter will be sent to prison until the trial."

Jennifer gasped. "How could that be? What if people are innocent? They spend two or even four years in prison before they are even on trial?"

He nodded. He'd heard Americans make this objection before and he had an answer that satisfied him, if not them. "The pretrial investigation is very thorough," he said. "I will keep you aware of any and all information as I receive it."

Jennifer gave a perfunctory nod and started to rise. She was eager to get to the jail to see Emma.

"One more thing," José added, holding up his hand. "The police are interested in finding a man named Paco Romero, who has been identified by several acquaintances of your daughter as her boyfriend. She claims she doesn't know where he is. Perhaps this is the case. I am not suggesting she is untruthful, but if you could communicate to her the importance of cooperating fully with the police, it would make a successful outcome more likely."

"Of course she will cooperate," Jennifer said coldly, and stood up.

He looked at his watch. "We can go to the police station now. Perhaps it will be better if they know we are there."

CHAPTER 3

At the station, José introduced Jennifer to Fernando Molina, the detective in charge of Emma's case. He was about fifty, tanned, with a tight, muscular build, a square jaw, black hair, and unusually bright blue eyes. He spoke softly but seemed tough, even scary. She also met Raul Gonzalez, the local lawyer who had accompanied Emma during her interrogation.

"When can I see my daughter?" Jennifer asked.

"Cuando puede ver a su hija?" José asked the detective.

"We've finished talking to her for now," Fernando answered in English. "We'll bring her soon." He walked to the front desk and spoke to the clerk, then turned again to Jennifer. "I'm sure you are very concerned, but this is just routine procedure in a homicide."

"But why are you holding her? She is the victim here."

"Ah, but she is alive, isn't she? And some of her story doesn't quite make sense yet. And she is a foreigner, you see. What would prevent her from taking the next plane back to the United States?"

"If you have no evidence against her, there is no reason for her not to do that," José said.

"Yes. So we need to be sure that we have no evidence against her."

"Please," Jennifer said, her eyes misting, "let me see my daughter."

"Of course." He led them to a lounge that was used as a visiting room. There was a knotted wood table in the middle and a few orange plastic chairs scattered around.

"Wait here, por favor."

It felt like hours, but about forty minutes later, they brought Emma into the room. She was handcuffed and walked slowly. Her long brown hair, the same shade as her mother's, hung limp and greasy around her pale face, accentuating her strikingly beautiful aqua eyes, each iris bordered in black. She looked strained and miserable, but she didn't run to her mother or embrace her. She stared determinedly at the floor.

"Mom," she said softly, closing her eyes for a second and letting out a deep sigh. "Thanks for coming."

Jennifer ran toward her and took her in her arms. "Of course, baby. I'm here. Daddy is coming too, as soon as he can. We love you." She hugged her tightly, and although Emma submitted, Jennifer could feel her body stiffen in her embrace.

Jennifer appealed to José. "Why is she handcuffed? Can't you ask them to take them off?"

José said something in Spanish and the police officer unlocked the cuffs and removed them. Emma shook out her hands and rubbed her wrists but didn't look at the policeman, focusing on her mother.

"As soon as he can?"

"He has to stay for a while to help Granny and Pops with Lily and Eric."

"And to do some more work?"

"He has to, Emma. We're going to need the money, especially now."

Emma swallowed and backed up a few feet. "Right," she said crisply. She turned her attention to José and, speaking sharply, asked when she would be released. "Cuando puedo irme? No puedo soportarlo más," she said. She turned to her mother. "I need to get out of here. I can't eat. I can't sleep. They questioned me all night with no break and nothing to eat. I can't think straight." She sat down at a small table. Her mother immediately sat across from her.

"All night?" Jennifer asked. She turned to José. "I thought you said they just asked her what happened and wrote it down."

"That is what they are supposed to do. Emma, did you talk to them without Raul?

"A little. At the beginning. Before he came. I felt so scared, and I couldn't even understand everything they were asking—they were talking so fast and so loud and there wasn't anyone to translate."

"What did you tell them?"

"Nothing. Just what I told you this morning. There is nothing more to tell. But they kept asking the same questions over and over until I got confused."

"What did they ask?"

She shrugged and looked exasperated. "I don't know. Everything. They wanted me to describe the guy who saved me. What did he look like, what kind of shoes was he wearing, as if I would have noticed. It was so fast and I was so scared, I don't remember very much, but I did the best I could."

"Emma, in the future, you are to say nothing to any policeman, psychologist, doctor, or judge unless Raul or I are in the room. Nada. Comprendes?"

"Sí," Emma said in a small voice.

Jennifer reached for Emma's hand, but Emma pulled it away. "We will straighten it out, honey, you'll see. Everything will be fine."

"Mom, please. You always think everything is going to be fine. This isn't a play. Someone is dead. I was there. Don't say things when you don't know what you're talking about." She noticed her mother's hurt face and José's surprise and said in a softer voice, "I'm sorry, it's just that I need to try very hard to stay calm and not get hysterical."

Jennifer drew back. She turned to the lawyer. "Is there any way to speed this up?"

"I don't know. I am going to speak to the investigating magistrate and find out what the plan is. It isn't clear if they plan to charge her."

"But what would they charge her with? Surely they don't think she killed him?"

Fernando walked in as she spoke.

"Actually, we don't think so, senora. In fact we have just received the early analysis of the crime scene and the pathologist's report which confirm that she did not . . . how do you say"—he mimed stabbing someone—"strike the knife."

"Wield," José said. "She didn't wield the knife."

"Sí, wield," he repeated carefully. "However, it is still not clear who did. We are looking for her mysterious savior. We will need to keep her passport, but she is free to go."

Enormously relieved, they signed some papers and left the police station. They were headed for her apartment, but Emma said she never wanted to see it again. Jennifer hesitated, but José insisted—it was the crime scene, he explained, and he needed Emma to show him exactly what had happened and where. As they drove, the charming brick and cobblestone alleyways gave way to poorly maintained streets. Emma didn't live in anything like the style Jennifer had imagined—and had been sending her rent money for. Emma had originally rented a room with a middle-class family in a good neighborhood. The idea was that she would improve her Spanish and the mother of the household would cook her meals and do her laundry. After two months, Emma told her parents that this wasn't working. She didn't like the family, which she said was too old-fashioned and rigid, and since none of her friends lived in those circumstances, she felt isolated. She wanted to live in the Residencia Universitaria los Bermejales, about four kilometers from the city center. It was expensive, but she told her parents it was safe and that it was where all her American friends lived. There was regular bus service back and forth from the university. Jennifer and Mark had hesitated—they liked the idea of their daughter having some adult supervision—but they wanted her to be happy and they gave in and supplied the extra funds.

The apartment Emma led her to, however, was a tawdry three rooms on the ground floor of a graffiti-scarred building. Jennifer looked at Emma as they approached, but Emma didn't meet her eye. The police had already finished their forensic work, but yellow tape still crossed the door and windows. Emma provided the key and they ducked under the tape, unlocked the door, and pushed it open.

"Is this student housing?" Jennifer asked, appalled.

"It's cheaper," Emma mumbled. "It's all I need."

She went straight into the bedroom and lay down. The double bed wasn't made and the sheets were rumpled and bunched at the foot. On the floor next to the bed was a tape outline of a body. The windows had been closed, and the oppressive hot air was stifling. "Would you two give me a few minutes?" she asked, closing her eyes.

Jennifer and José sat at a small table in the kitchen, which was equipped with a two-burner stove and a half-size refrigerator. There was no sink, but Jennifer could see through the open door of the adjoining lavatory that the bathroom sink was full of dishes. She was feeling worse and worse. How she wished Mark were with her. It was clear Emma had lied about her living arrangements, of course, but maybe that could be explained somehow, and it seemed like the least of her problems, given the circumstances. But Emma's mood was also confounding. Of course she'd expected her to be upset, maybe even in shock, but she thought her daughter would have been more relieved to see her, bolstered by her presence, comforted in the way she had been all her life. Instead, Emma almost seemed angry at her. She must be steeling herself, Jennifer thought, because if she allowed herself to express need or weakness, she would cry and then she would never be able to stop.

She opened the window and turned on the fan. She found a glass in the bathroom sink, washed it, and filled it with cold water. She knocked on Emma's door, and when there was no answer, she entered anyway.

"You need to come out now, Emma," she said, offering the water to her daughter, who took it and, habit overcoming mood, even mumbled a soft thank-you. Emma reluctantly led the way into the living room and plopped down on a faded, stained couch. José joined them and Jennifer offered him a glass of water and took one for herself. They found chairs and sat down. There was a brief, awkward silence.

"Now, Emma," José said quietly. "From the beginning. Tell us again. What happened?"

CHAPTER 4

Mark had made reservations at the Hotel Alfonso XIII, the oldest and most beautiful hotel in town, and José offered to drive Jennifer and Emma there. Jennifer suggested that Emma pack a few things and she complied, emptying her drawers into a duffel bag and adding items strewn around the apartment. As they got out of the car, José reminded them to contact him immediately if there was any further communication from the police.

The hotel was beautiful and gracious in an Old World way. In better times, Jennifer would have loved it. Now, she barely took in the Andalusian mosaics in the lobby and the central fountain with its romantic Arabian motif. They waited as the porter earned his tip by explaining the air-conditioning and other of the hotel's amenities. "At last," Jennifer said, when she had closed the door behind him. "We're alone."

Emma seemed glum. No wonder, Jennifer thought, but still, there was something else, an edge.

"How much is this place a day?" Emma asked, looking around disapprovingly at the formal floral curtains and matching bedspreads, the plush carpeting, high ceilings, and elaborately carved crown moldings.

"I'm not sure. Dad made the reservation."

"Well, I'll bet it's at least four hundred euros a day, more than many workers here earn in a month, if they're lucky enough to have any job at all. It's kind of obscene to pay that much in this economy."

Jennifer started to answer but thought better of it and said nothing.

When Emma noticed her duffel bag next to her mother's near the door, she looked surprised. "Don't I have a separate room?" she asked.

Jennifer couldn't suppress a sardonic reply. "No, honey, as you pointed out, that would be obscene."

Emma bristled. "Whatever. But I still have to have some privacy."

This was a throwback to adolescence, Jennifer thought: the irrationality of wanting contradictory things. Emma had almost never behaved this way, but Jennifer had seen it often in her friends' children. She was perplexed and beginning to lose her patience.

"Well, just think how long poor families could live on what it would cost for *two* rooms," she snapped. Emma glared at her and she held her temper and, speaking calmly and rationally, tried again. "We'll both lose our privacy, Emma, but we'll have to make the best of it until this is over. We don't know how long this will take, and we can't afford two rooms. You've made it clear that you don't want to go back to that apartment, and I don't blame you."

Emma sat on one of the beds, found the remote, and flicked on the television.

Jennifer asked her to turn it off, and Emma did, sighing as though much put upon. They sat in silence. Finally, Jennifer asked, "So what should we do now?"

"I don't know about you, but I need to sleep," Emma answered.

Of course, Jennifer thought. They'd been questioning her all night. No wonder she was behaving so badly. And Jennifer was tired too. She hadn't slept well on the plane. "Let's take a nap," she said. But Emma had already pulled the bedspread off her bed and curled up under the light blanket. Her eyes were closed.

Jennifer was so disturbed by Emma's behavior that she was sure she wouldn't be able to sleep, but she dozed off before she knew it and awoke two hours later. Emma was still in bed but beginning to stir. Jennifer asked her if she wanted to get a bite to eat.

Jennifer was too hungry to wander around searching for a café, so in spite of Emma's objections—"This restaurant is just for rich tourists and it won't even have good food"—she insisted they eat at the hotel coffee shop. After they ordered, Jennifer suggested that since they had some free time together, they ought to do something fun. "What's your favorite shop here?" she asked. "We'll go shopping."

This was a bonding activity of theirs, and Emma had never been known to turn it down, even when all she wanted was prewashed, pre-torn jeans and flannel shirts from J.Crew. Before Emma left for Spain they'd had a wonderful time shopping for warm-weather shirts and pants, skirts and spaghetti-strap dresses. As a special good-bye, Jennifer had secretly gone back to Emma's favorite shop on Germantown Avenue near their Chestnut Hill home. She'd bought a five-hundred-dollar Andrew Marc leather jacket that Emma had coveted and Jennifer had absolutely refused to buy because it was too expensive. She hid it and gave it to her as she was dressing for the plane. Emma had thrown her arms around her.

"Thanks so much, Mom; you're the best," she'd said. "You always know what I need."

But shopping didn't seem to be what she needed now. She thanked her mother in an offhand way but claimed she didn't want anything.

"Maybe you should, honey. If they question you again, you ought to dress nicely. It gives a good impression. We can get you one attractive, professional outfit."

"Professional what?" she said with a laugh. "Professional suspect?"

"Emma, stop it. There's nothing funny about this. What is going on with you? You're not yourself."

Emma shrugged. "Aren't I?" she asked softly. "I guess you would know." After that cryptic remark, she seemed to pick up.

"We need something to take our minds off all this," Emma said resolutely. "Maybe we should do a little sightseeing. I could show you around."

Jennifer gratefully accepted and they walked outside. The hotel was surrounded by palm trees, and the flower beds across the street on Calle San Fernando scented the air with the sweetness of oleander and jacaranda. She felt a little calmer just standing there. They faced the monument on the Puerta de Jerez and looked around. Jennifer knew that the university was just next door and suggested they go there so Emma could show her where she spent most of her days, but Emma wasn't interested. "Maybe some other time," she said. Jennifer was disappointed but she didn't insist. She suggested the cathedral. She could see the Giralda from where they stood.

"That's a big tourist thing. It'll be mobbed. And you don't need me for that. You can take a tour," Emma said.

"Okay. So where do you think we should go?" Jennifer asked.

"Triana," Emma replied immediately. "It's kind of a student hangout. I've spent lots of time there. I could take you around." She looked at her watch. "Well, it's still a little early, at least by Spanish standards. I guess we could go by the cathedral first and then walk across the bridge to Triana. Are you up for a walk?"

Jennifer said she was and they set off. As they approached the cathedral, Jennifer was stunned by its beauty—the massive golden beige stone, the majestic doorway with its intricate carvings, the spires that reached upward toward the heavens. Emma pointed out that it was an example of both Arab and Christian architecture. "You know, the people here are really proud of the fact that Muslims, Jews, and Christians coexisted here for centuries," she said. "Of course they leave out the Inquisition, but that's another story," she added, raising her eyebrows in a theatrical aside. "Anyway, it is true that first the Arabs ruled this place, then the Christians, and the architecture reflects it. The Giralda was once the minaret of a mosque. Then it became the bell tower of the Gothic cathedral they built to replace the mosque. It ended up becoming the symbol of the city. The Christians added their own symbolism to the tower—see the sculpted lilies on top?"

Jennifer looked at Emma and felt a flush of pride. She seemed so knowledgeable, so confident in her surroundings. She followed Emma's gaze upward and studied the Giralda. It looked like a wedding cake, with two square tiers topped by two graceful cylindrical ones, capped by what looked like a golden globe.

"See the very top, Mom?" Emma pointed. "It's a bronze statue of a woman and it moves because it's actually a weathercock. That's what 'Giralda' means. It's kind of funny that they named the whole tower after the weathercock when the statue isn't even of a saint or anything."

They wandered inside the cathedral, Emma talking all the while and Jennifer proudly listening. "How do you know all this?" she asked.

Emma shrugged. "I don't know. When I first came I was really into this tourist thing. I read all the guidebooks and spent lots of time looking around."

By the time they had finished their visit and Emma had deemed it an appropriate time to visit Triana, Jennifer wanted to get a cup of coffee and rest for a bit. They stopped at a café.

Jennifer ordered café con leche and Emma asked for a cortado. She explained that the Spaniards loved coffee so much they had specific names for at least six ways of drinking it—kind of like the Eskimos having more words than we do for snow, she said with a smile. Jennifer felt encouraged. She smiled back and reached over impulsively to tuck a stray lock of hair behind her daughter's ear.

"So . . . you seem very much at home here. Did you make lots of new friends?" Jennifer asked. "Do you hang out with the American kids on the program?"

Emma stiffened slightly and a tense, strained tone returned to her voice. "I did at the beginning. But it's stupid, don't you think, to come to a foreign country and hang out with your little ghetto of Americans? I wanted to meet Spanish kids and get involved in Spanish issues."

Jennifer immediately caught the signs of resistance, but she pressed forward anyway, pretending to have missed them.

"I can understand that. So how did you go about it?"

"It just kind of happened little by little." She paused as if considering whether to go on. Then she said, "I met someone. He helped."

Jennifer took her time. She sipped her coffee and answered casually, "Was that Paco?"

Emma was immediately on guard. "How do you know about Paco?" she asked accusingly. "Who have you been talking to?"

Jennifer tried to backtrack. "I don't know anything, Emma. I just . . . After you called to say you were in trouble we got another call from a friend of yours, a girl named Julia. She said that she wished your boyfriend, Paco, was around but he wasn't in town."

Emma nodded.

"I didn't even know you had a boyfriend," Jennifer said. "Do you want to tell me about him?"

"No," she shot back quickly, then seemed to collect herself. "I mean, I will, but not now." She seemed preoccupied. "It was nice of Julia to call," she murmured. "I didn't expect that." She got up abruptly and said, "Let's go, okay, Mom? I'm tired of sitting."

It was a fairly long walk to Triana. They walked on wide avenues and in and out of narrow cobbled streets and footpaths until they reached the Puente de Triana, which crossed the river. On the other side of the bridge was a wide staircase that led to Triana Square, a lovely public space surrounded by a church and several restaurants. The first street sign Jennifer noticed was CALLE RODRIGO DE TRIANA. "There's a story about that," Emma said. That guy Rodrigo, he was with Columbus. He was the one who saw land first. He shouted, 'Tierra a la vista'—'Land in sight'—and became famous forever after. Every Spanish school child has heard of him."

Jennifer saw young people sitting on the steps, laughing, talking, some swigging from bottles of beer. Emma looked around—a little nervously, Jennifer thought. Maybe she was reluctant after what had happened to run into anyone she knew. But she didn't seem to recognize anyone and no one greeted her, though Jennifer thought a few people seemed to stare at her and—was she imagining it?—some seemed to whisper together, looking in her direction. They wandered around for a while, looking at the houses, the architecture, the church, and finally, getting hungry, they found an outdoor table at one of a string of restaurants and sat down. Emma ordered chopitos—grilled baby squid—for an appetizer and followed it with cazón en adobo, which she said was marinated deep-fried fish wrapped in a cardboard cone, a Spanish version of the English fish and chips. The smell of sizzling olive oil and fried fish permeated the air. Emma was smiling. Jennifer felt relaxed, even happy. She almost forgot the tension between them since she'd arrived. Almost, but not quite.

She didn't bring up Paco again. She found that while Emma would chat easily about the sights of Seville and listen happily to stories about her sister and brother or friends back home, she became edgy, secretive, and prickly as soon as Jennifer asked anything about her personal life in Spain, her boyfriend, or, especially, the night of the murder. Thinking this was a form of shock, or at least a means of self-protection, Jennifer hoped it would slowly wear off and they would be able to make progress in planning their next steps before too long. In the meantime, she avoided subjects that set off Emma's hair trigger and tried to engage her in nonthreatening conversation.

They took a taxi back to the hotel. Jennifer hoped they would talk more the next day, but in the days that followed the pattern held. They saw the sights, ate in cafés and restaurants, walked all over the city, and spoke of anything that wasn't the one subject Jennifer wanted to engage.

They picked up the local paper every day and saw that there was a new feature: a box on the front page requesting the man they called *el buen samaritano* to step forward. But no one appeared. Emma translated, reading the story aloud to her mother. Although Emma's knowledge of the language wasn't perfect, she could make out most of the details. The police had offered to petition for the man to be granted asylum in Spain if he gave evidence. So far, however, he had still not appeared. "I'm sure he doesn't trust them," Emma said. "I wouldn't. Would you?"

There was one minor explosion when Jennifer admitted to Emma that it nagged at her that she had lied to her about staying at the Residencia when really she was living in a slum. "You had the money— what did you do with it?" Jennifer pressed. Emma turned on her

angrily, saying it was just like her to focus on the most trivial, material-
istic aspect of her situation. She refused to say anything else on the
subject.

Jennifer called Mark daily, spoke to the children, e-mailed back
and forth with Lily about her friends and school papers and extracur-
ricular activities, a life that more and more felt far away and foreign.
Mostly, she waited for whatever would come next. Then one day, just
when Jennifer was beginning to think the police silence meant they
must have found something to back up Emma's story and were pursu-
ing other leads, she got a call from José.

After the usual pleasantries, he said, "I'm afraid I have bad news."

Jennifer's stomach tightened as she waited for the rest. "The police
have informed me that they will be picking up Emma again for questioning. Apparently they are confused by some elements of her story
and need further clarification. I believe their questions will concern the
murder weapon, which they claim they have found. It would be best for
you to prepare Emma. Call me as soon as they arrive."

CHAPTER 5

Jennifer was surprised and distressed when the police showed up at 7:30 the next evening. She would never get accustomed to Spanish time. They didn't seem to respect day and night the way Americans did. She placed a hasty phone call to José, who said he and Raul would meet them at the police station. It worried Jennifer that both lawyers were coming. Emma too seemed very nervous. Of course, she would be—who wouldn't after what she'd been through? And then these relentless questions made everything worse. She reminded Emma not to say anything until José or Raul was at her side.

When they arrived, an officer once again showed Jennifer into the waiting room, and then he led Emma away. Emma looked over her shoulder as she left, almost reproachfully, as if she believed Jennifer was letting her down somehow, as if her world was broken and she expected her mother to be able to fix it. Jennifer's eyes followed her helplessly until she disappeared. There was nothing to do now but wait.

She picked up a local newspaper someone had left on a chair and was appalled to see a front-page photo of Emma. She couldn't understand the headline, but she saw the words *buen samaritano* and assumed they were sounding the call again for the Algerian to turn himself in. She stared at the photo. It was the same picture Emma had used on her Seville application. Jennifer looked sadly at her beloved daughter, this beautiful brunette in a floral dress smiling proudly at a dinner following her nineteenth birthday. They had gone shopping together for that dress. It had cost much more than she had wanted to spend, but Emma had begged her. She had loved it so much and looked so lovely in it, Jennifer couldn't resist. She well remembered that dinner—how happy they had been—and her heart lurched.

She continued to wait, her mind wandering. It seemed that motherhood for her had always entailed a lot of waiting. She was good at it by now. If you added it up, she must have waited hundreds of hours for Emma over the years—ballet lessons, piano, Model United Nations, soccer, tennis—and when she was in high school, waited past her 1:00 A.M. curfew, sometimes long past, sick with worry, until Emma walked in with some excuse or other. She had begged her to at least call to let her know when she'd be late so she wouldn't worry so much, but Emma never seemed able to remember. "Call on my cell; just leave a number," Jennifer would say, and each time Emma was late, Jennifer would check her cell phone for a message, but it was never there. She'd doze, then wake up automatically around 1:30 and peek into Emma's bedroom. When she hadn't come home, there was no going back to sleep. She'd wake Mark and he'd mumble that she'd be fine and tell her to go back to sleep before he turned over himself, but of course she couldn't until, finally, she'd hear the key in the lock and the door open and her anxiety would subside, replaced first by relief and then by anger.

There was a litany of fears about her children that sometimes tormented her, from the normal ups and downs of life—heartbreak, failure, disappointment, rejection—to the more serious dangers: illness, car crash, mugging, rape, even murder. She had read stories about crazy students who barged into dorm rooms and shot anyone in sight, and the thought that this might happen to one of her children terrified her for days after. But she never imagined her daughter would be suspected of being the person who caused another mother that kind of pain. And she knew with the kind of certainty that is unshakable that Emma didn't do this thing.

Mark would arrive tomorrow morning, and she felt it was important that she make some personal headway with Emma before he came. She had avoided confronting her daughter, hoping that she would open up to her in her own time, but that hadn't happened and it was time to bring things to a head. Emma would understand. Their family tradition was never to go to bed angry, without working things out. When Emma returned, she resolved, they would go out for dinner, order some wine, and talk to each other.

Finally, Emma appeared, looking pale and shaken. José, Raul, and Fernando, the same detective they'd met the first day Jennifer arrived, followed. Fernando shook hands with Jennifer and told her that Emma could leave, but should not travel out of Seville.

They found a restaurant near the police station and chose a table on the patio. It was nearly 11:00 P.M., and true to Spanish custom, the restaurant was just filling up. Jennifer started to question Emma even before they were seated.

"What happened? What did they ask you? What did you say?"

"They just kept repeating the same questions over and over."

"What questions?"

"What happened? When? What order? Stuff like that."

"But can you think of anything specific they asked? Was there any particular question they kept going back to?

Emma shook her head slowly. "I don't know, Mom. I'm tired. I got confused."

"Try, Emma. It's important." Jennifer put her hand on Emma's arm.

Emma pursed her lips and drew away. "Please, Mom, stop interrogating me. Give me some space, okay?"

They followed the hostess to a table and took their seats. Jennifer ordered a bottle of rioja to be brought over right away, then held herself in check as Emma translated from the menu. Emma decided on shrimp in garlic sauce and a Spanish omelet and Jennifer chose ham for the first course followed by the sole. "Gambas al ajillo y tortilla española aquí," Emma said, "y jamón serrano y filete de lenguado para mi madre." Jennifer was impressed once again with both her fluency and her self-confidence. She couldn't help but marvel that this crisis, from which Jennifer had rushed over to save her, was the first time Emma seemed in charge and independent.

"Your Spanish has gotten good," Jennifer said.

"Not really. But I'm getting better."

Silence again.

"Look at how crowded this place is," Jennifer said. "It's eleven o'clock. When do these people sleep?"

"They're used to it," Emma said.

"But don't they have to go to work in the morning? I mean, it's not healthy to go to sleep on a full stomach."

Emma's face registered annoyance. "Mom, you're so *American*."

"Yeah, I guess I am. . . ." Jennifer sipped at her wine. She picked at the ham, but realized she wasn't very hungry after all. They sat in awkward silence until the waitress brought the main course, clearing Jennifer's full plate and asking with a pained look if senora didn't like the food. Jennifer didn't understand, but once again Emma translated, saying that her mother loved it but just wasn't feeling well. Finally, as the waitress retreated in disappointment, Jennifer leaned across the table.

"Emma, what's the matter? I came all the way here the moment you called. I came to help you, but I can't if you don't talk to me. Are you mad at me for something? What am I missing?"

Emma sighed. She sounded very tired. "I'm not mad. I'm glad you're here. I said thank you for coming. It was the first thing I said."

"I know you said it. But you are acting as if something is wrong."

"Something *is* wrong, Mom." Emma's temper flared. "A guy almost raped me. He was killed in front of me in my apartment. The police don't believe me. Can you imagine how that feels? And on top of that, they seem to think I did it, or something. I don't know what I should do or say or feel." She paused and then continued quietly, as if talking to herself. "I'm kind of numb, I guess. I don't want to have to talk. I just want to *be* for a bit. You always think everything can be fixed by talking, but maybe some things get better if you just leave them alone."

"But we can't just leave this alone. You're involved in a murder. You could go to jail. We have to get you out of here. Then we can find someone to help you deal with all this when we get home."

"I don't need that kind of help. I don't think my reaction is abnormal."

"No, of course not. But you need comfort, and you aren't allowing it to come from me. You stiffen when I go to hug you. It's as if you blame me in some way."

Emma sighed again and shook her head in exasperation. "I don't blame you, Mom. I'm sorry if I stiffened." She was clearly exhausted. "Can't you understand that this isn't about you? I can't worry about your feelings now. It's all I can do to keep myself together. If you want to help me, let me do that."

"I want to do whatever helps you, but that means legally as well as emotionally. We need to help the lawyers prepare your case."

Emma averted her eyes. When she looked back, her expression was softer. "Look, you were the first person I thought of when this happened. I thought, I just want my mother. But then you came and I realized how upset and ashamed you are. You'll say you're not, but I know you so well. I could see it in your face, your body language, in everything you said and did. And that doesn't help me. It makes it worse."

Jennifer was shocked. "I'm not ashamed. There's nothing to be ashamed about. If you're ashamed, you shouldn't be. You're innocent. Why does shame come into this?"

Emma shook her head slowly. "You can't let it go, can you?" Speaking earnestly, she leaned across the table so only Jennifer would hear. "I just don't think you will understand, Mom. You've lived your whole life in this privileged cocoon. So did I—you provided that, I know, and you thought you were doing the right thing—but when I came here I realized how spoiled we are, how many people are suffering, and how we have a moral obligation to help. You know what the unemployment rate is here? It's twenty-five percent. None of the young people I know, people my age, have any hope of finding jobs if they stay in their country, and most of them have parents who are out of work and who they have to help support. And what about the immigrants? Especially the North Africans whose families sacrificed so much to send them here and now they can't find work and there is terrible prejudice against them."

It sounded so young, so naive, so *adolescent*, this ranting about the hardships of the poor without reference to or realization of the very real danger she might be in. It was all Jennifer could do to control her irritation.

"I know," she said in what she hoped was a sympathetic tone. "That's awful. But what has that got to do with your situation? You can't help anybody if you spend the next twenty-five years in a Spanish jail, and unless that Algerian guy turns himself in or they find your boyfriend, there's a chance you may do that."

Emma shook her head in exasperation. "You see what you do? You refer to him as 'that Algerian guy'—he's a decent human being who saved me from being raped. Of course he won't turn himself in. They'd deport him and his family would starve."

"I thought the police said they would help him stay."

"We already talked about that. And I tried to explain that there's no way that would happen. How can you be so naive?"

When Jennifer didn't reply, Emma continued. "And why mention Paco? He had nothing to do with any of this. It won't matter if he comes back or not."

Jennifer's frustration overcame her caution. "I don't know why you think that, Emma. What did they ask you when they questioned you? I don't think they're interested in your opinion on poverty or injustice."

"Thanks, Mom. Sarcasm is just what I need right now."

"You have no idea what you need, apparently, but I will tell you that you have some decisions to make and you need to make them fast. Daddy is coming in the morning. We're meeting him at José's office. If you want our help—and that's all we want is to help you—you have to cooperate with us and stop preaching and let us in."

Emma didn't respond. She finished her glass of wine and poured herself another and drank that. "It's just that I feel like a different person from the one you know."

Jennifer sighed. "Emma, you've only been here for eight months."

"I know that." Her voice expressed her irritation. "If you want me to talk to you, don't dismiss what I say, okay?"

"Okay. You're right. I'm sorry."

Emma leaned forward, speaking earnestly. "I've learned so much. You were shocked at my apartment."

Jennifer started to object.

"Don't deny it. I saw your face. You asked me why I didn't live in the Residencia. Well, that apartment is better than what lots of people have to live in for their whole lives. How could I live in some fancy, exploitive upper-class Residencia for rich foreigners when I know how all the others have to live, when I am in love with someone who came from the kind of poverty I'm talking about? I used that money to help him and he used it to help others—people in his village without jobs, without money for food. I'm not ashamed of it, but I knew you would condemn me for doing that. I'm going to devote my life to helping people who can't fight for themselves. And I know I can't do that from jail, but this whole case seems so crazy to me that I can't believe that's going to happen. I'm the victim, not the criminal."

Jennifer forced herself to sound calm. "Darling, I know you are. That's what I'm here to help you prove." She paused; her voice found the intimate tone she'd used in the past for their private conversations. "Do you really think you're in love with this man?"

"I don't *think* I am, Mom. I am."

Jennifer sighed. She knew she had to tread lightly. "Well, maybe later, you can tell me all about him."

"Yeah. Maybe."

"But, you know, you shouldn't be so quick to think you know what I would condemn."

Emma started to interrupt, but Jennifer brushed her objection aside.

"Anyway, that's not important. My only concern now is to stop you from behavior that will make you spend the best years of your life in jail, whatever you did or didn't do. At the very least, you are the only witness to a murder and, as the police must have told you, there is still no sign of your Good Samaritan. Without him, it's hard to verify your story. José said they found the murder weapon. What was that about? What did they want from you?"

"That's all they questioned me about. Over and over and over. Was I sure that that Spanish kid had a knife? Did I see it? What did it look like? They don't believe me; I can tell. But if they have no evidence to verify my story, they also have no evidence to disprove it. It doesn't matter what they believe; they need evidence. Paco knows all about the police."

"Paco? Have you been talking to him? Why isn't he here?"

Emma looked flustered. "No. I haven't," she said quickly, "and I don't know where he is, but he'll be back when he hears about this and he'll advise me."

"Emma, everyone in the country has heard about this. Your dad is a lawyer. And you have one of Spain's best criminal lawyers. They'll advise you."

Emma was through talking. "Yeah. Of course. Anyway, I'm tired; I need to get some sleep." She took a last sip of wine and started to get up, but Jennifer stopped her.

"In a minute," she said. "What do you mean that Paco knows about the police? Is he a lawyer?"

Emma laughed contemptuously. "No, he's not a *lawyer*, Mom."

"A policeman?"

"No. No. No. None of those things, none of what you and Dad could understand. That's what I meant. He knows about the police because he's always avoiding them, and he avoids them because he's been in jail and he knows how bad the conditions are," she blurted with a touch of pride, staring at her mother belligerently.

The other shoe had dropped. Jennifer nodded slowly and replied carefully, trying to keep her voice calm. "What has he been in jail for?"

"Nothing. I'm not sure. Probably disturbing the peace. He's a social activist, so they hate him. He's brilliant. He comes from this really poor family. His father is Moroccan and his mother is from a little town near Granada."

"Where did you meet him?"

"At school." Emma stood up. "Let's go. I really need to get some sleep if I'm going to have to face Dad in the morning."

"Face him? He's coming to help you, Emma."

"Yeah, I know. Let's go." She turned abruptly and Jennifer scrambled to follow.

"I have to pay, Emma. Wait a minute."

"La cuenta, por favor," Emma called to the waitress, the last words she spoke that evening.

CHAPTER 6

Jennifer and Emma were already seated in Raul's office drinking espresso when Mark arrived. He was carrying the morning edition of the *Diario de Sevilla*, which he had picked up at the airport but, not knowing Spanish, was unable to read. Another photo of Emma covered the front page, this time an informal snapshot probably taken by some friends. She was sitting on the steps at the Triana Bridge surrounded by other laughing students, smiling flirtatiously at the photographer. She looked beautiful, young, and very happy.

Jennifer rose to greet Mark and they embraced warmly. She introduced him to José and they shook hands. Emma hung back a bit, looking a little embarrassed, before she went to him and submitted to his bear hug. When he released her he held her at arm's length to get a better look.

"Honey, how are you? How are you bearing up?" he asked.

"I'm okay, Dad." Her voice was controlled, a little distant. "This isn't the way I meant to show you Seville. I'm sorry."

"Forget that. Let's just focus on getting you out of here."

He turned to the lawyer, dropping the newspaper on his desk. "I see the local papers wasted no time. What does it say?"

"I read it earlier. It's mostly a request for the Good Samaritan to appear. It recounts Emma's story about him to the police and repeats numerous offers to reward him if he shows his face. Today the paper promises to cover his legal expenses. On the whole, the incentive is not harmful to our case and, who knows"—he shrugged, closing his eyes momentarily and extending his palms upward—"it may encourage the man to appear."

"I don't think so," Emma said.

"We will see," José murmured. He offered Mark a seat and some espresso and Mark accepted.

"What worries me is the story inside the paper," Emma said. "Did you read the piece on the guy who tried to rape me?"

"You mean the murder victim," José added.

Emma didn't answer.

"I read it," he continued. "The reporter has interviewed dozens of fellow students and friends who maintain that this boy was incapable of such aggressive behavior. He was a good student and they claim he was respectful toward women. They can't believe he would force a woman into her apartment at knifepoint and try to rape her."

"Well, that's exactly what he did. So I guess he had them fooled," Emma shot back. "I mean, what do they expect his friends to say?"

Mark leaned over and put his hand on Emma's. "Calm down, honey," he said. He took a sip of his espresso and addressed José. "We need someone to help us do our own investigation—talk to the students the police talked to, and hopefully others who might talk to him but not to the police. Do you know anyone like that?"

José said he did and had thought of approaching him as soon as Jennifer had mentioned her desire to find a private investigator. He was a former policeman with an excellent record and good relations with the department. Mark asked why he had left the force, and José explained that the detective had been divorced and found it hard to maintain two households on a policeman's salary—he simply made more money on his own. Mark nodded and accepted the business card José offered.

"There's one more thing," José said. "The newspaper story claims that there is no record of Rodrigo Pérez—the victim," he went on, seeing the questioning look on Mark's face, "ever owning or carrying a knife. No one ever saw one and all who knew him found it inconceivable that he would carry one because he was particularly opposed to the use of deadly weapons to settle disputes. He had studied karate for self-defense but hadn't advanced."

He looked at Emma, as did Jennifer and Mark, but her face showed no emotion. She shrugged. "I didn't know him. All I know is he had a weapon that night."

Mark turned again to José. "You told Jennifer they found the murder weapon."

José crossed the room to pour himself another cup of coffee. "They think they have," he said slowly. He looked uncomfortable. "Frankly, this presents a serious problem for us."

Mark shifted in his chair. His eyes sought Jennifer's and they exchanged worried looks. He asked José to explain.

"A knife was found in Emma's kitchen whose blade matches the wounds in the deceased," José said, using a formal mode of expression. "Emma told the investigators that the intruder held a knife to her to force entry into her apartment. But it appears that the knife was already there."

"How do they know it was there?"

"It was part of a set of kitchen knives in graduated sizes."

"What makes them believe that was the murder weapon?" Emma asked. "I mean, how can they tell that it matches the wounds?"

"The blade is serrated and matches exactly the serrations in the wounds."

"Were there prints on it?" Mark asked.

"No. The police say it had been wiped clean."

"'Wiped clean' is a supposition. Maybe they were never there," Mark said. He turned to Emma. "Emma, are you absolutely certain that Rodrigo Pérez had a knife when he forced you inside?"

"Yes, yes, yes!" Emma exploded. "How many times do I have to tell everyone that?" She looked tearfully at her father. "Don't you believe me, Daddy?"

"Please, honey. Of course I believe you. I believe you think he had a knife. But that doesn't mean he did. During crimes, during terrifying circumstances, witnesses and victims are often guided by their panic. Maybe he pretended to have a knife."

"I felt it in my back. He pushed it against me." She put her face in her hands and pressed her eyes.

"Maybe it was his finger or his keys. Maybe he wanted you to think it was a knife. You were scared. Isn't that possible?"

Emma stopped and thought. "Well, yes, I guess it's possible," she said in a small voice.

Jennifer let her breath out. She looked gratefully at Mark. How relieved she was that he was here. Mark looked at José and both men nodded.

"But then how did the Samaritan get the knife?" José asked.

"I don't know," Emma said. "I'm pretty sure that the Spanish kid pulled it out first. The guy who helped me fought him, and at the last minute he grabbed it from him. I was screaming for them to stop, but the Spanish kid kept coming at him and the Algerian fended him off with the knife. I think the Spanish kid tried to take it back and got stabbed accidentally; I'm not sure—but it was definitely self-defense." Emma had worked herself up to a frenzy, and now, turning toward her father, she burst into tears. "I can't think about it anymore, Daddy. I keep dreaming about it and seeing the blood. I don't want to talk about it anymore. Please."

"Let's stop for today," José said as Mark put his arm around Emma. Jennifer got up to embrace her, but she curled tighter into her father's arms. Jennifer watched Mark comfort Emma, relieved that Emma accepted it and sad that she had rejected comfort from her. Emma had been so close to her just a few months ago, she thought again; the thought kept recurring and tormenting her. She knew that Emma had admired her. She remembered how, when she was young, Emma used to want to model herself after her. Jennifer had been her prototype of the perfect woman. She thought of all those birthday and Mother's Day cards addressed to "The Most Wonderful Mother in the World." As a young teenager, when Emma happened to see Jennifer change shirts and noticed the softness and slight droop of her breasts, Emma had worried. "Do you think there's something wrong with me?" she had asked. "I mean, mine just stick straight out." Jennifer had looked at her daughter's young firm breasts and smiled to think how beautiful they were. She told her that, of course, but secretly felt touched at Emma's innocence and flattered by her adulation.

Well, those days were certainly over, and she told herself that was as it should be. But why had it changed to this? It seemed so unfair. All those years of coddling and sacrifice and making excuses for Daddy, who wasn't always home or at every event. She'd consciously built him up so the kids would appreciate him even if he had left most of the parenting to her, immersed in his work and his golf and his world outside the home. And now he was the one she turned to. And not her. Not her. She reprimanded herself severely for being so petty, for allowing herself to feel this hurt and, she had to admit, anger, when the important thing was to get Emma home and comfort her in whatever way worked.

As they gathered their personal belongings and got ready to leave, Mark pulled José aside. "Did they question her about the knife yet?"

"Yes. Last night."

"What did she say?"

"She said she bought that knife set here in Sevilla and there must be people all over town who have similar ones."

Mark nodded and shook José's hand, thanking him for his help.

They went straight to the Alfonso XIII and booked another room. Emma went to what was now her own room to rest, and Jennifer and Mark checked in to the new room together.

"Well, what do you think?" Jennifer asked as soon as the door closed behind them.

"I don't know. I'm worried. This knife business is not good."

"Anyone could have had a knife just like it. And the Spanish kid could have had it in his pocket and used it to get entry, just as Emma said. Especially if his friends say he would never carry a knife—then if he had one it would more likely be a kitchen knife than a switchblade, for example."

"But why would a nice kid who's a good student suddenly decide to put a kitchen knife in his pocket and rape another student? It doesn't make sense."

Jennifer had been pouring a drink from the bar, but now she put down the bottle and whirled around. Her voice was sharp. "What do you mean? You believe Emma, don't you?"

"I didn't say I don't believe her. I'm trying to think like a jury. Or a policeman."

"I don't know why. Obviously we don't know everything about this Spanish kid. We need to call our own investigator and not rely on the police."

Mark fished around in his pocket for the card José had given him. "Do you want to call him, or should I?"

"How long will you be here?" Jennifer asked.

"Just a few days. I have to get back to this case. Jerry can handle it for now, but I'll need to be there when it goes to court."

"Well, then, I guess I'd better be the one to call, since I'll clearly be the one to deal with him," she said coldly. "You'd better tell Emma."

"Jen, you know I have to finish this case. It's not my choice. Even if Emma doesn't understand that, I'd have thought you would."

She looked down. Her eyes filled with tears she had a hard time holding back. Her emotional state had been unbearably volatile since she'd arrived. She rubbed her eyes hard, and when she looked up they were red and moist.

"I do understand. I'm sorry. I just feel so worried," she said. "And so alone." She stopped fighting and let the tears come, sobbing as he took her in his arms.

She let herself be comforted, but she held on to a residual sense of anxiety, a gnawing feeling in her solar plexus. This was caused, she knew, by the horror of Emma's plight and worry about what the future would hold. But it was also something more, something she didn't expect: her own scary, vague sense of loss.

She looked at the card. "Roberto Ortiz," she read. "Investigationes Privadas." She reached for the phone.

CHAPTER 7

Roberto Ortiz was nothing like Jennifer had expected. She had formed her image of private detectives from stories and films, especially her favorites, which dated from the middle years of the twentieth century: Dashiell Hammett's Sam Spade, Mickey Spillane's Mike Hammer, and Raymond Chandler's Philip Marlowe. They were tough, straight-talking men who could sniff out deception like bloodhounds and didn't waste words.

But Roberto Ortiz didn't fit that mold. His face was almost feminine in its beauty—more Johnny Depp than Humphrey Bogart—and he was elegant in his dress and manners. He was soft-spoken and polite and seemed acutely sensitive to Jennifer's concerns. On top of that, he was a painter—a very good one, judging from a striking abstract work that hung in his waiting room with his signature on it.

She met him in his office a few days after Mark returned to the States. The upscale Avenida de la Constitución was not far from town hall. A perfect view of the Giralda was complemented by beautifully appointed, sleek modern furniture and a few Spanish and French antiques carefully placed by someone with a defined, spare aesthetic. It was late in the afternoon and he offered her coffee. She said she'd appreciate a Scotch, if he had one, and he opened an inlaid teak cabinet to reveal a well-stocked bar. He poured the Scotch into a leaded crystal glass and looked inquiringly at her. "Ice, please," she said, "and a little water." Taking a cup of coffee for himself, he sat down at his desk and gestured for her to sit opposite him.

"And now," he said in only slightly accented English, "perhaps you will tell me how I can help you, senora."

She told him. When she said she hoped he would reinterview the sources the police had contacted and find ones they hadn't, he nodded. "Of course, senora. That is what I do," he said. "I think you were wise to come to me. I will be able to help you in many ways. Do you speak Spanish?"

"No, I'm afraid not. I speak some French."

"Yes, that would perhaps be more helpful in Paris." He smiled, but she didn't smile back. He looked at her with apparent sympathy. "I understand how difficult this is for you, a mother whose daughter is charged with a terrible crime in a strange country, unable to communicate or even understand much of what is happening."

Jennifer was surprised at the direction he was taking. "I'm okay," she said, with a short, slightly embarrassed laugh. "I'm managing. And, you know, this isn't about me. It's about her. And, by the way, she hasn't been charged."

He got up to refill his coffee cup. "Ah, yes, senora. But I think she will be. And you must be ready for it."

Jennifer started to object, but he cut her off and spoke with quiet authority. "Let me be precise. I speak of you and your emotions because if I take this case, I will need them to be very controlled. From everything you've told me and from what I've read in the papers, this isn't going to go away quickly. You will need to be strong and you will need to do everything I tell you if we are to have success in helping your daughter."

She frowned. "I'm confused," she said. "I thought you were a private detective. Now you are sounding more like a lawyer."

He smiled. "Sí, comprendo. You have seen *The Maltese Falcon*, correct? An old film but a great one. And perhaps too you have seen *Columbo* on American television. I like very much this Columbo. I have known detectives like him."

Jennifer waited for him to continue. Her frown deepened.

"But I am different, senora. Think of me more as a case manager.

I work with the lawyer—José, in this case, and if I may say so, he is a very good choice—and we investigate, we do many investigations, but we also build a narrative that is plausible and different from the story the police will assemble. I will not promise to find this Algerian for you—to be frank, I doubt he exists—and I will not promise to find the real murderer. But if you do everything I tell you to, I will do my best to free your daughter—although for all I know she may in fact be guilty."

At this, Jennifer stiffened. "Of course she's not guilty. I believe her completely. She says the Algerian was there, so he was there, I assure you. You don't know her, but when you meet her you will see for yourself. You must see. How can you help to free her if you don't believe in her?"

"I don't believe things that are not proven, senora. If belief is what you seek, you must find a priest. There are many of them in Spain."

Jennifer was silent. For the first time, she felt a slight easing of the fear that had gripped her from the moment Emma had called. This man seemed to know what to do, and he seemed fearless.

"You said, 'If I take the case.' Is there a problem?"

"No. I don't think so."

"What do we do now?" she asked.

He smiled and walked to his filing cabinet, from which he withdrew a bound printed document containing several pages. He handed it to Jennifer.

"This is an employment contract," he said. "It is in Spanish, but I have included an English translation for you. You and your husband should read it. My terms are clearly stated. To begin, as a goodwill gesture, I ask for my first payment of five thousand euros in advance. This goes toward both salary and my expenses, which I will enumerate and give you weekly. After these formalities are concluded, I will begin."

Jennifer started to read.

"Excuse me, senora," Roberto said.

She looked up.

"I apologize, but I have another appointment. Would you please read this later and discuss it with your husband?"

She folded the papers and put them in her bag. "Yes, of course. But I would like you to start right away and my husband is not here. I will read the papers, and if we go forward, I will sign myself."

"As you like . . . May I ask why your husband is not here?"

She was about to answer when he added, "I have a little girl. If she was in trouble, I would be there with her." He spoke sadly, with quiet sincerity.

Jennifer bristled with the outrage one feels when someone says something one has thought but tried to stifle. "I'm sure you would try to be with her, as he has," she said in a cold tone. "Perhaps you think we are rich Americans. We are not. We are not poor, but we are not independently wealthy. My husband has to work to pay all these bills, including yours. And we have two other children who need at least one of us at home. I don't think it's right to find fault with him."

Roberto was contrite. "You are right, senora. I meant no harm. I apologize. I misspoke because of my own sadness." He waited for her to politely inquire what that was, but she was silent.

"I am divorced," he said finally. "My child lives with my former wife in another city. I find the separation very painful."

She resisted her natural impulse for compassion. She didn't want to swerve from her main concern. This man offered some hope, yet his manner was both peremptory and surprisingly intimate and, she thought, inappropriate. She put this down to cultural differences, but she was determined to stay strictly on an American business-only basis. "I'm sure it is," she murmured. Then she gathered her belongings, said good-bye, and told him she would be in touch very soon.

Jennifer went straight to the hotel to tell Emma that she had found someone who seemed like he could help them. She took the elevator to the third floor and knocked on the door of the room they had reverted to sharing after Mark left. Emma had been sleeping a lot lately, or just hanging around in her pajamas—signs, Jennifer knew, of depression.

Not that Jennifer blamed her, under the circumstances. Still . . . She used her key to let herself in, calling Emma's name as she entered. There was no sign of her daughter but rumpled sheets and some of her clothes flung around the room. At least Emma was awake, Jennifer thought, and was probably out getting a bite to eat. It would have been nice if she'd left a note, though.

She sat down in one of the comfortable armchairs. She had pulled out the contract, turned to the English translation, and started to read when she noticed that the hotel phone was flashing. The message was from José. He had bad news. The pathology report was completed. The investigators had determined that the victim's wounds could not possibly have been made by a person who fit the description Emma had given the police. They were pressing forward with the theory that Emma had invented the story of the Good Samaritan, that there was no Algerian. Along with the knife found in her kitchen, they felt they had enough to hold her. Jennifer took a deep breath and called José. He answered on the first ring.

"I got your message," she blurted as soon as she heard his voice. "But it doesn't make sense. It's all circumstantial. Maybe her description was wrong. She was traumatized; she can't be expected to have an accurate memory of what he looked like."

"We can argue that point in court, if necessary. But they have enough to suspect she is withholding evidence. They believe she knows more than she says. . . ." He paused, then continued quietly, "And there is another problem. The boy's parents have arrived from Madrid. In Spain, even if the police don't think they have enough evidence to press charges against a suspect, they must hold her and continue to investigate if the victim's family makes an accusation. Emma has already been picked up and is at the police station."

"Where are you?"

"I am with her. She is very upset. You should come quickly. And one more thing—the reporter for the *Diario* is here. Whatever she asks, don't answer."

Jennifer headed for the door but then stopped. She rummaged through her bag until she found Roberto's card and quickly dialed his number. "Habla Roberto," his recorded voice sounded. "Digame lo que quiera."

"Roberto, this is Mrs. Lewis. I haven't read your terms, but I agree to whatever they are. My daughter is in jail at the police station. I don't know what to do. Please, can you come?"

He picked up the phone. "I will meet you there, senora."

CHAPTER 8

When Jennifer got to the police station José and Raul were waiting for her, but Roberto had not yet arrived. José continued to fill her in. Emma was being held as a material witness who was a flight risk and ineligible for bail. The police now believed that she was covering for someone, probably her boyfriend. "They do not have a motive, of course," he explained, "since they still have not located the boyfriend, but they are speculating that Emma was cheating on him, that he walked in and found them in bed and killed him in a jealous rage."

At this point Jennifer interrupted, outraged. She was frankly astounded that the police would build this murderous fantasy out of such scant evidence, and she told him so. "Do they have even one shred of evidence to support this theory?" she asked. "It just sounds so cliché, like they've seen too many bad movies."

José allowed that they did not—at least not yet. But he pointed out that these scenarios were cliché because they often occurred. And there was something else, he offered with a sigh. They had discovered that the Spanish boy had gone to the bank that day and withdrawn one thousand euros in cash. It was the last night of the *feria* and his family sponsored one of the many tents, or *casetas*, that had sprung up on the fairgrounds illuminated with thousands of brilliant lights. According to his roommate, he had been asked to buy supplies and pay some of the workers. He definitely had the money in his pocket when he left to go out that night, his roommate said. His pocket was empty when the police searched his body. When Jennifer countered that he must have spent it, José said the police checked and none of the supplies had been paid for and the workers still awaited their pay.

"He could have lost it," Jennifer countered. "He could have spent it on something else."

"Si, senora. Or it could have been stolen."

Jennifer paused. "What are you saying? You don't think Emma had anything to do with this, do you?"

"What matters is what the police think. And for the moment they are not saying anything about that. Their first priority is to find her boyfriend"—he scanned his notebook—"this Paco Romero, and they believe Emma knows where he is and refuses to tell them. They will hold her and try to convince her to change her mind. As I said from the beginning, if you can encourage her to tell what she knows, it will help her."

Jennifer felt hopelessly frustrated. They all insisted on seeing Emma as a liar at the least and possibly much worse. Even her lawyer seemed to have that mind-set. "She doesn't *refuse*," she practically shouted. "She doesn't *know* where he is."

José suppressed his obvious discomfort, but pressed on. "We have to assume that some of what she says may not be true. According to the police, she was seen with him at the *feria* hours before the murder. This directly contradicts her claim that she hadn't seen him for a few days."

Jennifer was unfazed. "I don't know about that. Who said she was with him? Why believe that person over Emma? And I'm sure she'd love to know where he is now. Don't you think she wishes he were here, that she feels abandoned by him, upset that he doesn't come back?"

José asked Jennifer to sit down, but she was too nervous to comply. He lowered his voice and spoke kindly. "I think she should not expect that kind of consideration from this man. He is not perhaps what she is used to. He is . . . we call it here . . . *un golfo*."

Jennifer looked perplexed. José's unmasked sympathy made her even more nervous. "What is that, please?"

"I think in English you say a thug. A bad egg. Trouble."

"What? How? What are you talking about?"

"The police have investigated him, starting with his arrest record. He is older—thirty-five, to be exact, and though he used to be a student and is still well-known among them, he dropped out and never completed university."

Jennifer waited.

"He sells drugs, senora," José blurted. "Bad drugs—heroin, cocaine, ecstasy, methamphetamine."

Jennifer could feel an almost physical sense of dizziness but pushed past it.

"Emma certainly would not have known that, or she wouldn't be with him," she said, almost to herself, sitting down heavily. She turned to José, who had sat down beside her. "She is against drug use of any kind," she continued. She spoke fiercely, running her sentences together, gaining speed as she talked. "She was the president of a club she founded in high school. They called themselves the Perfect Squares. They only ate organic foods and avoided all drugs, even medicine. I had to fight with her to take an aspirin if she had a headache. That's why this is so ridiculous, you see, she couldn't have—"

"I believe you, senora," José interrupted with a sigh. "But be that as it may, her boyfriend was a drug dealer, and she and everyone else knew it." He tentatively put his hand on her shoulder and said, "Children grow up. Sometimes it doesn't turn out the way we thought."

She shook off his hand and stood up. "You don't understand. I know my daughter," she snapped. "I need to see her. Where is she?"

She stormed over to the front desk to ask if she could visit Emma. Just as she got there, Roberto walked in. In that moment, before she could stop herself, not knowing why and certainly not intending to, she ran to him and burst into tears.

"No, senora," he said firmly. "This is not the way." He turned to José, who had followed her and was standing by helplessly. The men exchanged exasperated looks.

Jennifer, embarrassed, pulled herself together. "I'm sorry. I don't usually behave this way."

"It's all right, senora," Roberto said in a loud voice. "Everyone understands a mother's tears." He lowered his voice so only she could hear him. "But you must control them for the time being. Can you do that?"

She looked down and nodded.

He turned to José. "What has happened?"

"The girl is being interviewed. Mrs. Lewis wants to see her."

"Of course. Is that a problem?"

"No."

"Good." He led Jennifer back to the waiting room, then withdrew for a few private words with José before both men returned to Jennifer's side.

"She is in an interrogation room. An officer will bring you to her," Roberto said. "You must convince her to cooperate."

"She is cooperating," Jennifer protested. "Just because she isn't telling them what they want to hear doesn't mean she isn't telling the truth."

"I understand that," José said. He turned to Roberto. "But she refuses to talk about her boyfriend. If we are to help her, he must be found."

"And if she doesn't know where he is?" Jennifer also addressed Roberto.

"She refuses to acknowledge that she saw him the night of the murder," Raul added. "The police have spoken to several students who saw them together in a bar earlier that night."

Jennifer had a hazy memory of Julia saying something like that.

"I'll talk to her. Please, let me see her."

When Jennifer entered the interrogation room, Emma was sitting at the table, her head resting on her arms. She looked up and her face brightened. "Mom," she breathed with relief. "I'm so glad you're here."

In spite of the gravity of the situation, Jennifer felt relief at those words. She sat down next to her daughter and tentatively stroked her arm. "Of course I'm here, darling. I'll always be here."

Now it was Emma's turn to break down. "I'm so sorry, Mama, for the way I've been acting. I've just been so scared and worried, and I thought you and Daddy must be so angry at me, so disappointed in me, I didn't know what to do." She was crying so hard, it was difficult to catch all her words.

"It's okay. It's okay, I understand," Jennifer said, pulling her close and hugging her.

"No, it isn't okay. It will never be okay again."

"Whatever happened, we'll face it together. All of us. But you have to tell me everything so I can help you."

Emma pulled away. "I've told you. I've told everyone. They say someone who is short couldn't have made this wound. I don't know. I didn't measure him. He was there." She burst into a new flood of tears. "Why doesn't anyone believe me?"

"Forget that, Emma. Let's just talk about Paco."

Emma stopped crying. "Why?" She sniffled and wiped her eyes. "That's their obsession. He had nothing to do with any of this."

"I know. I believe you. But we need to find him. They say you deny seeing him the day of the murder, but others—"

Emma interrupted. "It wasn't murder. It was self-defense."

"Yes. Well, whatever it was that ended that boy's life. They know you did see Paco that day. Others saw you together. Don't you understand that if you lie about that, they think you lied about everything?"

Emma looked down. Her nails had been painted blue and the polish was peeling. She seemed to be studying them and concentrating on using the thumbnail of one hand to scrape off the remaining polish on the other. She didn't speak.

"Listen, Emma, I've found a really good person to help us. He's a detective but also a kind of trial manager who knows how to act and what to do. He'll find other people to talk to and try to verify your side of the story. But everyone is helpless if you don't tell us how to find Paco. If he's not involved, as you say, what are you afraid of?"

Emma sighed deeply. She spoke so softly Jennifer could barely hear her. "I don't actually know where he is. I've e-mailed him, but he hasn't written back."

"Did you tell the police that?"

"No."

"Will you tell them now? And will you tell them the truth about your relationship and the fact that you were with him earlier that night?"

Emma shot a sharp look at her mother, then stood up and paced the room. "I wasn't with him that night. There's a lot you don't know, Mom. A lot you'll never be able to understand. It's going to start coming out and I know they'll put the worst spin on it. Will you try to not judge me too harshly? Will you take my side?"

"Of course I will. But what are you referring to? How bad can it be?"

"I can't tell you. You'll hate me."

"I'll never hate you. Tell me, Emma. Whatever it is, it's better if I hear it from you."

"I can't. I really can't. Not yet. But if you hear bad things, please remember that I didn't do anything for bad reasons." Her eyes brimmed again with tears. "I'm not a bad person, Mom. I swear I'm not. You know who I am. And Paco isn't bad either. You've got to believe me."

Jennifer was frightened. "I trust you. But you need to tell me what to expect. I already know more than you think I do. He's a drug dealer, right? He dropped out of school and makes money by selling drugs to students. Is that what you don't want me to know?" She deliberately kept her voice even and, she hoped, nonjudgmental.

Rather than helping clear the air, this seemed to make Emma angry. Her voice rose and her body stiffened. "You see? I knew you wouldn't understand. You can't even say it in a neutral way. Just listen to your voice. You make him sound so evil, like he takes advantage of poor innocent students."

Now Jennifer was angry. "Well, what does he do, Emma? How else can you characterize what he does?"

"These students are not little kids. They know exactly what they're doing and what they want. You know these kids that come here from all over Europe? They come on scholarships; they're called Erasmus scholars. You know what everyone calls them? They call them *Orgasmus*—that's a play on their word for orgasm, in case you missed it, because they are so promiscuous and wild and take so many drugs. If it wasn't Paco, it would be someone else they'd get their drugs from. And Paco doesn't do it for himself. He uses the money for good causes— to help poor people, people who can't find jobs and can't feed their families."

"Yes, so you said." Jennifer wanted to know how deeply Emma was involved, but she realized that wouldn't be productive. What was important now was for Emma to lead them to him. The rest could come later.

"I think I understand," she said slowly. "Is this what you were worried we would find out?"

"Partly."

"Partly? What else? Please tell me. Trust me, Emma."

Emma sat down. She took a deep breath and let it out through her mouth, making a slight whistling noise.

"I can't, Mom. I'm sorry. You'd better go now. But I promise I'll tell the police what I can."

Jennifer wanted to make one last plea before leaving. "Emma, I hope you know what you're facing. You want to protect him and that's loyal and I admire the impulse. But are you willing to go to jail here, in Spain, for years, for something you didn't do? If Paco is innocent and he is a good person, he should be here to help you. If he's guilty and he's a good person, he shouldn't let you take the blame for his crime. Either way, he should be here."

"Guilty of what, Mom?" Emma shouted in frustration. "I keep telling you he wasn't even there."

Jennifer tried to calm her. "Okay, I believe you. But the police need to speak to him. And they'll find him eventually. If you help them, it will help you."

Emma seemed to have collected herself. "I love you, Mom," she murmured. "But I think you'd better go now. Don't worry about me. I know what I'm doing. I'll be okay."

She turned around and faced the opposite wall. Jennifer kissed the back of her head. Speaking softly into her ear, she tenderly stroked her hair. She begged her again to talk to the police more openly and reminded her to first talk to José and give him leads that would help Roberto in his investigation. Without turning around, Emma nodded her agreement and reached behind to squeeze her mother's hand. Jennifer walked slowly and reluctantly toward the door, but before she got there Emma was on her feet and running to her, hugging her and resting her head for a moment on her chest. Jennifer put her arm around her and held her close in a familiar gesture of comfort. How many times in how many circumstances had she held her child in this way to help heal hurts large and small? This physical act set off a rush of sense memory and maternal protectiveness so strong she felt it as pain. She left much more worried than before but also, somehow, less empty and confused. She knew what to do. Emma was back and she needed her mother. That, at least, was a familiar dynamic. Jennifer couldn't disappoint her.

CHAPTER 9

After visiting Emma, Jennifer returned to the hotel to call Mark and fill him in. He was upset, but not completely surprised, to learn that Emma's boyfriend was a drug dealer. He could see how she would be vulnerable to someone who played upon her naïveté and what he called her "middle-class American guilt" to convince her he was doing it to help the poor. "Maybe she wasn't ready, wasn't mature enough, to be on her own, Jen. We shouldn't have let her go."

"That's taking an unfair, negative view," Jennifer said. "She has always had a big heart and a strong sense of injustice and it sounds like she was taken advantage of and misled by this guy. But how could we know? Lots of kids her age travel to Europe in their junior year. Emma seemed like the perfect candidate." She reminded him that they had been proud of Emma because of her sensitivity to the needs of less fortunate people. "Remember when she got involved in the Innocence Project?" she asked. "And how she always believed everyone who claimed to be unjustly convicted?"

"I know," he said. "I used to think that was sweet. It looks more worrisome given what you've just told me."

She was unhappy with the direction the conversation was taking. She felt uneasy after hanging up and wondered what she should do. It was 12:45, too early for lunch, which usually started closer to 2:00, and a bit late for *aperitivos*, the midmorning snack. She left the hotel and wandered. She passed a café and stopped in, taking a table by the window. Glancing around, she saw a woman eating what looked like strips of deep-fried dough, which she dipped in hot chocolate. When the waitress approached, Jennifer asked for the same. They were called churros, she was told. When they came, they were sizzling hot, covered in powdered sugar, and delicious.

Maybe it was the sugar, and maybe it was taking a moment for herself, but her mood improved and she started to think of her next step. She wanted to do something more to help Emma's case. She remembered Emma's concerned friend from the Princeton program and took out her cell phone to check the contact information Julia had e-mailed to her. There it was: Julia Zimmerman. She lived in Triana on Calle Betis, the same student-friendly neighborhood just over the Triana Bridge that she had visited with Emma. Julia had included two phone numbers; Jennifer randomly punched in one of them.

"Diga," she heard someone answer.

She didn't recognize the voice, so she asked for Julia, and when she explained who she was, the speaker switched to unaccented English. "I'm her roommate," she said. "You've reached my cell phone. Julia's in class, but I know she really wants to talk to you. The class is almost over. Do you have her number?"

Jennifer thanked her and said she did.

"Mrs. Lewis, my name is Melanie. I, umm, I also know Emma. I'm really sorry about what happened."

"Don't worry, dear. I'm sure this is all a terrible mistake. Emma will be back in school in a few days."

There was an uncomfortable pause before Melanie murmured a soft "I hope so" and hung up.

Jennifer immediately tapped in the other cell number and heard a whispered hello. The class was about to end and Julia suggested they meet at the university. Since Jennifer's hotel was just next door and Jennifer was eager to see where Emma had been in school, she agreed to meet in front of the fountain in the courtyard.

As she stepped out of the air-conditioned café, the jolt of the hot, humid air and glaring sunshine was softened by the pale pink and amber tones of the surrounding buildings and tempered by the pervasive smell of orange blossoms and frangipani. She inhaled deeply. How had she not noticed that fragrance before? It was similar to the oleander she had remarked upon, but even sweeter. She walked until she reached the outermost university courtyard, pushed open a heavy engraved metal door, and entered an adjoining courtyard. There were several students walking past or resting on the edge of the central fountain, some reading books, others chatting to each other in an animated way. She noticed one young woman sitting apart.

Julia was petite with delicate features and wore her hair, so dark brown it appeared almost black, in a long ponytail. She was dressed in jeans and a T-shirt on which SEVILLA was printed in large block letters over the profile of a bull, a tourist getup that surprised Jennifer because Emma, by contrast, was more interested in trying to fit in with the locals. Julia slipped gracefully off the fountain's edge and met her halfway.

"Mrs. Lewis?" she asked in English. Her pale skin looked as if it had never been touched by the sun, accentuating her dark eyes, which were heavily made up with black liner and mascara, immediately commanding attention. Jennifer greeted her and wondered aloud where they could talk privately.

"I live in Triana," Julia said. "Have you been there?" Jennifer said she had but would be happy to go again. "Maybe you'd like to see my apartment," Julia offered. "We could talk there."

"That would be lovely," Jennifer said. "But I don't want you to go to any trouble."

"It's no trouble, Mrs. Lewis. But the place is kind of messy. I hope you won't mind."

Jennifer laughed. "No, not at all. I'm used to that." She felt a pang of nostalgia remembering the mess Emma and her friends used to leave in their frequent sleepovers at home. She had loved her relationship with Emma's high school friends in Philadelphia. She was the mother they all talked to, the one they thought would understand what their parents didn't, the one they told their problems to. Although Julia was a new Princeton friend, not someone Jennifer had met before, she could easily have been one of those girls. Pretty, polite, intelligent, they had come and gone over the years. After all, most of their mothers hadn't been around as much; they were busy with their jobs. It was left to Jennifer to have the neighborhood kids over for cookies and milk after school when they were little, and to provide the safe hangout when they were teenagers. She had taken great pride in their affection for her and she knew that Emma had too. She was about to ask her where she was from, but Julia had started talking about the university.

"While we're here, maybe you'd just like to look around a bit," she said. "This is where we have all our classes. You know, this building was constructed in the eighteenth century. It's an old tobacco factory. At one time, Spain had a big monopoly on manufacturing tobacco and their industry was centered here. They say it was Bizet's inspiration for *Carmen*. But maybe it came from a book about that period that was set in Seville." She paused, politely ignoring Jennifer's silence. "When we first arrived, Emma and I used to talk a lot about *Carmen* and the passion of that story and say now that we were here, we could understand it. Something about the heat and the direct quality of the light inspires passion, color, vibrancy; we all felt it, feel it still. When I saw these beautiful Spanish women dressed in their gorgeous flamenco costumes during the *feria*, I couldn't help imagining Carmen right here, maybe in this very courtyard." She gestured toward the fountain, where students still gathered with their books, chattering animatedly.

Jennifer smiled stiffly and Julia seemed embarrassed. She abruptly changed the subject, reminding Jennifer that Triana was about a twenty-minute walk and asking if she wanted to take a tram. Jennifer said she could use a good walk, so the two set out, passing the Alfonso XIII and the fragrant Jardines de Cristina and walking along the bank of the river on the Paseo Alcalde Marqués del Contadero until they reached the Triana Bridge. Crossing it, they came to the Plaza del

Altozano, and Jennifer saw again the staircase caught in the photo she had seen in the newspaper. There Emma was, sitting on the steps with friends, holding a beer and turning to laugh just as someone snapped her picture. A few more streets and they were at the Calle Virgen del Valle, where Julia lived. Jennifer marveled at the lovely brick alleyways that twisted and turned, and Julia pointed out how many of the window boxes of the cream-colored houses were festooned with flowers. Occasionally they were able to peer into a space between buildings or through an open doorway, which revealed a beautiful courtyard hiding behind the facade.

Julia finally stopped in front of one of these buildings and entered the front door with her key. Inside was a small two-bedroom apartment furnished with the kind of inexpensive student furniture characteristic of young people everywhere. Julia offered her a cup of coffee and, not wanting to be rude, Jennifer accepted. As Julia busied herself boiling water for Nescafé, Jennifer looked around. This was the kind of lodging she had pictured Emma in. There were books scattered about the table and floor and posters of flamenco dancers and a Miró print taped on the wall. The sink was piled high with unwashed dishes, but otherwise it wasn't as messy as she'd expected.

"It's a lovely place," she said, as Julia offered her a chair. "It's so different from Emma's apartment. . . . I . . ."

"Emma and I actually shared it for a while," Julia said, spooning the Nescafé into two tall mugs, "until . . ." She trailed off.

"Until when?"

"Until she moved in with Paco."

"Ah."

Julia produced a packet of biscuits. "Has Paco come back yet?" she asked.

"No. The police are looking for him. Do you have any idea where he might be?"

Julia poured the water into the mugs. One had a broken handle. She gave the undamaged one to Jennifer. "Sugar or milk?"

"Neither, thank you."

Julia sat down across from her. "Mrs. Lewis, I want to do whatever I can to help Emma. I didn't know her very well at Princeton, but we became friends once we were here. I don't know how much you know about Paco. . . ."

"I know a bit," she said. "And none of it good. What do you know about him?"

"He's an older guy. He's kind of a political activist."

"I've heard he's a drug dealer."

Julia shifted uncomfortably. "Well, I think he did sell some drugs to finance his activities."

"I see. And did Emma take them?"

"No. I don't think so," she said hastily. "Emma got involved with his causes. It kind of overshadowed everything else. She said he opened her eyes. He showed her how much the poor people were suffering, especially in his village. It made her feel guilty to be who she was. She wanted to help, and, you know, they became kind of a couple."

"So I've heard. When did she move in with him?"

"A few months ago." Julia paused, carefully choosing her words. "Look, I've been wondering what to tell you, but I think everything is going to come out, and I'd better tell you the truth."

Jennifer stiffened. "Yes, please."

"She dropped out of school. She moved in with him and stopped going to class and worked with him full-time."

"Oh, God," Jennifer murmured, biting her upper lip. She collected herself quickly, however, and tried not to show the extent of her anxiety, for fear Julia would stop talking. "Worked with him? How? What did he do?"

"I don't know, Mrs. Lewis." She was staring at the table, picking off some dried syrup with her fingernail. "I think he just sold drugs."

Jennifer nodded slowly. It was getting harder to hide her agitation.

"Look, Mrs. Lewis, Emma believed in him. She thought he was this kind of Robin Hood. He was trying to form an activist group among the students to influence politics. He wanted to lead a raid on supermarkets—stealing the food and giving it to the poor. They tried to organize the students and got a few, but nothing came of it. She thought that kind of thing was more important than anything she could learn in school. I argued with her. We all did. But she only listened to him and she felt she was doing the right thing."

"The right thing," Jennifer repeated as if by rote. "And now someone is dead and she is in jail."

"In jail?" Julia was indignant. "Why? She was almost raped. I'm sorry that kid got killed, but how can they blame her for that?"

"I don't know," Jennifer answered. She hadn't touched her Nescafé or the biscuits Julia had put on the table, but she stood to go. "Thank you, Julia. I need to go now and try to make sense of all this. You've been a big help."

Julia walked her to the door. "I'm so sorry, Mrs. Lewis. I hope I did the right thing telling you. I know this will all work out. Please let me know if I can do anything to help."

"Maybe it would help Emma if you'd visit her."

Julia hesitated. "I don't know. We weren't on great terms recently."

"I see." She opened the door. "Thank you," she said again, and walked back into the bright perfumed air.

CHAPTER 10

Was this what Emma had meant when she said Jennifer would hear things about her that she wouldn't understand? Well, she was right. She didn't understand. How could Emma be so stupid? How could she, a girl who was so smart and so seemingly together, have gotten herself into this much trouble? What the hell was she doing with a drug dealer? Hadn't they talked about drugs a thousand times? Hadn't she assured her mother that she would never use them or hang out with people who did? She should have been like this Julia—living in a pretty apartment on a cobbled street and studying at the university. Instead she was in jail, for God's sake, and her Robin Hood boyfriend was missing.

She tried to calm herself. This was all peripheral. The biggest problem was that a man had tried to rape her daughter and somehow, thankfully, a stranger had saved her, but unless they found him, her daughter was implicated in a murder. But where was he? Was there anything more they could do? If he would just step forward, she could take Emma home and they could speak to her about the foolish mistake she had made by getting involved with this Paco character and dropping out of school. Maybe they ought to consult a psychologist. She was so innocent, Jennifer thought, softening again toward her daughter. She believed everyone was as good as she was. But how had that led to this?

She walked back to the hotel in a rising panic, not paying attention to where she was going and finally realizing she was lost. She took out her map but couldn't concentrate and kept taking wrong turns, which led her farther away from her hotel. Finally, she gave up and hailed a cab. When she got to her room, she sat on her bed and stared at the wall for several minutes, trying to gather her thoughts. She called Mark, but June, his secretary, said he was in court. She wanted to talk to Eric and Lily, but she knew they were in school. She paced around the room. She hadn't eaten anything since she'd stopped for churros, and she was hungry, but she didn't feel like going to a restaurant. She turned on the television, looking for the English-language channel. There was nothing she wanted to see—just a cooking show—so she turned it off. Finally, she picked up the phone and called Roberto.

His voice mail answered and she left a message: "Roberto, this is Jennifer Lewis. I really need to talk to you. It's urgent. Please call back at the hotel."

She heard a click. "No need, senora. I'm here." He said.

"Do you always screen your calls?"

"Yes."

"I have just met with a friend and classmate of my daughter. I have heard very distressing news. I'd like to talk to you if you have time."

There was a pause as he checked his calendar.

"I can meet you in two hours. Would you like to come to my office?"

"Yes, sure, wherever it is convenient."

"Bueno. I will see you at five."

She had two hours to kill. She freshened up and left the hotel again. At a kiosk, she bought a copy of the *International New York Times*, then stopped at an outdoor café for a coffee and some jamón serrano. Though she had trouble concentrating on the news, she scanned the paper to satisfy herself that there was no story about Emma. Studying the crowd at the café and watching the passing pedestrians as they went about their lives, she imagined stories about who they were and where they were going. Thus the time passed, and looking at her watch she saw it was time to leave.

Someone was with Roberto when she arrived, so she sat in the waiting room for fifteen minutes, until a fashionable woman dressed entirely in black and exuding a sense of money and privilege exited. Jennifer wondered if she was hiring Roberto to find out if her husband was having an affair. He closed his door after the woman left and re-opened it a few minutes later to invite Jennifer in. Having heard the urgency in her voice when she phoned, he was prepared. He spoke be fore she did.

"I think perhaps you have discovered that your daughter had left school, am I correct?"

"You knew? And did you know that she had moved in with her boyfriend?"

"Sí, senora."

She felt a flash of anger. "And when were you going to inform me?"

"When I felt it was the right time," he said calmly. "I have many things to tell you and that is perhaps not the most important."

"Maybe I should be the judge of that."

"If you were an adequate judge, you would not need me. Come, this is wasting time. I will tell you what I know." He got up and poured himself a glass of sherry, offering her one, which she declined.

"Do you know what the *feria* is?" he asked.

"Not exactly," she said impatiently. "Some kind of traditional celebration?"

"Yes. It is a ten-day fiesta that we celebrate every year about two weeks after Easter, our *semana santa*, or holy week. This is a tradition throughout Andalusia—in Granada, Córdoba, all over the south of Spain. There is a great parade of horses with caballeros—these are men in traditional costumes demonstrating their riding skills—and bull-fighters on their way to the ring. The fairgrounds are covered in fabu-lously decorated brightly colored private tents—we call them *casetas*—and there are more than a thousand of them. They belong to the wealthy families of Sevilla who host the private parties and some community and religious organizations. The parties spill into the streets all night and end up in the *casetas*, which you can enter only by invitation. The women dress in flamenco costumes, the men wear *trajes cortos*, short jackets and tight pants and boots, and everyone dances *sevillanas* and drinks sherry or wine. This fair, this *feria*, has been going on for about a hundred and fifty years."

Jennifer interrupted. "Look, I'm sorry, and I don't mean to be rude. I wish I were here as a tourist and could appreciate these customs and traditions. But I'm here for my daughter, and I've just learned some disturbing news about her. Can we please talk about that?"

Roberto smiled. "I understand your impatience. But trust me. This concerns you. Please allow me to continue."

Jennifer nodded.

"The Spanish boy who was killed—Rodrigo Pérez—is a member of a very wealthy, important old Sevilla family. He grew up in Almeria, where the father worked, but his roots are here. They put up and host a grand *caseta* every year. Their son was killed on the last night of the *feria*. He had over a thousand euros in his pocket to pay some of the staff and expenses. When his body was found in your daughter's apartment, his pockets were empty. The police believe he was robbed."

Jennifer looked up quickly. "Yes, I have already been told this. But I've been thinking. Maybe the Algerian immigrant who helped Emma is the one who took the money; isn't that possible? Maybe that's why he doesn't come forward."

"At this point, anything is possible. The police don't know. The boy could have been robbed before he got to Emma's *piso*. He could have lost it. What they know is that he never paid the staff or the bills and the money disappeared. It is possible Emma knows something about this."

"Have they asked her?"

"Yes. She says she knows nothing."

Jennifer shifted in her chair. "Well, that's that, then. She would have been so shaken by the whole experience and by the fight and the murder that she wouldn't have noticed if the Algerian had taken the money. He might never turn up. If he had enough money to go away, maybe he went back to Algeria."

Roberto stared at her for what felt like a long time without speaking. "Perhaps," he said finally.

"I would like that glass of sherry," Jennifer said. "I'll go to see Emma again tomorrow so I can ask her myself. She wouldn't lie to me."

Roberto seemed lost in thought. Jennifer was fidgety. She downed the last of the sherry, asked for another, and got one.

"Emma claims she didn't see Paco the night of the murder," Roberto said slowly. "She says she was out in the streets with some friends and they confirm this. But we have found several other students who swear they saw her at a bar with Paco earlier that night. Why do you think she would lie about this?"

Jennifer had been staring at the swirls in the carpet. Her mind was wandering to Lily, whose practice college boards were today. First she wondered how Lily had done on them and if, without her there, Mark had gotten her to study. And then she felt how small, how unimportant that was compared to what her eldest child was now enduring. And Eric? Was he missing her? Did he feel abandoned? Her thoughts shifted again. What if the American papers got hold of this story? How would the kids at home react? How would Mark deal with their friends? And what about her parents, heroically holding down the fort in Philadelphia? How would they feel if this terrible mess became public? And what about Princeton? Would they expel Emma?

"Mrs. Lewis?" Roberto interrupted her thoughts. "Did you hear me?"

She looked up sharply. "I'm sorry. What did you say?"

"I asked you why Emma would say she didn't see Paco the night of the murder if she did."

She snapped to attention. "I don't know. I don't think the word of a few drunken kids on party night can be taken so seriously. But there is something I've been wondering. I mean, why is Paco missing? Maybe Emma contacted him somehow after the boy was killed to ask for his help. Maybe he took the Algerian somewhere to hide him. Maybe that's why Paco isn't here now and no one can find him."

Roberto considered this. "That is certainly possible," he said. He thought for a moment, then got up and withdrew a sheet of paper with some notes he had taken from a pile on his desk, handing it to Jennifer. "We will know very soon."

She couldn't read the Spanish, and she looked up, confused. "How?" she asked.

"He will tell us. The police have located him. He will arrive in Sevilla tomorrow."

CHAPTER 11

Roberto explained that there would be no information to be gleaned that day. The police would book Paco and start interrogating him, but they would not share any of what he said until they were ready. Roberto assumed Paco would have a lawyer, probably one assigned by the court. José could find out who it was and perhaps they could talk to him, but not until the next day at the earliest. For the moment, there was nothing to do but wait.

"And eat, of course," Roberto said. "Why not join me for dinner? It will be better than pacing around your room and calling room service, no?"

Jennifer felt grateful. "Yes, much better. Thank you. But please don't feel obligated. I mean, if you have something else to do . . ."

"If I had something else to do, I wouldn't have suggested it," he said, smiling. "I would be delighted to dine with you for the same reasons you are glad to join me: I too need distraction and would welcome not moping in my apartment and eating alone."

She knew it was a cue for her to ask why, but she assumed she knew: His marriage had broken up and his daughter wasn't with him. He had mentioned all that the first time she met him, and it seemed clear he needed to talk to someone about it. She didn't follow up with the expected question, but thought that if it came up again later, perhaps she would.

"Besides," he said, "we have several other issues to discuss about this case. It will be more congenial to have that conversation over dinner."

She nodded. It was 6:00 P.M.—still the afternoon by Spanish standards—so she returned to the Alfonso XIII by taxi, determined to get some rest before meeting him at the designated restaurant. He had suggested 10:00, but she persuaded him that 9:30 would be better—she still wasn't used to these late Spanish hours, she said—and he had acquiesced. At the hotel, she kicked off her shoes and lay down on the bed. She closed her eyes and tried to nap, but sleep wouldn't come. She tried counting backward from one hundred—a strategy that rarely worked—and it was as unsuccessful as usual. She finally gave up and phoned Mark to tell him about Paco. She used her cell phone, and although she stepped into the bathroom and turned on the faucet to avoid being overheard, she did it self-consciously and felt slightly foolish and paranoid. She reached his office, but his secretary told her he had just left for a lunch appointment, so she sent him a quick e-mail and promised to fill him in as soon as she learned anything new.

She was about to put her phone away, but thought better of it and punched in the cell number of her closest friend, Suzie Berenstein. She was going to tell her that she'd lied in her e-mail—that everything wasn't fine, in fact nothing was and she was worried and afraid and needed her. She was going to swear her to secrecy. She was sure Suzie would keep her confidence—she always had over the years, everything from her doubts before marrying Mark to her suspicion a few years ago that he was having an affair. That suspicion had turned out to be baseless. He was just going through a difficult time at work, he'd said, and had withdrawn from her in a palpable way, but talking it through with Suzie had helped her see that she needed to try to bridge the distance between them and restore some of their former intimacy. She'd been so tied up with the kids, so centered on them that naturally she and Mark had drifted apart a bit, Suzie had suggested. Jennifer had agreed, but she didn't worry too much about it at the time. Their children were doing so well, and their shared pride in them would sustain their marriage too, she had believed. There'd be time to work on their relationship when there was just the two of them left, she'd decided, imagining the day when even little Eric would go off to college and her daily mothering would come to an end.

She'd promised Mark not to talk to others about Emma's predicament, but it was simply too hard, with him not here and Emma acting so strangely, to go through this without Suzie's help. Besides, she thought, Suzie was Emma's godmother. She had a right to know. The phone rang a long time, but there was no answer, so she left a message: "Suze, it's me. I need to talk to you. I haven't been honest. I'm in Spain with Emma, but she's not fine and neither am I. Please call me. My cell works here."

Mark still hadn't called back when it was time for her to leave to meet Roberto. She'd told him that she'd fill him in tomorrow, she knew, but she still felt he should have called. He should be calling all the time, she thought, not just for information but to share this experience with her, to console her and shore her up. After all, she was here and he was in Philadelphia. She had to live with the day-to-day developments and both her own and Emma's worry, anger, and frustration.

She was glad she was going out for dinner. She showered, changed into a navy blue sleeveless dress, did her makeup, and left her room, taking the elevator down to the lobby, where she asked the doorman to get her a cab. She had written the name and address of the restaurant on a piece of paper and she gave this to the driver, who nodded and stepped on the gas.

Roberto was already there when she arrived; the hostess showed her to his table. He sprang up to hold her chair. He had already ordered a bottle of Marqués de Riscal rioja, and he filled her glass. She scanned the menu, suddenly feeling slightly ill at ease.

She chose fish—the *merluza*—as did he. After the waitress took the order, Roberto leaned forward slightly.

"Senora, I must talk to you about what may be a delicate subject. It is the media."

Jennifer looked puzzled.

"You do not read Spanish, so you have not perhaps followed it, but every day there is a story about this affair."

He opened his briefcase and extracted several copies of the *Diario*. Each had front-page headlines about the death of the Spanish boy, who was the son, after all, of a prominent Seville family and therefore a major local story. On the jump page there was always the same picture of Emma, the one she'd used for her application to the Seville program, looking serious and beautiful. He read two of the articles aloud. Each included a plea for the Algerian to show himself and a promise to support his immigration appeal.

"This was the way they covered it until now," he said. Then he pulled out that day's paper. There was a front-page photo of Emma dressed in a low-cut tight-fitting black minidress and stiletto heels, her weight on her left leg, with her hip jutting out over it. Her lips were parted in a provocative expression. It was clear even in black-and-white that she was heavily made up, with dark lipstick and black eyeliner.

"Oh, my God. What is this? She looks like a . . ."

"Like a *puta*. I know."

"A prostitute. That's what she looks like."

"Yes, that's why they printed it. The headline says, 'Innocent American?' The story says, 'This is the "innocent" American who claims our Spanish honors student tried to rape her.'" He continued to read to himself and then looked up. "It says that the picture shows a side of the American—they keep referring to her as *la americana*—that makes her story of the Spaniard's actions suspect." He turned the page, leafing through the paper to see if there was anything else. "There is an interview with Rodrigo Pérez's parents telling what a fine boy their son was and accusing Emma of seducing him, robbing, and killing him herself."

Roberto handed Jennifer the paper and she stared at the picture of Emma in disbelief. "I don't understand. Where did they get this? Where did it come from?" She put the paper down and looked pleadingly at Roberto. "Look, I understand the parents of the boy. How could I not?

This is a tragedy for everyone, and of course they can't believe their son is capable of trying to rape someone. And they've endured a terrible, tragic loss. But their conclusion about Emma is wrong. You have to believe me."

Roberto didn't respond.

He thinks I'm pathetic, Jennifer thought. He thinks we all are.

But Roberto was just planning his next move. Finally he looked at her. "We need to speak to Emma. She must explain this picture so we can respond to it. Clearly there is a good deal more she hasn't told you. They have stopped access to her until they finish questioning Paco. We'll have to wait until tomorrow. I will accompany you there in the morning. I'm afraid you may find press and television reporters at the police station. Remember that you will not speak to them or answer any of their questions. I will be with you and help you pass through the crowd."

"The crowd?"

"Probably. You must tell your husband to come immediately."

"I have already told him."

What she had feared had happened. Now surely the story would get out beyond Spain. How long before the American media picked it up and it became a circus with them, all of them, in the center ring? "I won't be able to bear it," she murmured.

"You will. You must."

She felt a wave of anger. "That's very easy to say."

"Easy to say, yes. Easy to do, no. I know that."

She closed her eyes and tried to collect herself. "I'd like a drink," she said.

They ate dinner and finished the bottle of rioja. Jennifer, who drank rarely and was already pretty far past her limit, asked for another glass, and Roberto ordered another bottle.

"It's so strange," she said. "I always thought I knew Emma so well, as if I was inside her head, anticipating her needs and desires and mostly, to be honest, trying to satisfy them, to help her along, and so proud of how she was doing. And, I'll admit it, proud of myself too, crediting my mothering at least partly for her success. I mean, I didn't go back to work. I stayed with my children. I didn't let babysitters raise them. I remember when I gave birth to her and I nursed her, you know, and I wondered how I'd be able to wake up often enough to feed her. But it wasn't a problem because my body knew when she was hungry; the milk started to seep out of my breasts before she woke up, so when she finally did awaken, a few minutes after I did, I was all ready for her. It kind of stayed like that."

Roberto nodded. "I understand. I felt a bond like that with my daughter. . . . Without the nursing," he added with a smile. "But that was before."

"Before? You don't anymore?"

"Of course I do. But I haven't seen her in eight years. I don't even know where she is."

Jennifer put her glass down and stared at him. "Oh, Roberto, I'm so sorry. What happened?"

"Her mother kidnapped her when she was five years old—took her away, probably out of the country, and disappeared. I have looked everywhere for her, hired other private detectives, and asked the police, but no one has found her. I don't even know if she is alive."

"But why? Why did she do that?"

"Who knows? It's strange. When something this extreme happens to you, people always ask you why, like you know the reason, like maybe you did something terrible enough to deserve it. But the truth is that my wife was very ill, had been for a long time. She is delusional and impulsive and I kept hoping the doctors and drugs and treatment would help her. But none of it did and she ran away. I make my living partly by tracking missing people, but she has simply disappeared." He took another swallow and put his glass down heavily. "So maybe it was my fault. I should have stopped her before. I should have taken Christina away from her before she could take her away from me."

Jennifer didn't know what to say. Her lips felt heavy from the wine and she had trouble forming words, but she wanted to tell him that it wasn't his fault. That we don't always see things that are right in front of us. That we don't know people as well as we think we do.

He raised his hand to call the waitress over for the check. When it came, they both put their credit cards on the tray and Jennifer asked the waitress to split it. Roberto took her card and handed it back to her with a reproachful look. "It is for me to pay," he said. "I invited you, and you are in my country. Please do not offend me." She didn't argue.

"I'm sorry, senora. I am here to help you with your problem and not to tell you mine. But I wanted to show you that I too understand grief and loss and the strength needed to confront them. You must, how do you say, muster"—he clenched both fists in front of him as he said this—"yes, muster all your resources and then you will have a chance to bring your daughter home. I ask you to trust me." He paused and waited for his words to sink in. She didn't say anything. "Estás de acuerdo?" he continued.

"'De acuerdo'?"

"It means do you agree?"

"Yes," Jennifer said, her voice heavy with drink and emotion. "I agree."

CHAPTER 12

Jennifer couldn't fall asleep. She tossed and turned, restless and agitated, and when finally she took an Ambien and fell into a drugged slumber, she was troubled by fragments of worrying dreams. The pill offered only a brief respite—four hours later she was awake again. She glanced at the clock: 5:30 A.M. She sighed and lay still for a while, staring at the ceiling. It would be 11:30 P.M. in Philadelphia. The kids would be asleep. Mark would be up, probably working in his study. She reached for the phone.

Her mother answered on the first ring. Mark was out for dinner, she said, and not home yet. Jennifer felt a stab of discomfort. "Who is he with?" she asked casually, but her mother didn't know. "Someone from the office, I think," she said. "I don't know where he is. He said he'd be home early."

"Did he come home first to say good night to the kids?" Jennifer wanted to know.

"No, honey. He didn't need to. Everything here is fine. Don't worry. How is Emma?"

The time had come to tell her what was going on, and Jennifer girded herself for a hysterical reaction. She told her enough so that if the story came out in the media it wouldn't be a complete shock, but she didn't go into details. She emphasized that of course Emma was completely innocent and would soon be cleared but in the meantime she was being held in the "detention cell" at the police station. Her mother was silent as she spoke, and when she stopped she expected an explosion, but it didn't come. She asked Jennifer's father to pick up the phone and asked Jennifer to repeat what she had told her. She spoke soothingly, telling Jennifer that she must stay as long as was necessary to help Emma, that everything would be fine at home and she was convinced that Emma would soon be freed. Her father echoed her remarks and asked some specific questions: Did they have a good lawyer? Was Emma being treated well? Jennifer had expected this calm reaction from her father, but her mother surprised her. Her mother became frantic with worry when one of the kids had a cold or a slight fever, so much so that Jennifer usually shielded her from that information. Yet she seemed unruffled by the news of her eldest granddaughter's incarceration in a murder case. Thinking about it, Jennifer realized that her mother had done this before. When Eric was hospitalized as a baby with a mold allergy that closed his trachea and required him to be intubated to save his life, her mother arrived the next day, cooked the meals, helped with the girls, and took over so completely that Jennifer could sleep at the hospital. Clearly, her mother rallied in emergencies—thank God, Jennifer thought. She hoped she was doing the same for her daughter.

"Tell Mark he must come right away," Jennifer said. "There's been a new development—I can't go into it on the phone—but I think this story may reach the papers soon and he needs to be here. Tell him to call or e-mail me when he's booked his flight."

It was now 6:30 A.M. and the sky was still pitch-black. In a little while it would fade to gray and soon after that the rising sun would flood the room with light. She thought about going back to bed, but more sleep was clearly out of the question; her mind was racing with both worries and plans to head off new problems before they arose. She picked up the phone again and called Suzie. Her friend's voice sounded groggy and she knew she'd awakened her, but Suzie came to life quickly when she realized who was calling.

"Oh, thank God," she said. "I've been trying to call you back on your cell. No one answered."

"I'm sorry. I was busy and didn't check. But listen, I need your help."

"Yeah. I know. I got that from your message. What is going on?"

She told her, adding a little more detail than she had for her parents.

"I don't understand that suggestive picture," Suzie said. "It can't be true. Could it have been photoshopped? Was someone trying to frame her? Ruin her reputation? Is there someone who hates her? Someone who's jealous of her?"

"I don't know, Suze. I never thought of that. I think it's far-fetched."

"You don't think a photo of Emma looking like a prostitute is far-fetched?"

"Yes, of course I do. I'm horrified and I need to talk to her about it. But the thing is, tomorrow I have to go see her in jail, and I have been told to expect a press presence. I'm really scared that this will become a big story and be picked up by the American media too. If that happens, it's a circus. We need to do something to control the story in the States. Can you help with that?"

"Of course. We need to hire a firm to help show the world the real Emma and to make it clear that she is being unfairly targeted in a foreign country, maybe partly because she's an American."

Jennifer hesitated. "I don't know if that's true. I should ask the guy we hired here to manage her case and see if he thinks that approach is helpful."

"Look, Jen, I'll take care of the U.S. side. You worry about Spain."

"Okay. But there's something else. If it does go public there's going to be a lot of people—friends, family, acquaintances—who will want to follow it, to know what's happening. I can't take that on. Can you start a blog or something, and can I forward all the e-mails I get on this to you? Will you be the spokesperson for the family?"

"Yes. Absolutely. Now try to calm down. We will beat this. She's going to be all right, you'll see. Is Mark with you?'

"No. He's coming soon."

"I'll call him. I'll talk to you tomorrow, okay?"

"Yeah. Thanks, Suze. Thanks so much. I love you."

"Love you too."

She hung up. The sun was just beginning to break the horizon, ushering in another blindingly bright Seville day. Jennifer felt the tight fist of anxiety relax a little. She showered, dressed, and ordered breakfast. Soon Roberto and José would come to escort her to the police station.

In a black-and-white tailored suit with black pumps and her long hair up in a twist, she looked as though she might have been a lawyer going to try a case. She carried a black shoulder bag and had carefully folded the newspaper with the damning photo of Emma and placed it inside. They ushered her into the backseat of a hired car, Roberto climbing in beside her and José sitting in the front passenger seat. As the driver wove in and out of traffic, Roberto reminded her that the media would make this a different experience than before.

She could see how right he was even before they pulled up in front of the police station. There was a small mob assembled—at least twenty people milling around, some with cameras, others with microphones, and still more with notebooks or electronic devices. As the car pulled over she could hear someone shout, "That's the mother!" and the whole group moved as one to the car, crowding around it, making it difficult to open the door. Roberto got out first and led her through the throng, where she found herself in the middle of a scene she'd only ever seen before on television crime shows. Questions were hurled at her like lightning bolts. At first they spoke Spanish, but they soon realized she didn't understand them and switched to English: "Did you know your daughter was a call girl?" "The police say she invented the Algerian— what do you think?" "Has she told lies before?" "Do you think she thinks an American can do anything she wants and get away with it?" "Have you seen the mother of the victim? What message do you want to send to her?"

Jennifer put her head down and clutched Roberto's hand, trying to listen only to him as he whispered into her ear. "Don't answer," he told her. "Don't listen. Keep walking."

Once inside, she stared at him, aghast.

"This is what I meant, senora. This is only the beginning. You must be strong," he said crisply. She nodded, swallowing hard.

José approached the desk officer and requested a meeting with Emma. They were told to wait until Fernando, the detective in charge, came to fetch them. Roberto occupied himself with Jennifer, showing her where she should sit, bringing her a cup of coffee from the machine in the hallway. She felt grateful and more and more dependent on him, looking to him for how to react, what to say, what to do next.

They waited for more than an hour, during which time José and Roberto tried to impress upon her, as if she didn't already know, the importance of convincing Emma to cooperate with the police. When Fernando appeared, he greeted them politely and told them they had concluded their interrogation of Paco for the moment. They all noticed that Fernando looked exhausted. His clothes were disheveled, his hair greasy, and he had a five o'clock shadow.

"We have questioned Paco all night," he said, rubbing his hand across his eyes. "He has begun to be cooperative." This news sent a chill down Jennifer's spine. What did he mean? she wondered. What had they done to him to make him cooperate? He turned to Jennifer. "Your daughter doesn't know he is here. You will tell her, of course. We will question her again later. I suggest you explain to her, as we will, that one of them will tell us the truth first. That is the person who will have the advantage and testify against the other. It is beginning to look like that person may be Paco."

Jennifer bristled before Roberto could stop her. "I see that you do not have the belief that a person is innocent until proven guilty here. My daughter did nothing that anyone could accuse her of."

"We will see," Fernando said with a tired smile. "Would you and your lawyer like to see her now?"

"Sí, por supuesto," José said.

"I should tell you that Paco confirms what we have already heard from several witnesses: He was with Emma earlier on the night of the murder. Only Emma denies it," Fernando said. He looked sympathetically at Jennifer. "I am a father. I understand the pain this must cause you. I have said it before and I repeat it: You must convince your daughter to tell the truth about everything. It is her best hope."

He turned to go and José followed. Jennifer stopped for a moment and turned to Roberto. "Will you come with me?" she asked.

Roberto looked at Fernando, who nodded.

"Yes, of course," Roberto answered. "In any case, it is important that we meet."

Emma was sitting on her bed reading a copy of *The New Yorker* that Jennifer had brought her on an earlier visit. She tossed the magazine aside and jumped up when she saw her mother. She hugged her distractedly, greeted José politely in Spanish, and looked inquisitively at Roberto. Jennifer introduced them, reminding her who he was. She shook his hand and said something Jennifer didn't understand in Spanish. They sat down around the table and Emma asked when she could get out. Roberto spoke first. "That isn't so easy, Emma. But the answer depends very much on you. I need to tell you first that Paco has been found and is in custody here. They—"

Emma didn't let him finish. She jumped up. "Oh, no. They will try to pin this whole thing on him. I need to talk to him right away. When can I see him?"

"You can't see him," José said. "They are not through interrogating him, although they have questioned him throughout the night, and they will start again with you probably after we leave. They won't let you talk to him until they find out what they want to know. Apparently he has begun to talk to them."

Emma looked at her mother. Her voice sounded desperate. "Mama, isn't there anything you can do?"

How many times had Jennifer heard those words? And in the

past, there often had been something she could do. How easy that had been. She could talk to the school if Emma wasn't in the same class as her best friend and get it changed. She could get her a tutor when she didn't understand math. As she got older, it was a little harder, but she still managed. She remembered when Emma was caught in tenth grade including in an essay two verbatim paragraphs from a published source. The teacher called it plagiarism and wanted to fail her for the course as punishment. Emma swore she hadn't done it purposely and Jennifer believed her. These things happen.

Jennifer went in and talked to the teacher. She pointed out how easy it was when writing and copying notes from other writers to confuse them and inadvertently use them. She reminded her that even Doris Kearns Goodwin, the famous historian, had done it, for heaven's sake. Finally, she managed to convince the teacher to relent. "She's learned," Jennifer said. "She's so sorry and will be much more careful next time. This was an important lesson." She begged her not to "ruin her whole life" or her chances of getting into the college of her choice. The teacher had caved in and had assigned Emma to detention for two weeks instead.

But now she was helpless. It was more like the time Emma had been bitten in the face by a friend's German shepherd. Jennifer had been in the next room and she had heard Emma cooing at the dog. "Hi, Denny," she had said, and then a growl followed by a terrible scream. "Mommy help me, help me!" Emma had shouted, and there was the blood running down her face and the dog's teeth deep in her cheek, and finally the dog being dragged away and Emma still screaming, a scream Jennifer would never forget. She had felt helpless then, but she was still able to call the hospital, arrange for a plastic surgeon to meet them in the emergency room, carry Emma to the car, and talk soothingly to her, holding cloth over the bleeding bite and stroking her hair until they reached the hospital and Emma was wheeled into the operating room with Jennifer right behind her. But this time, she really was helpless.

"No, darling, I can't," she said, her voice breaking. "But *you* can do something. You can stop protecting Paco. He has already told them that you were with him the night of the murder. They have other witnesses. You have to tell them what part he played in all this. The case against you has exploded. The press is turning against you. The police must have leaked their suspicion that the Algerian doesn't exist."

Emma started to object.

"No, wait, Emma," Jennifer continued. "I believe he does, of course. If you say he does, then he does; I know that. But you can understand, as I've tried to tell you before, that now that they know you were lying about seeing Paco the night of the murder, they are reluctant to believe anything you say." Her voice was rising and her mouth felt so dry she had trouble swallowing her saliva.

"The Spanish media is surrounding this jail, and if it hasn't happened yet, soon the international press will join them," she continued in a tight, tense voice. "We have had to prepare Pops and Granny and Lily and Eric."

"There is something else," Roberto added. "Once the media is involved they start digging up information that might put you in a negative light. Up until now, the press view of you has been positive—a pretty, naive American caught in a web of drugs and murder. They might have been willing to give you the benefit of the doubt about your lie concerning seeing your boyfriend. But now that they have been doing some research, all that has changed."

"Changed? Why? What negative things could they have dug up?" She looked again at Jennifer, her voice rising in agitation. "Mom?"

Jennifer rummaged in her bag and pulled out the newspaper. She was overwrought and her hand was shaking as she tossed it onto the table. "That, Emma. What is that? What in God's name were you doing dressed like that?" She fought back tears. "Oh, my God, what has this Paco done to you?"

Emma picked up the newspaper, seemingly bewildered. She looked at it for a long time, during which everyone seemed frozen. Then she laughed—a hard, bitter laugh that Jennifer barely recognized as belonging to her daughter.

"That was Halloween, Mom. That was a costume for Halloween. What did you think? That I was a hooker? God, Mom, don't you know me at all?"

CHAPTER 13

Jennifer felt she had made a serious mistake. She should have known that there would be a good explanation for that photograph. Her trust in Emma had wavered, and of course Emma had felt betrayed. She was determined never to let that happen again. She told Roberto to be sure he explained Halloween to the Spanish media in order to defang them, and she called Suzie and told her to make much of it with the public relations people, telling them it was a perfect example of a typical innocent American custom being turned into ugly innuendo and used against Emma.

Mark was scheduled to arrive in three days. But before he did, yet another blow struck. José called to say that the police had decided to charge Emma as an accomplice to murder. She had already been moved from the cell in the police station to a prison out of town. Jennifer called Mark to alert him and beg him to come sooner, but she didn't reach him and his secretary said he was in court. She fired off an e-mail giving him the news and telling him to call right away, but she didn't hear anything until she received a voice mail the next day saying he got her message and wished he was with her. "Only two more days," he said.

He arrived, as scheduled, greeted by the crowd of journalists that now gathered around the hotel and hounded Jennifer every time she appeared. A big man and an angry one, he barreled through the crowd with large strides and pointy elbows and flicked away their badgering questions with contemptuous looks and curt replies.

Jennifer was waiting for him inside where the doormen were able to keep the journalists away. They walked together to the elevator, riding up and then entering their room without a word.

Jennifer was so angry she could hardly look at him. He knew her well and saw at once, by her refusal to make eye contact, how upset she was.

"I couldn't come sooner," he said. "I couldn't even reach you to talk. I was in court all day yesterday."

She shot him a long-suffering look. This was an explanation she'd heard before; she couldn't even count how many times. It was word-for-word the excuse for everything he had missed that mattered to her or the kids throughout the years. He understood her meaning without a word passing between them.

"I'm sorry, honey. I know how important this is. But I have an obligation to my client too."

This was the wrong thing to say. She exploded.

"An obligation to your client? You put that on the same level as your obligation to your daughter, to your wife? Do you have any idea what's been going on here? Emma is now viewed as some kind of promiscuous, entitled American whose lies are damaging the name and honor of a murdered Spanish boy. Some journalists have speculated that she killed him herself, ridiculous though that is." Jennifer was just warming up, and now she talked more rapidly as she listed the recent terrible developments in their case.

"Last night the boy's mother was interviewed on television. She talked about the kindness, intelligence, and promise of her son. She wept and said this '*bruja americana*' had killed him twice—first his body, then his name. She denied there ever was a rape attempt or an Algerian savior. She publically accused Emma and her boyfriend of killing him while robbing him of the thousand euros he had just withdrawn from the bank." She stopped the onslaught and continued in a tired, heartbroken murmur. "And that seems to be what the police believe too. I left you a message that Emma has been charged as an accomplice and they've moved her from the jail to a prison out of town. Did you get it?"

He nodded grimly. "How is she doing?"

"I haven't been allowed to see her yet. They've charged her boyfriend with the actual stabbing, but they say she helped him. It's terrifying. You see why I'm so upset, don't you, Mark? I know the practical reasons you had to stay. I am trying to be understanding. But all this was happening while you were defending your client against insider trading that you know he did. How can it be possible that you can't get someone else in the office to handle that, Mark?"

Her husband sighed and shook his head. "I don't know how many times I have to tell you that it doesn't work that way, Jennifer. My cases are the ones I get paid for, and we need the money. What do you want me to do? We have two other children, school fees, college ahead of us, a mortgage, and then this case—the lawyer and case manager here, the public-relations firm in New York, the hotels, the airfare—do you think we have enough money to take it all from savings? Because we don't. Do you think I wouldn't rather be here? I am working with only half my mind; the rest is always worrying about what is happening here."

Jennifer didn't answer. She saw that he was right and she felt ashamed. The tension, she realized, was getting to both of them.

Mark sat down heavily on the edge of the bed. "I need to see Emma as soon as possible," he said.

"They don't allow free access to her anymore. The rules state we can visit for forty-five minutes twice a week, but it seems they can cut off access to her whenever they feel like it. I haven't been let in yet. Maybe we can go tomorrow."

She tried to fill him in on the case, reviewing with him that the police claimed the wounds Rodrigo sustained were made by a taller and heavier man than Emma had described.

"What does this Paco look like?" Mark asked.

"I've never seen him."

"You know what I'm asking, Jennifer. What have you heard?"

"The police say that the wounds would have been made by a man about Paco's size." Jennifer said this without looking at him and without any expression in her voice, as coolly and objectively as possible. She went on to report that Emma had practically admitted to her that she had been with Paco earlier on the night of the murder, but she continued to deny he ever came back to the apartment and was sticking to her story that she had been saved from an attempted rape. Jennifer sat down next to him and put her hand on his knee. "The police have suggested their own scenario—something so cliché, and so unlikely for Emma to be involved in that I can hardly bear to repeat it."

Mark stood up, crossed the room, and sat in a chair near the desk. He took a piece of paper from the desk drawer and removed his pen from his inside jacket pocket, ready to take notes.

"Repeat it, Jennifer. I will hear it soon enough anyway. I need to be prepared."

She paced nervously around the room as she spoke.

"According to José and Roberto, the police think this is a typical story of a jealous lover. They think Emma somehow met Rodrigo that night, liked him, and invited him back to her apartment. In their version, Paco walked in, found them in bed together, and killed Rodrigo in a jealous rage. They claim Paco went through the dead boy's pockets, took the thousand euros he was carrying, and fled. They say Emma and Paco cooked up this story about the Algerian together to throw the police off track, and they are charging her as an accomplice." She waited for an outraged reaction from Mark, but it didn't come. "It's absolutely ridiculous," she added. "They can't prove any of it, and they just invented it because they are too incompetent to find the Algerian who helped her. And of course they don't want to admit that a rich local Spanish boy could be capable of rape. It's easier to imagine a spoiled American and her drug-dealer boyfriend, who also just happens to be half-Moroccan, by the way." She paused again. Mark still said nothing. "It's absurd," she added.

Mark finally broke his silence. "Is it?" he asked softly. Jennifer stared at him.

"I mean, Emma's story doesn't make sense, Jennifer. We have to face the possibility that there is a lot she isn't telling us."

Jennifer had stopped pacing. Now she sat down on the bed, incredulous. "What are you saying, Mark? She's your daughter. You love her. Don't you trust her?"

He walked over to her, sat down next to her on the bed, and put his arm around her. He spoke gently. "Of course I love her, Jennifer. But I'm not blind and deaf. Loving her and believing her aren't the same thing. I've tried to explain this to you before. I'm a lawyer and I have to look at this as objectively as possible. That's my best chance of helping her. I need to know what evidence they've found. I've spoken daily to José but I haven't heard of any unusual DNA turning up—nothing; no fingerprints of anyone but Rodrigo, Emma, and Paco. If the Algerian was there, where are his traces?"

Jennifer pulled away sharply. Her voice was angry and accusing. "I don't know. I suppose he cleaned them up. You aren't prosecuting her, Mark. It's your job to defend her. I can't listen to this."

"No. It's my job to find out the truth and to figure out how to save her, whatever that truth is," he shot back. He collected himself but didn't relent.

"You pretend, Jennifer. You cover over and ignore or deny anything you don't like. You never confront what is real and in front of you, only what you think ought to be there. You do that with the kids and you have done it forever with me too."

He stopped himself, but his words hung in the air. They both realized they were on the brink of a dangerous conversation that neither was ready for.

Jennifer turned away, squelching her reply. It was hot in the room and she realized she was perspiring. She wiped the beads of moisture off her upper lip and walked over to the air conditioner, turning down the temperature to let in more cold air. It wasn't enough. The room felt too small and cramped. She needed to get out.

She grabbed her key from the tray on top of the dresser. "I'm going to take a walk," she said.

"No, Jennifer. Not yet. I have something else to say."

She reluctantly turned around to hear him out.

"Remember when Emma was in eighth grade and her teacher called to report her copying during a test?"

Emma interrupted him. "I remember it all," she snapped. "I remember that, as usual, you were on a business trip and I had to handle it alone. And I did and it turned out okay, and what possible relevance does that have now? Are you going to bring in everything she ever did, every normal teenage misstep, and use it as evidence against her? Maybe you should stop thinking like a lawyer and start thinking like a father."

She left the room, letting the door slam behind her. She slowed down in the hallway on the way to the elevator, expecting him to follow, but he didn't come after her.

It was hotter outside than it had been in the room, so she didn't walk for long. She ended up going to the coffee shop in the hotel and ordering a cup of hot chocolate and some churros. She always craved sweets when she was upset. In the past, she'd joked with friends about this, bemoaning aloud her observation that some women lost their appetite when under duress but trouble always made her gain weight. She hoped Mark would worry about her, so she stayed away for about an hour before returning.

Of course she remembered that call from Emma's eighth-grade teacher. Her name was Mrs. Resnikoff and she had claimed that Emma had copied during a history test. Emma had denied it, but the teacher had claimed she had seen it herself, and besides, the friend she had copied from had gotten the answer wrong and Emma had the exact same mistake on her paper. Emma had gotten a zero averaged into her grade and was forced to apologize. Mark had wanted to punish Emma when he came home, not only for copying but also for lying about it, but Jennifer had convinced him that one punishment was enough. This was an important learning experience, she had said, and she was sure Emma would never do anything like it again. Emma was proud and stubborn,

Jennifer had argued, making those characteristics sound like virtues instead of faults, and she was also probably so very ashamed, Jennifer had continued, she simply couldn't admit it. Jennifer had even wondered if the teacher had made a mistake. In the end, Mark had gone along with her, as he usually did.

She always thought there was a sense in which she was lucky that Mark wasn't more involved in household matters. It gave her pretty complete control—when she objected to an idea of his, he quickly retreated back to his work and let her handle it. In that way, she'd managed to determine the style of their furnishings, the paintings on the wall, their social calendar, and every major decision about the children. She sometimes complained about it to friends—saying that she wished he took more of an interest and contributed more—but she knew she wouldn't really have wanted it any other way.

Mark was on the phone when she returned to the room. He quickly signed off and turned to her. "Feeling better?"

"Not particularly. Who were you talking to?"

"I called José to see when I could see Emma."

"When *we* could see her, you mean," she said coldly. "What did he say?"

"He hopes he can arrange it for tomorrow morning around ten o'clock. He'll pick us up and take us there. Of course you'll see her too, but I'll need to spend some time talking to her alone."

Jennifer nodded and started to turn away. Mark reached for her hand. "I didn't mean to upset you," he said. "I didn't sleep at all on the plane. I'm exhausted."

She looked down to avoid eye contact. He hugged her and she kissed him primly on the cheek before wriggling away. She didn't want to argue, but she didn't really feel better either.

Since they couldn't see Emma until the next day, they had some free time, and Mark wanted to see the site of the murder. He wanted José or Roberto or both to accompany him and go over all the details known so far, both those revealed by Emma and those sometimes contradictory clues uncovered by forensic evidence and police work. José was unavailable, but Roberto said he could meet them at the apartment in two hours. Mark told Jennifer she didn't have to come, that she might find it too difficult, but although she sensed he actually would prefer to go without her, she wanted to be there.

Jennifer had shared with Mark her distress at the conditions their daughter had been living in, but he still seemed surprised when he saw it for himself. Aside from the shabbiness of the neighborhood and the grimy walls, peeling paint, and chipped plaster inside, the apartment still looked like a crime scene, because no one had removed the yellow tape that sealed off the door or the outline of the body taped onto the bedroom floor. It was clear that nobody had been inside since Jennifer's visit when she had first arrived—or at least nothing had been touched—and no one had cleared out the garbage, so the acrid smell of decay hit their nostrils as soon as they entered. They had to cover their noses with their hands. Mark handed his handkerchief to Jennifer, who placed it over her nose and mouth and gagged anyway. He threw open all the windows and held his breath as he grabbed the garbage bag under the bathroom sink, threw the few bits of rotten food in the fridge into it, and took it outside. Jennifer left the door open to air out the apartment and joined Mark outside, where they waited for Roberto.

Jennifer saw him first, alighting from a taxi across the street, looking out of place in his elegant linen suit and shiny black shoes. As he neared, she noticed how crisp and cool he appeared and wondered how he managed it. His pace quickened as he approached and saw them. Before Jennifer could introduce him to Mark, Roberto smiled and grasped his hand in greeting. "Ah, Senor Lewis," he said softly, looking him directly in the eyes. "Por fin." By now, even Jennifer understood that. It meant "At last."

CHAPTER 14

Mark wasted no time. He wanted to know everything the police knew and more. Even before they entered the apartment, he told Roberto that he was going to visit Emma the next day and that after talking to her, he hoped to be able to work with him and José on planning her defense. He emphasized that he would value their honest opinion of how the case was shaping up so far. Then he turned and entered the apartment. The others followed.

The stench had subsided considerably, but a faintly putrid smell still permeated the room. Mixed with the stifling heat, it seemed to give the air an oppressive texture. Roberto noticed a fan in the kitchen, plugged it in, and turned it on. He picked a glass out of the bathroom sink gingerly, with two fingers, hesitant to touch it, and washed it with dish detergent that had been left near the sink. Then he did the same with two other glasses, all the while running the water until the rust ran off. Finally he filled the glasses and, keeping one for himself, gave the others to Jennifer and Mark.

He took a long swig, put down the glass, and sighed. "There are many contradictions and problems with your daughter's story, senor, as I am sure your wife has already told you."

Mark nodded attentively, encouraging him to go on.

"Let us begin with the attempted rape." He looked ruefully at Jennifer, who stiffened visibly. "You already know that Emma refused to allow a rape kit because she claimed it was only an attempt; the boy was not successful. She could legally insist that she not be examined internally, but she was sent to the hospital and examined externally and a medical report of her condition was made. When she was questioned they asked her, Where did he grab you? Was it the hair? The arm? Did he shove you against the floor, against the wall? The detective then looked at the medical report and compared it to what she told him. Was she bruised? Were there any signs of a struggle? Were her nails broken? Were there any scratches on the corpse? They asked her if she screamed. How many times? Was it loud or low? They asked where exactly she was standing. Where did the knife come from? Where did he fall? They checked the neighbors and asked what they heard and when."

Roberto was dragging out his explanation, infusing it with as much drama as possible, and Mark seemed impatient.

"Yes, I know what an interrogation of an alleged rape victim looks like," he said with some irritation. "What did they find?"

Roberto looked at him. "Nothing, senor." He sat across from him at the kitchen table. "Nothing at all. But finding nothing doesn't mean they have no answers, only that the answers contradict your daughter's story. She had no bruises, no broken nails, no signs on her body of any struggle. She says she screamed loud enough to cause this passing stranger to barge through the door, but no neighbor in or around the courtyard saw or heard anything until at least forty minutes after she says she came home, when one neighbor thinks he heard sounds of fighting."

Jennifer interrupted to say that this proved nothing because Emma said she screamed and the Algerian came in to help her. Maybe that happened right away and there was no time for her to have bruises and broken nails. She looked at Mark for support, but he ignored her and continued to direct questions to Roberto.

"There is something else," Roberto said. "There are, as you probably know, senor, wounds of attack and wounds of defense. Attack wounds are usually overhead, strong and with force. Defense wounds are on the arms, the hands, as the victim tries to hold off the assailant. Rodrigo had mainly defense wounds, as though he tried to defend himself from an attack, and one major attack wound that finally killed him."

Mark nodded again. He pointed out that if that was all, there was nothing definitive, nothing that proved beyond doubt that Emma was lying.

"No, señor. But in certain cases, where there is no definitive proof, the police, and later the jury, must look for what the evidence suggests."

Mark took this in and then got up and walked into the bedroom. He looked at the tape on the floor outlining where the body had fallen, a few feet from the bed. He wanted to know exactly how Emma had described the scene to the police.

Roberto joined him. "She said the Algerian burst in and dragged Rodrigo from the bed here"—he put his hand on the unmade bed—"while she put her shirt back on and huddled in the corner there." He pointed to the opposite side of the room.

"Her shirt? There was time for him to take her shirt off?"

"That's what she said. She said he tore it off, and it is true that several buttons were actually torn open."

"Please continue."

"She said the Algerian simply tried to force Rodrigo to leave, but he was crazed with drink and maybe drugs. The toxicology report does not support this, by the way. She said then Rodrigo lunged at the Algerian with the knife, and so he had to fight back to defend himself. She claimed the Algerian was very fast and he grabbed the knife. They struggled, she was screaming, she said—again, no one heard these screams—and finally the Algerian secured the knife, and as Rodrigo came at him, he plunged it into his chest in self-defense. She reports seeing only one strike with the knife. This explanation does not account for the fact that the wounds matched the pattern of a knife found in her kitchen, nor does it explain the defensive wounds on Rodrigo's hands and arms. And you already know that the depth and angle of the mortal wounds don't coincide with the height and weight description Emma provided."

"Is it true that Paco is the right size and weight for those wounds?" Mark asked.

"I'm afraid so."

Mark jotted something in his notebook and looked up. "Is there anything else? What about the hashish? She told her mother that she had eaten brownies laced with hashish on that night."

"This is the first I have heard of that. There was nothing in the report to indicate that she was acting as if she had taken drugs. I'm not sure of its relevance." He looked at Jennifer. "Where did she say she was when she ate them?"

"I think she said she was at a bar," Jennifer replied.

Roberto looked thoughtful. "That might help us determine a time sequence."

Mark nodded and Roberto paused. Mark and Jennifer looked inquisitively at him, waiting for him to go on.

"There is something else," Roberto said slowly. "There is a problem about the blood. It isn't clear yet so I hesitate to report it, but perhaps you should know what they are doing."

Mark leaned forward, alert. "Please go on."

"You know the police have a substance which tells them if bloodstains have been washed or rubbed away. Blood always leaves a trace," he said ominously.

"You mean luminol?" Mark said.

"Yes. They have covered the floor of every room with it as well as all the kitchen knives. They already know those results, but we don't. They are analyzing them to decide their relevance."

Jennifer was listening carefully. "Like what?" she asked. "What are they looking for?"

"I don't know."

"And what does Emma say when confronted with all this?" Mark asked.

Roberto shook his head. "She is stubborn, this girl. She doggedly insists that everything happened the way she said it did in spite of any evidence to the contrary. She cries, she accuses the police of trying to railroad her, she spouts figures about unemployment and lectures the police about poverty. She gives up nothing." He paused. "Well, that's not completely true. She does now admit that she was with Paco earlier in the evening. She says they had a fight and she went home alone. Maybe that was when she was in the bar and ate the brownies. She gave this information only when told that Paco had given it first."

"Did he?"

"Yes."

Roberto sat down again and took another gulp of water. He took a white handkerchief from his pocket and wiped his brow, which was beginning to perspire. Addressing both of them, he tried to explain that although the police didn't have definite proof of their charges, they did have a reasonable, believable narrative that was supported by some evidence. Emma's narrative was looking more and more suspect. It was the narrative, ultimately, he claimed, that in a case like this was on trial. Who would the judge and jury believe?

"How is the jury constituted?" Mark asked.

"There are nine jurors and a judge. The verdict is by majority; it does not need to be unanimous."

Mark looked thoughtful and took several minutes to review his notes. He asked Roberto if he agreed that in order for the police narrative to succeed, they would have to prove that Emma somehow either knew Rodrigo before or met him the night of the murder and brought him home; otherwise how would they wind up in bed together? If she knew him before, wouldn't someone have seen them together? The night of the murder the fair was going on. If she met him then, someone would have seen them together—at a party, a bar, a meeting place, somewhere.

"They have no evidence of this, do they?" Mark asked. "These are all just their own suppositions."

Roberto agreed and admitted that up until now no one had surfaced who had ever seen them together. They had no common friends, studied in different programs, frequented different bars, and might well never have encountered each other. Jennifer hung on to this—it was the first hopeful news she'd heard that day.

They thanked Roberto and left the apartment, locking the door after closing the windows. Before they left, Roberto gave a last warning.

"You're right; it is just supposition," he said, addressing Jennifer. "But there is always one cop who gets an idea and doesn't let it go, who keeps asking questions until he gets the answer he knows is there. In this case, that cop is Fernando."

"He can keep asking," Jennifer said. "He can't find it if it's not there."

"I hope you are right, senora."

Before they parted, Roberto phoned for a taxi, explaining that there were few in that neighborhood. He offered to order one for them, but they said they'd prefer to walk for a bit.

As they headed off, Jennifer tried to sound upbeat. "You see, Mark, she didn't know this Rodrigo. It's crazy to think she would just meet him and sleep with him when she already had a boyfriend. We know her. We know what she's capable of."

Mark walked silently, staring at the ground. He seemed far away. "I wish I knew that," he said. "I don't think I do. And I know you don't."

She let it go. She couldn't allow him to turn this into a verdict on her either as a wife or as a mother, although she felt accused on both fronts.

They passed a café and Jennifer suggested they stop for coffee. They had walked for fifteen minutes and were hot and tired. They took a table inside, where it was air-conditioned, and both ordered café con leche and a pastry. It was hard to overcome the tension between them, and Jennifer felt an unaccustomed awkwardness.

"Are you tired, Mark?" she asked gently, reaching for something to talk about that was not so fraught. "You said you didn't sleep on the plane. Would you like to go back to the hotel and take a nap?"

He shrugged and shook his head, and there was another awkward silence.

"What did you think of Roberto?" she asked. "He seems very good and competent to me, and he's been an amazing help during the tough times."

"Jennifer, I think you should come home for a while," Mark said.

She was surprised and taken aback. "What? Why?"

"Because Lily and Eric miss you and need you too. Because you are too intensely involved here and I don't think that's good for you or maybe even for Emma. Because you have to get some perspective back. This is bad. It's terrible. But we are doing whatever we can to help, and it doesn't sound like Emma is either cooperating or appreciating it. And we have two other children who are confused by all this and need their mother."

She had spoken to Lily and Eric the night before and knew he was right. They wanted her home. They were frightened by what they now knew had really happened to Emma, and it was going to get worse when stories started appearing in the newspapers and on television. Even if they could keep some of it away from Eric, there was no way to protect Lily. Jennifer ached for them, but what she said was, "Right. And you'll take my place here, is that it?"

"You know I can't do that."

"Then you know I can't leave. Lily and Eric have you and my parents and their friends and teachers. Emma is alone here and in danger." She was bristling with indignation. "But don't worry. You go home. Don't rush back. I'll take care of things here myself. Why should this be different from anything else in our family?"

He paid the check and got up angrily, stalking out to the street and striding ahead, barely looking to see if she was behind him. She followed and caught up with him. They kept walking, and after a while she saw a taxi. It wasn't at a designated stand, the usual place to find taxis in Seville, but it stopped anyway when Mark hailed it. They rode back to the hotel, both lost in private thoughts.

CHAPTER 15

José was scheduled to arrive at 9:00 A.M. to take them to the prison. They woke early without an alarm and went about their morning ablutions in relative silence. Mark retrieved the *International New York Times* from the floor in front of their door and scanned it nervously as Jennifer ordered coffee from room service and went into the bathroom to brush her teeth.

"Shit!" she heard Mark exclaim, and knowing with a sinking feeling that he had found what they both hoped he wouldn't, she wiped her mouth and rushed back into the room.

He tossed the paper with the offending article over to her. It was short, stating simply that an American exchange student named Emma Lewis from Princeton University was being held in connection with the murder of a Spanish student in Seville. No further details were given, but it was enough. It would bring the rest as surely as threatening clouds bring electrical storms.

Jennifer sank down on the bed and looked helplessly at Mark. Usually, she would take comfort in his presence, gain strength from their dual purpose, from his arm around her. But now? She felt alienated, criticized, hurt, but mostly alone. Sitting next to her on the bed, he did put his arm around her shoulders, his habitual gesture in times of trouble, but he did it absentmindedly, dutifully, and she sensed the difference.

"What do we do now?" she asked.

"We knew this was coming. We have prepared. This doesn't change anything." His voice reflected a confidence she didn't believe he felt.

That must be the voice he uses with his clients, she thought.

They went downstairs intending to grab a quick bite in the hotel dining room. They were surprised to see that a lavish buffet was spread out and, hungry in spite of themselves, they decided to take part in it. Once again, the bad news had the effect of making Jennifer ravenous—a perfect example of using food for comfort instead of sustenance, a habit that was completely out of her conscious control. Mark browsed the various offerings, judiciously filling his plate, while Jennifer went straight to the egg station and ordered a cheese omelet. She added bread and several pieces of bacon, and at the last moment, having only briefly hesitated, she put a puff pastry on her plate.

Neither mentioned the anger of the day before, but neither forgot it either. It sat between them, an unwelcome visitor in front of whom they needed to make polite small talk.

At nine sharp they stood in the courtyard outside the hotel waiting for their ride. José pulled up a few minutes later. Jennifer waved to him, and when he pulled over in front of them, she climbed in the back, letting Mark, with his longer legs, sit in the passenger seat.

"I thought Roberto might come," she said.

"He couldn't. Only one nonfamily member is allowed at a time."

Mark asked José to tell them what they should expect about the place where Emma was being held.

He didn't respond immediately, concentrating on pulling out of the driveway onto the street crowded with rush-hour cars. After navigating a difficult turn, he said he planned to explain exactly what the protocol was and was ready to start now.

He told them that Emma was in a women's prison—the Centro Penitenciario de Mujeres—in a small town about thirty miles from Seville. She was there on remand after a preliminary hearing by the investigating magistrate determined she needed to be held until trial. She had been charged as an accomplice and as a hostile witness, but no trial date had yet been set. He reminded them that it could take two to four years for her case to go to trial and said it would still be possible—and obviously preferable—to clear her without a trial if she provided them with exculpating evidence.

This was her first permitted visit since arriving at the new location, and José went on to tell them how it would go. He spoke in his usual businesslike manner, as if he were reading a brochure, not speaking directly to a prisoner's worried parents. She and Mark would be finger-printed and photographed. Their passports would be taken and the numbers recorded. The visit would take place in a booth with a glass partition. He rattled off the restrictions mechanically.

"Wait. Stop. You mean we won't be able to touch her?" Jennifer asked.

"I'm afraid not."

This was too much. She exploded. "What do they think she is, for God's sake? A murderer?"

There was an uncomfortable silence as her words hung in the air. She grimaced, realizing what she had said.

Mark reached behind him to comfort her. She gratefully took his hand.

"I am sorry, senora," José said softly. "I do not make the rules. Let me continue."

He said the visit could last thirty-five to forty-five minutes, not lon-ger. He explained that prisoners are divided into three levels in Spain, with the first being the most restricted. Usually only aggressive or dan-gerous criminals are classified as Level One offenders. Most prisoners are in the second level, he emphasized, and the prison is a Level Two facility, which should have allowed Emma a certain amount of free-dom, including one monthly visit with family members in a private room without direct police supervision. He pointed out that Level Two prisoners also have more phone use, access to art classes, and other priv-ileges denied to those in Level One. At the moment, however, he ex-plained, Emma was being denied some of these privileges, but he was confident he could get her status changed.

"You can't mean that Emma is classified as a Level One offender," Jennifer interrupted. "That just doesn't make sense."

José gave a helpless shrug. "In Emma's case, it appears the judge believes that a harsher regimen might encourage her to be more cooperative."

"Is this legal?" Mark asked, indignant.

"No, not officially," José said. "It was a private arrangement between the investigating magistrate and the prison administrator. That is why I think I can get it changed."

Mark asked what the third and most liberal level entailed and wondered if that could be arranged for Emma.

José explained that Level Three is reserved for prisoners who have shown exemplary behavior while they are incarcerated. Those women are even allowed weekend passes to a known address. "I hope she will not be imprisoned long enough to require that kind of intervention," José said.

Mark and Jennifer each faced the realization that Emma might be there much longer than they had hoped. Jennifer looked out the window. They had passed out of the city and had entered a flat desert landscape of baked red earth and scrub cacti. It stretched as far as the eye could see, punctuated here and there with goats, horned sheep, and, occasionally, a few black-and-white cows, listless in the humid air. The sun was shining with a blinding, almost intolerable brightness over a landscape that looked parched and lonely, adding to the uneasiness inside the car.

In the distance the old red brick facade of the Centro Penitenciario de Mujeres came into view, a solitary building in the middle of what felt like nowhere. José drove up to the guardhouse, showed his credentials, and passed into the parking lot outside the prison wall. He led them through the formalities for which he had prepared them: They showed their passports to a prison official, who would keep them, they were told, until after the visit. They were then searched and photographed and, finally, led by a guard who opened a locked door and conducted them to the visiting room. The glass partition looked to

Jennifer like the plexiglass separating the driver and passenger in New York taxis, with a grille running the length of the glass just large enough to allow prisoner and visitor to hear each other. On one side they could see several women prisoners sitting on stools and talking to their visitors, who were seated on chairs lined up on the other side. It was clear that privacy in this setup was not an option. They had been informed that they could only speak to her one at a time. The other parent would be able to sit in a chair against the back wall until it was his or her turn. Jennifer turned to Mark and pleaded with him.

"Please, Mark, we have so little time. Let me talk to her first. I want to find out how she is before you start interrogating her." Mark's expression showed his annoyance with that characterization of his intentions, but he nodded his assent and moved to the designated spot.

Jennifer peered through the glass, looking for Emma, whom she didn't see. She caught José's attention as he was leaving to join Mark; he signaled that they were bringing her in shortly.

Emma appeared at the entry and looked around for her visitors. When she spotted Jennifer, her face broke into a small, sad smile, and she hurried to the empty stool on her side of the partition. The first thing Jennifer noticed was her hair. The beautiful long dark hair she had worn since childhood was gone. In its place were ragged locks unevenly chopped to her ears. It hurt her to look at it, but she stopped herself from commenting.

"Oh, Emma, I'm so glad to see you," she said after a brief pause. "They wouldn't let me come sooner."

Emma was still looking around, as though searching for someone. "Is Daddy here?" she asked.

"Yes. He's here. They won't let us talk to you together. He'll come when I finish." She leaned forward and lowered her voice. "How are you? Is it awful here?"

Emma shook her head. She shrugged and even uttered a single laugh, but it was not a joyful sound. "God, Mom, you're always so dramatic," she said. "Really. You don't have to worry about me on that front. It's actually an amazing place. It's more like a strict boarding school than what you'd think of as a prison. I mean, it's overcrowded and noisy and sometimes the echoes drive you crazy." She lowered her voice and leaned closer to the partition. "And, you know, the women are kind of tough, and you have to be careful not to offend anyone or step on any toes, if you know what I mean, but they really seem to believe in rehab. If I'd been guilty of something, I'd feel lucky to be sentenced here. As it is, of course, I feel pretty pissed off."

If only she could touch her, Jennifer thought. It was so hard to comfort her with only words. She told her she was relieved to hear it wasn't terrible and assured her they were doing everything they could to get her out as soon as possible. She asked if there was anything she needed, anything she could bring that was permitted. And, finally, unable to contain herself a moment longer, she asked what had happened to her hair.

"Oh, they have a hairdresser here, believe it or not. I decided to get it cut 'cause it's easier since we don't get to wash it every day," she explained casually. She went on to say that they needed to put some money into an account for her to pay for extras like the haircut, which she had traded cigarettes to procure.

This was another unpleasant surprise. "I didn't know you had started smoking," Jennifer said.

Emma shrugged. "I think that's the least of my problems right now."

Her manner was provocative—Jennifer knew Emma was trying to both shock and hurt her, and she had succeeded.

"Anything else?" she asked.

Emma also told her there was a library in the prison and that she had been trying to read, but all the books were in Spanish so she was having a hard time with it. Jennifer promised to get her some English-language books and bring them on her next visit.

There was an awkward pause in which both seemed to have run out of things to say. Finally, reluctant to leave and searching for a topic, Jennifer asked about her daily routine. Emma reported that the prisoners would take turns cleaning and doing the laundry, each with an assigned job—"The more they think you are cooperating, the better the job," she said, giving another of those bitter laughs. "I get the toilets, of course." But she said that even though in some ways they were treating her as a Level One offender, they allowed her to go to art classes and to decorate her room with the pictures she made. She had produced a painting that hung in the hall outside her room. "There are three of us to a room, so we have to decide what to hang where and I sort of just let them pick first," she said.

Seeing her mother's worried face, she seemed to soften a little and added that there was even a lounge in the prison where they could occasionally congregate. "My Spanish is improving every day, you'll be happy to know. Though I suppose the vocabulary might not be as useful in Princeton as it is here—not that I expect I'll ever get back to Princeton again. Anyway, it's not that bad. The other day, some of the women even got to go on a field trip to Seville. Not me, of course. It's so weird. There are women here from all over Spain and Latin America, there are lots of gypsies and drug addicts and thieves and murderers, but I'm the one they restrict the most. I really don't get it. Maybe they just don't like Americans."

Emma had been talking fast since they arrived, with a kind of manic energy she often lapsed into when she was nervous. Jennifer didn't know if all the news she was delivering was an attempt to make her feel better or an effort to overcome the tension and awkwardness between them.

Mark coughed loudly and Jennifer turned around. He gestured impatiently that it was his turn, so she stood up.

"Daddy wants to get a chance to talk to you now, honey. I'll sit right there"—she pointed behind her—"and I'll be back the first day they let me come. I'll also write to you and send you the books and the money for your account and whatever you need. Call me when they let you use the phone. I love you."

She ceded her place to Mark, who sat down in her chair while she took his next to José. She found that if she leaned forward and paid strict attention, she could hear most of the conversation between Emma and Mark.

"Hi, Daddy," Emma said in a small, sad voice.

"Hello, Emma." His voice sounded businesslike and he got right to the point. "Listen, we don't have a lot of time and we need to talk about something important. I wish we had more privacy, but we don't, so we have to deal with what we have."

"You sound so serious, Daddy."

"Yeah, well, I think visiting my daughter in a Spanish prison where she is being accused as an accomplice to a murder is serious business."

Emma blanched, surprised. "Are you mad at me, Daddy? You sound mad."

He said he wasn't mad, just worried, but he continued to sound mad. He told her that her situation was extremely serious and that whatever her reasons for protecting Paco, she had to start protecting herself, even if that meant withdrawing her protection from him. As soon as he mentioned Paco, she stiffened and angrily flung back her response, saying he didn't know what he was talking about. He looked at her sideways, surprised by the abrupt change, but he pushed on, telling her that there was no evidence at all that anyone had been in the room except for her, Paco, and the dead boy.

"I don't know what you mean by 'evidence,'" she spat out. "Paco and I live there together—of course he had fingerprints in the room. But he wasn't there that night, and I was. I am telling you what happened. I'm your daughter. You believe the police more than me?"

"I believe the evidence. Your story has too many holes in it."

"Well, I'm sorry, Dad. Life is sometimes full of holes. It is what it is."

Mark leaned back in his chair and surveyed his daughter's face. She was frowning, her eyes were narrowed, her lips pressed tight to fight off tears. She looked angry and hurt, as though she honestly felt betrayed. He softened his tone and leaned forward.

"Emma, honey. I'm not against you. I'm trying to help you. I don't want you to spend the next fifteen years in prison. I want you to think a little for a minute—not of Paco and not even of yourself, but of Ro-drigo's family."

Emma sighed and rolled her eyes.

"Don't you dare roll your eyes at me!" Mark exploded. "Those people have lost their only son, a boy they were very proud of and, from all I've heard, had a right to be. A good student. A devoted son. A kind person. That's all they have now, those memories and that reputation. When you say he tried to rape you and tried to kill the person who rescued you, you're taking away their last comfort. Have you thought of that? Is that really what you want to do?"

Emma's face scrunched up, and finally she burst into tears. But they were angry tears, not repentant ones. "How can you do this to me? How can you accuse me and try to make me feel guilty about someone who tried to hurt me? That's like the typical male reaction to rape, right? You want me to say he didn't do it. But he did. I don't know what you think happened, but the truth is—"

"I'll tell you what I think happened," he interrupted. His jaw was clenched, the color rose in his face, and the veins in his neck bulged slightly. "I think there was no Algerian, Emma. I think Paco killed Rodrigo. I don't know how Rodrigo got into your room or what he was doing there, but I don't think he tried to rape you."

Emma got up, sobbing uncontrollably. When she spoke, her voice was less bitter and more heartbroken. "I can't stay here. I'm sorry you think so badly of me, Daddy. I love you, and I wouldn't lie to you. I don't know how you don't know that." She turned around and walked to the exit, asking the guard to let her out.

Jennifer left first. José followed and Mark walked slowly behind him. They retrieved their passports without looking at each other. José led them outside, where they each, almost unconsciously, took a deep breath.

"Wow, Mark. That went well," Jennifer said furiously. "What is happening to you? How could you talk to her like that when she's so desperate and so alone?"

He looked straight at her. "She's lying through her teeth," he said.

CHAPTER 16

Mark's phone rang as he was getting into the car, and he spent most of the ride back in intense conversation with the caller while Jennifer fumed. José drove with his eyes fixed straight ahead of him, occasionally trying to overcome the tense atmosphere. "Ah, here we are, back in the city," he said as they left the expanse of desert and entered a more developed area. When they reached the hotel, Jennifer told José she'd be in touch and, not waiting for either him or the doorman to open her door, rushed out of the car and walked briskly into the lobby without looking back. Mark hurriedly ended his phone conversation, thanked José, and followed Jennifer inside.

She was in the room, lying on top of the bedspread with her shoes kicked off when he entered.

"I heard a little of your end of the conversation," she said. "I assume it means you need to go right back."

"I should get there pretty soon," he answered.

"That's fine. Why not see if you can get on a flight tonight?"

He went into the bathroom and closed the door. She could hear the water running, and when he came out he was drying his face.

"Did you need to cool off?" she asked.

"In more ways than one," he answered. "Listen, Jennifer, we need to talk."

"Do we? Are you sure? I mean, I know we need to talk about

whatever it is that's going on between us eventually, but do you think it's wise to open that particular can of worms now?"

"What did you think I meant? I meant we need to talk about Emma. But yes, I guess that also means we have to talk about us. I know you're mad and just want me to leave, and I know that's partly because you want to avoid this conversation, but honestly, I don't see how I can leave without our talking about what happened today."

She looked at him. He was so upright, so earnest. His boyish face, his sandy hair just beginning to fleck with gray, his conservative, loose-fitting dark blue suit, his Paul Stuart shirt—all made him look like the respectable, law-abiding, decent man and successful attorney he was. This was the package she had fallen in love with. It's funny, she thought, how the very things that first draw you to someone are often those that finally put you off. What she once saw as integrity she now saw as rigidity. He can't cut Emma any slack. He refuses to believe her, and now that he's turned on her, he blames me, she thought.

"What is there to talk about? I believe her; you don't. Let's hope the jury, if it comes to that, ends up agreeing with me."

Mark removed his jacket, loosened his tie, and pulled it off. "The point is that they won't. If you weren't so blinded by your defenses, you'd see that."

"What do you mean my defenses? You think I'm responsible for all this?"

"I think you believe you're responsible for everything our children do and that's why you don't let yourself see them honestly. I think you take too much credit for their successes and too much blame for their failures."

What Jennifer thought was that his words were really unfair. She had waited and waited for Mark to come, practically counting the days. She went over it in her mind. Though she knew he had to be in the States, she couldn't help feeling that it was wrong for her to be shoul-dering all the pressure by herself. She'd thought she was doing a pretty good job and that he'd thank her for it. She'd needed his partnership, his support. And now, instead of this crisis bringing them closer, which it might have, he was using it as a weapon against her. How could he? What a moment for him to start criticizing her.

"I don't know where this is coming from, Mark." Jennifer spoke quietly. "But I don't think this is the time for you to start psychoanalyzing me. Let's take care of Emma first, okay?"

He barely reacted to her. He had his own thoughts and his own agenda and he had come too far to stop. "Jennifer, do you remember when Emma was in high school and she was caught shoplifting?"

High school again. Was he really going to dredge up every last bit of mud from the past? Yes, she remembered it well and had herself begun to think about it, though she tried not to. Memories crept into her consciousness, even affecting her unconscious dreams, but she kept pushing them away. She felt strongly that doubting Emma was a kind of luxury she didn't have. She wasn't a fool, she thought; she saw the new hardness in Emma, the anger, the dangerous signs of a distorted morality—but that had to be the next phase. That would be about *fixing* Emma. Now had to be about *saving* her.

"Yes," she said. "I wondered when you'd get to that. Are you going to bring up her wetting her pants in kindergarten too?"

It was the one time in their lives before this that Emma had really worried and disappointed her. At sixteen, Emma was caught taking clothing from an upscale Chestnut Hill boutique. Jennifer and Mark had been deeply puzzled by her actions. Emma didn't need more clothes, and if she did, she had money to pay for them. She didn't even like expensive clothes. But the store owner found a silk party dress, price tags attached, in her backpack. He said he'd been watching her and saw her put it in. He'd suspected she'd done it before, he said, but this time he'd seen it with his own eyes. Jennifer was a good customer, so he didn't call the police, but he called her and Mark, who paid for the dress and confronted Emma. She had been with her friend Ashley when she was caught, and she claimed that Ashley had stuffed it into her backpack and she didn't know it was there. Ashley denied it and the two broke off their friendship.

Mark was talking, but Jennifer barely heard him. She was going over the shoplifting incident in her mind, step by step. He seemed to be waiting for an answer.

"What did you say?" she asked. "I'm afraid my mind was wandering."

"I said do you remember how cold she was, how she insisted it wasn't her fault? We thought she'd be crying and sorry, but she seemed angry rather than repentant. Remember?"

Jennifer remembered. She had talked Mark into going to see the owner. Mark had apologized and convinced him nothing like that would ever happen again.

"We had a big, tough talk with Emma, and we thought that ended it," Mark said.

"It did end it. It isn't the same, Mark. Lots of teenagers shoplift. That's not some deep character flaw. She learned from it."

"Really—what did she learn? I'll tell you what. She learned she could get away with anything by lying." He paused and changed his tone from anger to sadness. "She was willing to throw her best friend under a bus, Jennifer. They never spoke again. Didn't you ever wonder about that?"

She had. It had bothered her a lot. She'd known Ashley since the girls were in first grade together. Ashley's mother had been her friend, and they'd lost touch after the incident. But she had pushed her disquieting thoughts away. Now, without admitting it, she asked herself again if Emma had lied about Ashley.

"I don't know," she answered. "It's too long ago to remember. Why do we have to talk about it now?"

Those words had stopped Mark before, but there was no stopping him now.

"When was the last time you and I talked about anything important? We have been moving into separate lives little by little, and whenever I try to talk about the shift, you gloss over it and call it unimportant—it's not the right place; it's not the right time; we can discuss it at some later time that never comes. Let's be honest, our life has been about the kids and not much else for years, and you make no effort to change that. Does it never occur to you that I count too, Jennifer?"

She sighed with a trembling breath. "Of course you count, Mark." She was on the verge of tears and he softened slightly.

"Look, I've let it go, so maybe it's partly my fault. But ignoring upsetting things, refusing to confront them or talk about them—that won't work this time."

She thought about the affair she'd feared he'd had. She'd come to think it wasn't true, but now the thought flashed through her mind that maybe it was. She remembered Suzie telling her to pay more attention to him, not just the children. Maybe she should have. But not now. Now certainly anyone could see that Emma's problem had to come first.

She really wanted him to leave. For the first time, she was grateful for his demanding job. She spoke in a conciliatory tone. "Listen, Mark, I know you're right. We have to have a long talk about a lot of things. But we can't solve everything in a few tense hours before you have to get on a plane. Can you please hold off on this until next time? And can we decide what I should do next about Emma before you go?"

He hesitated, then nodded somberly. He knew he had to leave, and he didn't want to go with so much anger between them. He sat on the bed, took her hand, and gently pulled her down to sit next to him. He put his arm around her and tried not to react when he felt her stiffen and saw her turn her head away. "Let's not leave like this, Jen. I'm sorry it came out the way it did. I think we can fix it. I love you."

She slowly turned her head toward him, but she cast her eyes downward to avoid looking at him directly. "I love you too," she said mechanically. "I'll be okay. We'll be okay." She laughed suddenly. "I guess that just sounds like what you've been complaining about, me thinking all this will go away. But it's not because I can't or won't face it; I just think we can overcome it. Am I wrong there too?"

"I hope not," he said. "I don't think you're wrong, if you're willing to try."

She asked him what she needed to do about Emma until his next visit. He told her that the most important next step depended on her accepting that Emma was not telling the truth. "Even if you don't accept it, then you need to realize that her only defense lies in that direction. She needs to admit there was no Algerian—maybe even no attempted rape; I'm not sure about that—and tell us what really happened. It will mean implicating Paco, I'm fairly certain, and she won't want to do that. But if she really understands it's her or him, she may change her mind." His presentation had been unemotional and professional. Now he paused and, lowering his voice, added a more personal, bitter remark. "After all, she had a longer relationship with Ashley than she's had with Paco, and she didn't hesitate to turn on her for her own advantage."

Jennifer pulled away before she could stop herself. "Oh, Mark, you have such a low opinion of her, you frighten me."

He got up, walked to the desk, and picked up the phone. "I'm sorry. That was an unnecessary swipe, but I fear for her freedom."

He called the concierge to arrange a booking for that day's Iberia flight to JFK. Then he busied himself with packing his toiletries and the few other items he'd brought and called his car service in New York to arrange a pickup at the airport.

"Let's call the kids before I leave," he said. "I think they'd like to talk to you."

"I'm not up to it right now. It would be hard to put on any fake optimism."

"Maybe you should let them know you're blue. After all, you miss them, Emma is in trouble—they know all that."

"I don't think so. Anyway, I've spoken to them almost every day. I'll call them later when I'm feeling better."

What does he want me to do? she thought. Tell them that their father believes their sister is complicit in a murder? He knows nothing about how to talk to children. He never did. But he always thought I did. Now he doesn't trust either me or Emma.

The concierge called a few minutes later to tell him he was booked on a flight to Madrid that left in an hour. There was a two and a half hour layover in Madrid before his flight to New York. Mark said he'd be right down and asked for a taxi. He hurriedly put his tie and jacket on, grabbed his bag, and walked to the door. "I have to go," he said apologetically.

"I know. That's fine. Have a safe trip." She walked over to him and kissed him lightly on the cheek. He put his bag down and took her in his arms, which she passively allowed.

"I'm sorry this happened, Jen. I know you have your hands full here and I hate to upset you more. But I think this conversation was important. I think you'll see that eventually."

"I'm fine. Better hurry."

She waited for the door to close and the sound of his footsteps walking down the hall toward the elevator. Then she heaved a sigh of relief and lay on the bed staring at the ceiling. After a few minutes, she got up, walked to the desk, and picked up the phone. She punched in a telephone number. The phone rang four times before she heard the familiar message: "Digame lo que quiera."

"If you're there, please answer," she said. "I need to talk to you."

A few seconds and then she heard someone pick up. "Sí, senora," Roberto said. "I am here."

CHAPTER 17

They met at a tapas bar Roberto recommended on Calle Batis. Always precisely on time, Roberto had arrived first and was waiting at the counter. When Jennifer entered a few minutes later, his wasn't the only head that turned to stare. She looked beautiful, dressed in her favorite black dress and pointy, patent leather high heels. Her long chestnut hair was pulled into a knot with a few wisps that came loose and softly framed her face. She had put on a little makeup and her lips shone with a pale pink gloss that nearly matched the color of her pink quartz necklace and earrings. She could feel the approval of the appraising glances.

She had deliberately created this effect. Feeling upset and insecure after Mark left, worried about Emma and not sure what to believe, she needed what she had managed to produce: male attention, which restored a small sense of her own power. She spotted Roberto right away and joined him at the bar. He had already ordered and offered her some fried cheese croquetas and jamón serrano. She wanted a drink first, so she called the waiter over to order one. "Vino blanco, por favor," she said.

"Qué bueno," Roberto said with a big smile. "You are learning Spanish, senora. This experience will have taught you something, at least."

She looked past him, not meeting his eyes. "It has taught me many things. Spanish is the nicest of them."

He took a sip of his beer and peered at her over his glass. "That doesn't sound good. Has your husband gone home?"

"Yes, but that's okay. I'm actually relieved he left."

Roberto picked up his beer again and downed the rest in one large swig. He signaled to the waiter to bring him the check and took out his wallet to settle the bill. Jennifer's wine was just arriving, and he told the waiter they had changed their minds and had to go but would pay for the wine anyway since they had ordered it. Although she didn't understand his words, there was no missing his body language as he stood up, offered her his hand, and gently pulled her to her feet. She complied, confused, and let him lead her outside, where she asked him why he was suddenly in such a rush.

"From the way you have dressed and the way you are talking, I see this is not the night for a tapas bar," he said with a crooked smile. We will go to a quiet restaurant I know where we can talk, and after, if you like, we can take a walk and talk some more. Am I right in thinking you have something you want to discuss?"

She gratefully fell in step with him. He stopped at a taxi stand and they waited for a few minutes until an empty cab pulled up.

"Thank you," Jennifer said, leaning back into the seat and staring ahead of her. "You're right, of course. I do need to talk." She turned to look at him. "I saw Emma today."

"I know," he said soothingly. "But we will not discuss that here. We will soon be somewhere more appropriate. I will order a Scotch and you will order some wine—white, I believe—and we will ask for a private room and talk there."

"A private room? For only two people? Is that possible? Maybe you're a little optimistic."

He seemed almost offended, but she couldn't tell if it was real or if he was playing with her.

"I once told you I never do anything on faith, senora. My brother owns the restaurant. He will accommodate us."

"But what if the rooms are all taken?"

"Ah, you are very exacting. Good. We will need that kind of thinking for our case."

"But you haven't answered."

He smiled. "I planned to take you there after our tapas. I have reserved the room for the entire night since I wasn't sure what time we
would arrive. Are you satisfied?"

"More than satisfied. I'm impressed. And kind of astounded."

She leaned back again and looked out the window at the crowded
streets, all the people moving about, living their lives, hurrying to meet
someone or going home alone to empty apartments, happy or sad or angry or afraid. They were all coping with their own private crises or celebrating their own triumphs. And though she didn't know them and
could barely understand their language, she felt a kinship with them
somehow, a sense that they were all part of the same human drama and
that, though the cause might be different, her current unhappiness was
something they could understand. It would change, even pass one day,
and be replaced by other emotions, emotions they also had felt. It was a
strange sensation, kind of soppy, she thought, but it was salutary. It made
her feel connected to the life around her, less alone. The last time she'd
felt anything like it was in college when she'd smoked pot. Remembering
that made her think again of Emma. Maybe her involvement with Paco
was not so different from Jennifer's own college days when she had a
boyfriend who smoked joints every day and sometimes snorted cocaine.
He was always trying to get her to join him, but except for the pot once
or twice, she resisted everything else. She hadn't liked the sensation of
being high because she didn't like feeling out of control. And she hadn't
stayed with him or his crowd. She never approved of the drug scene.

Still, in retrospect, it seemed rather innocent. And that old boyfriend had ended up going to Harvard Business School and was now
the CEO of some big company. Maybe Paco wasn't so . . . But that's ridiculous, she thought. There's no comparison. No one died in that
group; no one was stabbed to death. And the detective had said that
Paco dealt serious drugs, the hard stuff. No. This was different.

The cab pulled over to the curb in front of a restaurant with several small round tables outside. They were all taken, and Jennifer noticed pitchers of sangria on some of them, while at others fried squid and beer were being consumed. It looked good, and she realized she was hungry. Roberto led her inside, and after a few pleasantries with the host, they were taken to a private room in the back. It was furnished with a heavy oak farmhouse table large enough for eight but set for two, a rustic buffet with a travertine marble top, and several side tables. A lavish bouquet of bright pink peonies sat atop one of the tables and white beeswax candles in brass candlesticks had been placed artfully around the room. The host showed them to their seats, lit the candles, and withdrew.

Roberto held her chair and sat down after she did. Almost immediately, the waiter appeared to take drink orders, and she asked if the bartender could do a Bellini. He told her he thought they had peach nectar and could therefore produce it. Roberto asked for a Scotch, neat. The waiter left the menu for them and she started to peruse it.

"There's no rush," Roberto said. "We can drink first, if you like. You can order whenever you're hungry."

"Actually, I'm hungry now," she said. "You whisked me out of that other place so fast I didn't get a chance to eat anything."

"Ah, then by all means . . ."

She looked at the menu while he called the waiter back and ordered some more croquetas and gambas. She had chosen the lamb for her main course and Roberto ordered that for both of them.

"Now that all of that is out of the way, you are perhaps ready to tell me what you wanted to talk to me about."

"I think I'd like to have my drink first," she said.

They waited, making small talk. She commented on the restaurant's decor and asked if his brother was the chef as well as the owner. He told her that his brother was both but unfortunately had taken a day off or Roberto would have liked to introduce him to her.

The waiter came back with their drinks and they held them up for a toast. "To Emma's release," Roberto said. They clinked glasses, but

Jennifer was not looking directly at him. "Ah, senora, we must lock eyes for a toast or it will bring bad luck."

She looked at him. "Then by all means . . ." They clinked again. "Roberto, you must call me Jennifer."

"Perhaps. But not yet."

She put her glass down and sat quietly for a few minutes, staring at the tabletop. At last she spoke. "Mark thinks that Emma is lying. He thinks there was no Algerian. He thinks Paco stabbed Rodrigo and Emma is protecting him."

Roberto hailed the waiter and ordered another Scotch. When they were alone again, he spoke. "But that is not a surprise. You think the same."

"What are you saying? Of course I don't think that. I believe Emma."

He shook his head and spoke gently. "No, senora, you don't. You want to believe her very much. You think you *should* believe her. But tell me the truth—or don't tell me but think about it yourself—do you really believe her? Hasn't she been lying to you from the beginning? Wasn't she lying even before you came—about what she was doing and where she was living?"

"Yes, but . . ."

"You resent your husband for saying it, but you have said it to yourself, I am sure."

She thought about what he had said and then nodded slowly and looked down as she spoke. "I resent him for saying it the way he said it. I resent him for bullying me, for accusing me, for expanding this whole nightmare so it includes my relationship with him too."

He reached out his hand and put it on top of hers. She didn't withdraw it. He spoke softly, almost in a whisper. She had to lean closer to understand him.

"But you have had the same thoughts, yes?"

Her answer was reluctant and very quiet. She did not look at him but continued to stare fixedly at the table. "Yes. Sometimes. I try not to."

"You think he blames you?"

She pulled away her hand and looked up. "No. Not really. But maybe. Maybe a little. Maybe I blame myself. I don't know what to think." She finished her Bellini. "Maybe you could order a bottle of wine," she suggested, and he obliged. She waited for the waiter to fill her glass, then drank in little sips until she drained it. She felt the warmth suffuse her body and her eyes get heavy while her mind became slightly clouded.

"Roberto, there is something else, something I understand but I don't think Mark does. Emma is many things, but one of them is a twenty-year-old young woman who is in love for the first time in her life. And in that early stage of first love the line between who she is and who he is sometimes becomes obscured, especially in someone who is at the same time breaking away from her parents, trying to establish her independence, at least psychologically if not economically. And because I think I understand this, I have an idea of how to help her."

The waiter stopped at the table to deliver their dinner. When he left, Roberto got up.

"I need to use the restroom. I'll be right back. What you are saying is intriguing. I want to hear what you have in mind."

She watched him go, pouring herself another glass of wine. She remembered how she and Emma had been amused by Emma's friend Mara, one of three suitemates who bunked with her during her freshman year at Princeton. They shared adjoining double rooms separated by a common bathroom and had all been very close friends. But once Mara met her boyfriend, Jules, he was constantly with her. It was awkward for the other two roommates in that cramped space. They kept bumping into him as they came out of the shower or when they were trying to study or get ready for bed, and they got tired of his being constantly around. When they complained, Mara told them, "What you say about him is what you say about me. If you say he's around too much, it's like saying I'm around too much."

"No, it isn't," the girls insisted. "You are you and he is him."

"You don't understand," Mara finally proclaimed with frustration. "I *am* Jules."

Emma and Jennifer had laughed and laughed over this, but now she wondered if this wasn't exactly what was happening to Emma.

If they wanted to separate her from Paco, if they had any hope of getting her to tell the truth about what had happened even if that would mean getting him into trouble in order to save herself, they had to find a way to demonstrate that she was separate from him, that his well-being wasn't necessarily hers.

She saw Roberto wending his way through the tables as he returned to their private room. He sat down, put his napkin on his lap, took a sip of his drink, and smiled at her.

"Bien. Now tell me your idea."

"We need to separate her from Paco psychologically."

"Por supuesto, pero cómo?" he mumbled.

"What?"

"I'm sorry. Of course we do. But how?"

"I think it's something you might investigate. For example, where does the money we have given her and she has given to him actually go? He tells her he does everything to help the poor and unemployed, but does he? Where does his drug money go? What organization? What individuals in what village? If we can show Emma that Paco has lied to her, that he isn't what he claims—and I don't know; I'm just guessing that he isn't—maybe she will stop trying to protect him. And there's another thing. Maybe you could find out if there's another girlfriend somewhere. I mean, if he was cheating on her, that would be the best."

Roberto laughed out loud. "Your daughter would not agree with you. But you are devious; I like that, senora. It may be just what we need. Will you tell Emma that you no longer believe her story?"

"No. Not yet."

"Will you tell your husband?"

"I haven't decided what I will tell my husband. For the moment, this is just between us. De acuerdo?"

"Sí, Jennifer, de acuerdo."

CHAPTER 18

Two days passed during which Roberto tied up some loose ends on his other cases and he and Jennifer met to discuss their strategy. She awoke on the morning of the third day optimistic and energized, even though she had once again been refused permission to visit Emma and couldn't reach her by phone. Still, she was a woman with a mission, and now she knew what it was. She would expose Paco, who she was sure was hiding something, and she would free her daughter, not only from prison but from the psychological stranglehold in which Paco held her. Once she was set on this plan, it simply did not occur to her that she might be wrong and that there might be nothing helpful to discover.

She glanced at the clock—it was 8:00 A.M. She stretched, turning over to lie on her back, where she stayed for a few minutes, a satisfied smile creasing her face as she recalled the plan she and Roberto had finally settled on. He would leave this morning for Paco's home village and find out whatever he could about Paco's background: parents, siblings, school reports, neighbors, whomever he could track down. José would check with his sources in the police department to see what they had found out. And Jennifer would try to contact Paco and Emma's friends.

In some ways Jennifer's job was the hardest. She had Julia as her contact to Emma's circle, but she had no idea who Paco's friends were. Still, she was eager to get started, and she figured she'd call Julia first.

She got up and made her way to the bathroom, trying to ignore the lethargy in her limbs and her aching head. She shouldn't have drunk so much wine, she thought as she splashed cold water on her face and reached into her medicine bag for some Advil. She showered and dressed and, feeling somewhat better, opened the door to pick up her copy of the *International New York Times*, which she intended to take with her to the breakfast room on the ground floor. The paper lay on her doorstep, front page up, and as she bent down to retrieve it her pulse quickened. In the lower half of the front page was a picture of Emma. And not just any picture. It was the incriminating shot of Emma dressed as a prostitute, the one the Spanish press had used and that Jennifer thought had been taken care of when Roberto had explained to the press that it was a costume for the American holiday of Halloween. But here it was again, with no explanation of its provenance, above a headline that read: PRINCETON CO-ED PRIME SUSPECT IN MURDER INVESTIGATION.

Her greatest immediate fear had been realized: The story was now the property of the international press. They would arrive in droves, she fretted; they would investigate, incriminate, sensationalize. They would turn an already painful situation into a circus. Most important, they would lessen any chance of getting Emma out quietly without a trial. And there was absolutely nothing she could do about it.

She grabbed up the paper and pulled it inside, her heart pounding. She hurriedly read the story, fear turning to despair. Her first thought was to call Roberto, who was on his way to Paco's village, about four hours away. She tried his mobile, but the phone went straight to voice mail without ringing, so either he was out of range of a signal or—unlikely, given his attention to detail—his phone needed to be charged. She hung up and tried Suzie, forgetting the time difference until she heard Suzie's thickened, groggy voice.

"Suze, I'm so sorry to wake you. What time is it there?"

"Jesus, Jennifer. It's two a.m. What's up? Did something happen to Emma?"

"No, not that. I'm sorry. But I don't know who else to call. I just saw today's *Times* and there's a picture of Emma in that prostitute costume on the front page. The reporter says she interviewed students in and out of Emma's program. She quotes people claiming Emma was crazed from the moment she arrived here, that she went to wild parties and slept around before she even met Paco. I mean, it's totally shoddy journalism. I don't see how they can use unidentified sources when it blackens someone's reputation and could even affect a verdict. And no one even called me for a comment on this. My lawyer didn't know it was coming or he'd have warned me."

"Well, there's nothing really new in those accusations," Suzie said. "They're all lies and gossip. You know that. You've heard most of it before."

"I know, but that was local, the Spanish press. Now this is an American story, an international one—everyone will turn against her."

"No. We have to get the spin doctors we hired to get to work on this. They have to counter it somehow. She was celebrating Halloween. They'll push the idea that this is an anti-American witch hunt."

Jennifer lowered her voice. "Suzie, I don't even know if it's true."

"Don't say that, Jennifer. Don't think it. It doesn't matter right now. We'll fight these rumors. The truth is, what if she did sleep around? So what? Maybe she went a little wild. That's like every college freshman in the U.S. Maybe they're not used to that there. Whatever it is, it's a long way from being a murderer. Or helping a murderer. We have to get back to the original story where she's the victim. Any luck in locating the Algerian?"

"No. No one believes there was an Algerian. No one. Not the police. Not her lawyer. Not the reporter who wrote this damn story. Not even her father."

"Mark doesn't believe her?"

"No. That's another story. Too long for now."

"Well, do you believe her?"

"I don't know anymore. There's lots of evidence pointing away from that story."

"Is any of that in the paper today?"

"No. But it will be. It's just a matter of time."

"What does Mark say about this?"

"I haven't called him."

"Call him, Jennifer. Whatever is going on between you two, he's her father. You have to call him. I'll get hold of the PR company and get back to you when I hear what they have in mind."

"Thank you, Suzie. I love you."

"Me too. Call Mark."

Jennifer hung up and sat motionless staring at the phone. She noticed it was blinking and realized there must be a message, so she picked it up and pushed 6, which connected to the hotel's individual message system. There was a voice mail from someone called Catherine Murphy asking her to please call back. The date was two days ago, meaning the delivery had somehow been delayed, since she checked her messages carefully these days and was sure the light wasn't blinking earlier. The name sounded familiar. She glanced at the byline on the story, and there it was: Catherine Murphy. The reporter had called for a comment. Small comfort that was, though it would at least have given her a chance to explain that the picture was misleading and the implication, in her opinion, libelous.

She broke the connection and punched in her home number. The phone rang four times before Mark picked it up. She could picture him first doubling his pillow over his ears, then rolling over to her side of the bed, where the phone was stationed, finally reaching for it, barely awake. He mumbled a sleepy hello.

She didn't bother to apologize for waking him, launching immediately into the story in the paper. He hadn't known about it, and they wondered if it would be in that day's *New York Times*, which would be delivered by 7:00 A.M.

"We always knew this was a possibility, Jennifer. We'll do everything we can to launch a counterattack, pushing our own narrative."

"I'm a little confused about what our own narrative is."

He answered quickly and fluently, making it clear he was ready for this question.

"Emma is a star student at Princeton, a believer in social justice, an innocent who lived a supervised, hardworking, busy life of study, friends, sports, and volunteer work. She was overwhelmed by the relative freedom she experienced this first time completely on her own, and may have gotten involved with the wrong people. But she is essentially a decent, honest person and would never be involved in either drug sales or violence."

"Well, *I* believe that."

He let that go. "There will probably be reporters trying to interview us," he continued. "Ask Roberto how to handle that. My gut says talk to no one."

"But maybe we should orchestrate an interview with the right publication or TV channel to give our side," she suggested.

"We can't do that until we know the truth or falsehood of their allegations and why they made them. Does this come from gossip or somebody's actual knowledge? You'll need to have Roberto talk to the same students and others, and you should go back to talk to Emma again."

She agreed, telling him that she would consult with Roberto, who was out of town at the moment but should return the following day. She didn't mention the errand Roberto was on, still intending to keep that secret until they found something. And she didn't say that she would try to find Emma's friends and fellow students herself while Roberto was away.

"I might be able to come back in four or five days. Can you hold on by yourself until then?"

"Of course. You don't really need to come at all."

"Jennifer—"

"Do what you think is best. I have to go."

She hung up. Already regretting her behavior, she reached for the phone and called him back to apologize but changed her mind and hung up after she heard the first ring. She knew she was wrong, but on another level, she felt better. It wouldn't kill him for her to stay mad awhile longer, and it helped her. She didn't want to waste time dealing with relationship issues between her and Mark. She had work to do for Emma today.

She went downstairs for some breakfast before calling Julia. The dining room was relatively empty. A few men and women in business suits sat alone at tables, and she noticed one woman with two little girls sitting nearby. The children—she reckoned they were about four and seven—were quarreling. She remembered when Emma and Lily were about that age. How they fought with each other! Emma had taken the birth of a sibling hard. She had so loved being the first and only child and was loath to share anything—her toys, her room, and especially her mother's attention. She was fine at first, even being protective of her baby sister and urging her mother to pick her up if she cried. But as soon as Lily got old enough to start wanting to play with Emma's toys, or break Emma's Lego creations, or sit on Jennifer's lap, Emma rebelled. After that, there was open hostility, and although they occasionally played together when neither had a playdate, most of their interactions were competitive and explosive. It was different when Eric was born, because by that time, Emma had resigned herself to not being an only child. In fact, she had taken it upon herself to mother him. She begged to let him sleep in her room and showered him with little presents, including her collection of stuffed animals. Mark had joked that Emma was actually sending Lily a message: "You see, I don't hate *all* my siblings. Just *you*." As they grew older, though, that relationship changed, and by the time Emma left for Spain, the girls were good friends.

The two sisters had stopped bickering, busying themselves with the coloring books and crayons their mother had handed them.

Jennifer ordered a continental breakfast with a basket of rolls, orange juice, and coffee, and ate a muffin when it came. Then she went back to her room to call Julia.

The message light on the room phone was flashing, and she picked up the phone to discover that she had missed two calls. Hoping that one of them was from Roberto, she hurriedly played the messages back. They were both from reporters—one from *El País* in Madrid, another from *Le Figaro* in Paris. They each left a number and asked her to call back. It had begun. She erased both messages and called Julia's cell phone.

Julia's voice mail picked up and Jennifer left a message asking her to call back. She figured Julia was probably at class and wondered if she should go to the university and try to meet her. But it seemed senseless—she didn't know what class she might be attending, or even if she was actually there. She decided to wait for Julia to return her call. She felt restless and anxious and didn't know what to do to pass the time. She tried calling Roberto again but was once more greeted by his voice mail. She called José but was told he was at a meeting. She hesitated, then called Mark on his cell phone so she could leave a message without waking him again.

"Mark, it's me. I'm sorry about before. Of course I want you to come and to come as soon as you possibly can. I've been rattled by everything that's been going on lately, but I know we can handle it best together. Call me later, when you're up and have a minute, okay?"

She tried to read the rest of the paper but couldn't concentrate and finally grabbed her bag and went downstairs. There was no point just sitting in her room and waiting, she thought, so she left the hotel and walked over to the university. It was a beautiful day: hot but not humid, with the bright sun illuminating the multicolored flowers, whose scent perfumed the air. How she would have loved it here under different circumstances. Even now, even after the shock of today's newspaper story, she felt her spirits lift just by stepping outside.

She was lucky; she spotted Julia as soon as she entered the university's courtyard. She was walking with a group of friends, chatting and laughing, carrying her books in front of her. It looked as though class had just let out. Jennifer called out to her and waved and Julia caught sight of her. After a slight pause in which Jennifer thought a flicker of reluctance crossed her face, she waved back, excused herself from her friends, and joined her.

"Hi, Mrs. Lewis. Are you looking for me?"

"Hi, Julia. I am, actually. I'm sorry to take you away from your friends."

"That's all right. I want to help Emma any way I can. A friend gave me a ride out to visit her. I wrote to her and she asked the prison for permission to let me in. It was so depressing. She seemed okay, but it was awful seeing her in jail with all those tough women. She's trying to be brave, but she looked so alone."

Jennifer sighed. "I know. But she's not. She has all of us. When did you see her? We saw her a few days ago, and I haven't been told when I can go again."

"I saw her the same day, right after you did. She told me you and her dad had just left." Julia hesitated and looked down. "She was really upset, Mrs. Lewis. I guess she had some kind of fight with her dad?"

Jennifer ignored the question and thanked her for going. She told her that all the people trying to help Emma thought that her case could be cleared up if she would just tell the truth and stop protecting Paco. "It's hard, because maybe she will have to admit that some of what she's been saying isn't true, but she won't consider changing her story, not if she thinks it will get Paco in trouble." She watched Julia's reaction carefully, hoping she might give something away.

Julia frowned and bit her lower lip. It seemed to Jennifer that she was deciding how much to reveal of what she knew.

"Julia, please, if you know anything about Paco that might help separate him from Emma, tell me. That's the best way to help her."

Julia avoided looking at her. "What if I know something that might hurt her case? Do you want me to tell you that?"

Jennifer tensed as she girded herself for bad news. "Yes," she said. "I need to know everything."

Julia glanced around uncomfortably to see if anyone was listening to them. Jennifer suggested they go out for a cup of coffee. They found a café nearby and Julia scanned the neighboring tables to be sure she didn't know anyone.

"Look, I think you're right about Paco. She's blind when it comes to him. You know he's a drug dealer, but she may be more involved in that than you think. I mean, I'm sorry to tell you this, and I don't even know if it's true, but some of the kids say she had kind of become his partner. They said they sold the drugs together."

Jennifer stopped her. "But you don't believe that, do you? That couldn't be true."

Julia blushed, stammering as she answered. "I don't . . . I mean, I'm not . . . Look, if she did, she justified it by believing the money was going to the poor people in his village who had no jobs and no hope of getting any in this economy. I'm sure that's what he told her, anyway."

"What do you mean? Do you think he was lying?"

"Who knows? Even if it was the truth, it's no excuse."

"I know. Of course. But who did he sell to?"

"I don't really know. Mostly students, I'd guess. A lot of the foreign students, the ones they call *los orgasmus*.

Jennifer vaguely remembered Emma mentioning something about this but couldn't recall the context. "What does that mean?"

Julia looked embarrassed. "You know, from orgasm. They're a group of foreign students who like to party and go to bars and take drugs and sleep around. That kind of thing."

"And Emma was involved in that too?"

"I don't know. But lots of them had money and they spent it on drugs."

The waiter came over and Julia ordered a café cortado. Jennifer asked for a café con leche. She sensed that Julia was holding something back. She leaned in and spoke in an intimate, confiding voice. "I'd like to know more about Paco, Julia. Has he been in Seville a long time? Who was his girlfriend before Emma? Who are his friends? Do you know anything about that?"

Julia looked uncomfortable. She seemed to be making up her

mind about something, and finally she blurted: "I know that he was not always nice to Emma. That's something else I wanted to tell you, but I wasn't sure if I should. I saw them together a lot before she moved in with him. He'd be with her and then break up with her. He'd criticize her and make her feel awful about herself. Then he'd be charming and make everyone think he was great. He'd berate her for being rich, for being privileged, for being an American. He always had some girl after him and he'd use that to make her jealous, but if anyone else looked at her, he'd go ballistic. He didn't like us and tried to get her to stop seeing so much of us, which she actually did for a while. He took the money you sent her, but he always said bad things about you and your values. We all thought it was kind of an abusive relationship, but she thought he was a saint or something."

Jennifer nodded slowly, taking it in, trying not to show any emotion. She asked again if she knew any of his friends or the name of even one former girlfriend. Julia said there was a guy she'd seen around them lots of times but she didn't know his name. He was Spanish. She thought he'd known Paco for a long time, maybe before he came to Seville. He hung out at the Triana Bridge almost every Saturday starting around midnight, and he was always stoned.

"I need to speak to him," Jennifer said, her voice rising in excitement. "Today is Thursday. Do you think he'll be there this Saturday?

"I don't know. Probably."

"Would you go there with me so you can point him out?"

Julia hesitated. "I wouldn't want him to know I mentioned him."

"He won't know. I promise. Just point him out and I won't even talk to him right away. I'll bring a friend of mine who used to be a cop."

"I don't know, Mrs. Lewis. I shouldn't have said anything."

"Please, Julia. It's the only lead I've got."

Julia reluctantly agreed and they made a date to meet at the bridge a little before midnight on Saturday. Then Julia rummaged in her bag to pay for her coffee, but Jennifer stopped her, saying this was definitely her treat. Julia thanked her, gathered her books, and left quickly.

As soon as she was alone, Jennifer pulled out her cell phone and tried Roberto again. This time he answered.

"Diga."

"Oh, Roberto, I'm so glad to hear your voice. I need to talk to you. A lot has happened."

"I know. I saw the papers and there's a lot of online traffic."

"Not only that. I also have some news. Someone for us to talk to about Paco."

"Bueno. I have some news about our friend Paco too. I have to make another stop, but I'll be back early tomorrow morning and come straight to your hotel. Please don't go anywhere. Wait for me."

"I will."

CHAPTER 19

The morning was long gone and still Roberto hadn't come. She'd been up for hours, had ordered room service for coffee and sweet rolls and, having decided that presenting Emma's side might be better than saying nothing, had fielded half a dozen phone calls from reporters all over Europe. Finally she'd called the hotel operator and told her not to put through any more calls. She could look over her messages later. Anyone she wanted to talk to would reach her on her cell phone anyway, she thought. Calls to the hotel would almost certainly be from people she didn't know.

She had read with dismay the follow-up article in the *International New York Times* and had also had the London *Times* delivered to her room, and she couldn't believe what they had already dug up. She read again that Emma had been a "party girl" who lived a fast, sexually promiscuous life; that she had dropped out of school and eventually moved in with Paco, who was also in custody, in a shabby apartment far from the usual student section; and that Paco was known as the local drug dealer. There were quotes from unidentified students in the program suggesting that Emma was more interested in partying than studying and others saying that she always seemed cold and unfriendly. One young woman said that her impression was that Emma was so enthralled with Paco she would have done whatever he wanted. That story was in the *Times*, and the reporter was at least honest enough to follow up with a question about how well her informant actually knew Emma.

"Well, I didn't actually know her personally," the young woman said. "But I knew many people who did." The reporters had also interviewed friends and professors at Princeton who were shocked and disbelieving that the serious, hardworking student they knew could be involved in this kind of scandal. It was as if Jennifer were reading about two completely different people.

Her cell phone rang, and although she didn't recognize the number, she answered the call.

"Hello, Mrs. Lewis. This is Theodora Aspek from the London *Times*. Please don't hang up."

"How did you get my private number?" Jennifer asked.

"I just want to ask you one question. I want to give you a chance to tell your side, your daughter's side. The police say that the victim's body was found in the bedroom near the bed, but they were able to ascertain that the victim wasn't killed there. They say the body was dragged from the kitchen, leaving a trail of blood. Do you have any response to that?"

Jennifer felt her face flush with anger. "There were two victims that night. One was my daughter. Please don't call me again." She hung up.

But she wondered about the information. Did that reporter get a leak from the police? Was what she had said true? She called José and asked him. He said that the information was correct. She asked how they could possibly know unless Emma had told them, and he said that the chemical luminol could detect blood even when it had been wiped away. The detectives were able to see the path the body was dragged along by the reconstituted blood evidence, which glowed in the darkened room once the luminol was applied. She had heard of this chemical earlier from Roberto, she remembered. She hadn't known enough to fear the results.

"Emma's story didn't account for that," José pointed out, "and they will now of course go back to her and Paco and try to get them to admit what really happened." He was surprised that the reporter already knew, because he had only just been informed of this development himself. He suggested that Jennifer change her cell phone number immediately and give it only to close friends and family. "There's one more thing," José added. "They applied the luminol to the kitchen knife. They found traces of blood on it and incomplete fingerprints in the blood that might be Emma's."

"Might be? And might not, right? Besides, she lives there. Of course the knife might have her fingerprints. The blood might have been hers—she probably cut herself. At home, she was always cutting herself when she sliced tomatoes. That's probably what happened."

"Perhaps."

Her anxiety was mounting again. "Have you heard anything from Roberto?" she asked. "He was supposed to be here this morning and he hasn't arrived and hasn't called. It's not like him."

José said he didn't have any information but assured her that if Roberto said he'd be there and wasn't, there was a good reason. She asked if he could arrange another visit to Emma, saying that when she called, they told her a visit was not possible at this time.

"They have told me her visiting privileges were under review," he said, his voice apologetic.

"But why? I don't understand. They originally said she was permitted two visits a week."

José sighed. "They report that she has continued to be uncooperative and they have decided to put her on a restricted visitation schedule," he said. "But I will try to get that reversed. I don't know how much I can do."

Saddened and frustrated, Jennifer didn't respond.

"You can call her," José added. "They still allow her to use the phone."

"I tried; she won't take my calls."

"Oh?"

"I think she's still angry at what Mark said in our last visit. But she won't talk to me either. I don't know what to do."

"I suggest you keep trying, senora," José said in a sympathetic tone. "And soon you will be able to visit her, I hope."

She felt caged in the hotel room, every impulse thwarted. Not only was she blocked from reaching Emma; she was also unable, because of the time difference, to reach her children in Philadelphia, who would surely be needing her help to get through all of this now that it was public. They would still be sleeping now, but she would call them before they left for school, which was still two hours away. She didn't know what to do to pass the time. Why didn't Roberto come?

She decided to take a walk—maybe she'd shop for some presents for Lily and Eric—and went downstairs. As she exited the elevator and walked through the lobby toward the entrance she heard a commotion and someone outside shout, "There she is!" She tried to ignore this and make her way out of the hotel, but a throng of at least fifteen reporters shouting questions crowded around her as she exited. "Did she do it?" "Is she getting fair treatment?" "Does she feel remorse?" "Do you believe her story?" "Was she a problem at home?" She backed up and took shelter inside the lobby, where hotel guards prevented the reporters from entering. She felt flustered and her heart was pounding. She turned to go back upstairs but was stopped by the hotel manager, who asked if he could have a word with her in his office.

She settled into a black leather chair as the manager sat behind his desk. It was quiet and cool in the air-conditioned office and she felt herself calm down a bit.

"I'm sorry, senora. I understand that this situation is difficult for you," he said kindly.

"Yes," she answered, "but I am convinced it will get better."

He looked uncomfortable and shuffled some papers. "I hope you are right, senora. But in the meantime, I'm afraid I must reluctantly ask you to make other arrangements."

"I don't know what you mean."

"I mean, we are a tourist hotel and the best in the city. We cannot afford to have scenes outside our door such as the one you just participated in."

"I hardly participated. I was accosted."

"Yes, I am not saying it is your fault. But it will continue until you leave, and so I am forced to ask you to find another place to stay while you are here in Sevilla."

She didn't beg him or argue with him. She simply rose and walked to the door with as much dignity as she could muster. "How long do I have?" she asked.

"It would be best if you could leave by tomorrow, but if that is impossible, you could stay until Monday."

She nodded and walked out. When she was back in her room, she sat on the bed and allowed herself to cry. Afterward, she splashed cold water on her face and tried calling Roberto again. Still no answer. She called José again—she thought his voice sounded weary; he must be tired of her—and told him what had happened, and he suggested she rent an apartment instead of a hotel room. He said he would ask his secretary to find something and she thanked him. It was time to call the kids in Philadelphia, but she felt so disheartened that she knew it would be hard to sound the note of confidence she thought they needed. Still, she reminded herself, she'd been an actress; she could fake it.

But she put it off, deciding to check the Internet first to see if there were any updates. There were probably lots of tweets about all this, she realized, but she didn't have a Twitter account and wouldn't know how to use it if she did. She'd have to ask Roberto when he came. In the meantime, she used her iPad to log on and typed in the URL for the *Huffington Post*. As she had feared, the story about Emma was on their home page and included the damning photograph that was in yesterday's *NYT* and all the British papers. She quickly scrolled through it, ascertaining that it didn't add anything new. But when she reached the end, she was shocked to see dozens of comments from readers. It seemed that everyone had an opinion, and every opinion was negative. Many were cruel and insulting and some gave links to blogs that, when she opened them, opined freely about Emma's behavior without a shred of credible evidence. One person, who signed herself "tellall," claimed that Emma had slept around promiscuously at Princeton and had seduced her best friend's fiancé. How could that be? Jennifer thought.

She knew Emma's best friend. She wasn't engaged—didn't even have a boyfriend. Was it someone else? Was it a lie? No way to tell. Another, from Spain, asked what did anyone expect? Emma was known, this person wrote, as the "*reina de los orgasmus.*" Jennifer had only recently heard about them, she thought. Now Emma was supposed to be their queen. This was absurd. A guy calling himself "spanishstud" said he had gone to Paco's to buy drugs and Emma had been there. He said she had looked stoned and was watching cartoons while he concluded the transaction. Cartoons? Emma? Still others wrote outraged comments condemning Emma as a rich, entitled American who was ruining the reputation of American foreign students and deserved to "rot in jail." Someone else suggested that the government close the program altogether, as it was bringing bad publicity to Spain. Many other posts were in Spanish, so Jennifer couldn't make them out.

She read what she could voraciously, hypnotically, overwhelmed. Her reactions ranged from despair to fury. Who were these people? How could anyone possibly tell who was lying and who was telling the truth? And how could others feel entitled to have such strong, condemnatory opinions on a subject they knew nothing about? Where did all the bile come from?

She had to talk to Lily right away, she realized, feeling guilty that she had put it off. She would see all this on the Internet and she had to be armed against it. And maybe even Eric needed to be prepared. Kids at school would have heard their parents talking and might well repeat what they had heard. She hoped Mark and her parents were talking to the kids, helping them through this, but everything that had happened to her since she had been a mother told her that only she could adequately handle something of this magnitude. She didn't—she couldn't—trust anyone else. She decided she would go home for a few days. She couldn't get in to see Emma for another week anyway, and Roberto would track down the background of the elusive Paco Romero.

With that resolution, she picked up the phone and punched in her home number. As she expected, Lily was distraught. She said reporters had been calling the house and were camped out in front of it and at her school. Mark had instructed them not to talk to anyone, but the kids at school seemed to like the attention and she saw them standing in groups talking to the same reporters she had ignored.

"I just don't understand," she said plaintively. "Did Emma do this? Everyone seems to think she did, but I can't believe it."

"Of course Emma didn't do this. This is an injustice and you have to stand up for your sister, darling. You know her. You know what she's capable of, no matter what people are saying."

Jennifer asked about Eric, and the news there was no better. The kids in his class had been hearing gossip from their families for days. Where they had learned of it was a mystery; it had only just made the international news. But somehow the word had gotten out, or some version of it was being bandied about. Jennifer had no way of knowing what they were saying, but Lily said the effect was disturbing. Eric was being treated with either scorn and attacks or discomfort and pity from formerly close friends and even their parents. He was miserable and acting out at school.

"Should I come home for a while?" Jennifer asked. "I could get away for a week and it wouldn't hurt Emma."

Lily thought about it. "No," she said finally. "We've got Dad and Pops and Granny, and Emma only has you. And besides, it will only get worse if you're here."

Jennifer was stung. "Worse? Why?"

"Because all those reporters will follow you. There will be even more of them."

She was right. She told Lily she was proud of her and asked her to be brave and then asked to speak to Eric. He didn't want to come to the phone and she could hear Lily and Mark in the background urging, cajoling, and finally ordering him to pick up.

"Hello," he said sullenly.

"Eric, honey, I know you're mad. I'm so sorry this is happening. But I'll be back before long and so will Emma. We're a family and we do these things for each other. I need you to be brave and loyal, like I know you are, and to remember that by being here, I'm helping your sister when she most needs it. Okay?"

He didn't answer.

"Okay, Eric?"

"Yeah," he said, barely audible. "But I gotta go."

"Okay. Let me talk to Daddy."

She updated Mark on the recent call from the London *Times* and they agreed that now that things had heated up he would be more valuable staying where he was and helping to manage the story on that end. They had to get their side out, to stress Emma's longtime empathy for the poor, her volunteer work, her good grades and hard work. When they hung up, there was less tension between them than before.

She thought about what she had said to Eric, that her being there was helping Emma. But was it? Emma seemed mostly inured to any comfort Jennifer might give, too caught up in the idea that she and Paco were engaged in some kind of class war in which her parents were on the wrong side. The by now familiar ache stabbed at her chest. Oh, Emma, Emma. She had to find a way to break through to her somehow. She latched on again to the idea that if only they could find something to discredit Paco, that would be a start.

She wanted to avoid reading any more stories about Emma but was drawn to them like a gambler who has already lost almost everything and can't stop herself from risking what was left on the slim chance of hitting the jackpot the very next time. Maybe someone would report something that would give her hope. She turned on CNN. The news report had just started. The top story was about the rash nuclear threats coming out of North Korea and the American reaction. She listened absentmindedly, knowing it was important but not able to focus on it. The newscaster followed with stories about Cyprus and Spain's economic outlook. She was relieved there was nothing about Emma, until the anchor announced that next up would be an interview with the parents of the Spanish student killed in Seville. She felt an internal plunge, like going downhill in a roller coaster, and her heart rate sped up. She wanted to turn it off but couldn't make herself do it.

The parents looked to be in their midfifties. The mother wore a trim black suit. Her dark brown hair was swept up into a bun and she wore large silver earrings. She'd have looked like many well-groomed Spanish women one passed on the street, except for her face. She didn't seem to be wearing makeup. Her eyes looked lined and puffy and—there was no way to avoid it—she had the look of a person who was ravaged by grief. The father wore a dark blue suit, white shirt, and gray tie. He sat by his wife's side, serious, looking as much angry as bereft. They spoke in Spanish and then English, saying they wanted to reach Emma's family and friends. They said they wanted to go on television to tell the world that their son was not a rapist. He was a good boy. He would have been a lawyer, maybe even a judge, they said. He respected the law. The American girl was lying. There was no Algerian. No one had tried to rape her. The mother began to cry. Saying she wanted to speak to Emma, she looked straight at the camera. "Please, if you are watching this, please tell the truth. You took my only son. Don't take the honor of my family." She covered her face as she began to cry. Her husband put his arm around her and glared at the camera as the interview ended.

Jennifer didn't know what to think. Her ability to block out any argument that led to Emma's guilt was disintegrating. She wasn't sure about anything anymore, especially about whether she had ever really known her daughter.

She tried calling Roberto one more time, not really expecting an answer and not getting one. She was beginning to seriously worry about him. Cars here typically moved along at breakneck speed; Spanish drivers were more aggressive than those in the States. Maybe he'd had an accident. She couldn't imagine what else would prevent him from at least calling her to say he had been delayed. She hoped he'd show up the next day. Aside from his investigative talents, she needed him as a translator, and she had counted on his being back in time to go to the Triana Bridge steps with her on Saturday. Now she faced the possibility that she might have to meet Julia and Paco's friend alone.

CHAPTER 20

A strident ring awoke her early the next morning. Still half-asleep, she thought it was her alarm clock, but it continued after she pressed the Off button. Groggily feeling around for the phone on her bedside table, she picked it up without looking at it, sure that the call was finally from Roberto.

"Where were you?" she asked with relief, her voice still thick with sleep. "I was so worried."

"It is José, senora."

Embarrassed, she apologized. He spoke formally, saying that he regretted that he seemed to have awakened her, but his secretary had found a place for her to stay and he thought she'd want to make arrangements as soon as possible. She hadn't gone out since the previous day's fracas and had almost forgotten the need to move. She thanked him and asked where it was.

"It is a small but I think adequate apartment in the *judería*," he said. "Only a few streets away from Las Casas de la Judería. Do you know it?"

She didn't, and she asked what *judería* meant.

"Ah, it means 'Jewish quarter,'" he said pleasantly. He laughed. "You will be comfortable there. You are Jewish, are you not?"

She was shocked. "Do you mean there is still a special section of town for Jews here?" she asked.

Now he laughed louder. "Oh, no, senora, of course not," he said.

He explained that the area, which was now the Barrio de Santa Cruz and the chief tourist section of the city, had indeed been a Jewish ghetto in the fifteenth century, cut off from the rest of the city by a wall. "You can still see what is left of that wall today," he said. He encouraged her to read about it and recommended an article in English she could find online. It recounted, he said, that in a much lauded historical restoration, the Duke of Segorbe had spent the past thirty years trying to return parts of the quarter to its original architecture.

"Las Casas de la Judería is the duke's special project," José continued. "A massive renovation of a former mansion into a hotel that is like a small village of connecting houses, patios, and gardens, each with its own personality. You will like it; you will see. Tourists find it very appealing." He told her that the apartment he had found was modern and comfortable, while the neighborhood retained the feel of an old European city.

"But you mentioned that I am Jewish. Is this area mostly settled by Jews?"

"No, no," he said. "Forgive me. I was making a joke. Perhaps a bad one. There are, sadly, very few Jews in Seville now and certainly not congregated in any area."

She thanked him and said she'd certainly like to see the apartment. Could she visit it before committing herself? He assured her that she could and arranged for his secretary to meet her in an hour at the address, 54 Calle de la Madre de Dios. She smiled at the name. "Madre de Dios—Mother of God." Well, it certainly had shed its Jewish origins.

She showered and dressed, wondering in passing how José knew she was Jewish. Not that it mattered, she thought. She'd been to the Barrio de Santa Cruz, she realized, not knowing its history. She'd visited those sites with Emma—she remembered the Alcázar, the royal palace that used to be a Moorish fort, and the cathedral with the Giralda looking like the top of a wedding cake. She had noted the beautiful labyrinthian narrow stone streets, shielded from the hot sun by the facades of the white and mustard-colored houses that lined them, many decorated with flower boxes overflowing with fragrant blooms.

She stopped at the hotel restaurant for breakfast and then took the elevator up to the lobby. She approached the exit warily but was relieved to see that the crush of reporters had diminished. She exited carefully, her head down, and was able to leave unaccosted, slipping into a waiting taxi and giving the address of what she hoped would be her new apartment. She arrived early and so had time to wander the alleyways and look in shop windows. Passing by, she peered into the stone courtyard of the Casas de la Judería. It was charming, with its white columns supporting an arcade of graceful arches that surrounded a blue-and-white-tiled fountain. Continuing her explorations, she saw a café near the Plaza de Santa Cruz that beckoned her, and she stopped to order a coffee, even though she had just had one at breakfast. It was so pleasant to sit there, shaded from the sun while enjoying its light.

Checking her watch, she saw it was time to walk to the meeting place, and having paid her bill, she made her way there. She recognized José's secretary, Rosa, even though she hadn't met her before, by her agitated look as she scanned the passing women to see if the American had arrived. Rosa seemed to know her as soon as she laid eyes on her; she bustled over enthusiastically, a broad-hipped middle-aged woman in a blue-and-white business suit, with bright red lacquered nails and matching lipstick. "Senora Lewis?" she asked. "I am Rosa. I am very happy to see you," she said in heavily accented English. "Let us go quickly. The landlord, he waits already."

Jennifer apologized for being late, even though her watch told her she was exactly on time, and followed Rosa into the building.

The apartment was perfect—modern, comfortable, and simple at less than half the price she'd been paying at the hotel. She took it quickly, leaving the paperwork to be handled by José. The landlord handed over the keys and she told him she planned to move in later that day.

After thanking Rosa, she walked briskly in the direction of the hotel. It was, as usual, a beautiful day. She tried Roberto's number again, but when she still heard only his voice mail greeting, she didn't bother to leave another message. The heaviness, the sense of dread that had accompanied her since she arrived in Seville and had lifted so briefly as she wandered the barrio and rented the apartment, settled in again, and she stopped at a taxi stand and wearily climbed into a waiting cab.

Passing the manager in the lobby at the hotel, she asked him to prepare her bill in advance of her imminent departure, and to ensure that her messages were forwarded. Then she went to her room to pack.

When she was ready, before leaving the room, she sat at the desk and called the prison. This time, Emma came to the phone. Jennifer could tell from the moment her daughter greeted her that something was wrong. "Emma, what happened? Are you okay? I've tried to call you many times, but you never took the call."

Emma's answer was soft and slow. "I know. I'm sorry. I've been kind of out of it."

"What do you mean? What's happened?"

"I've just been kind of anxious, I guess. I didn't feel like talking to anyone. They gave me something."

"What did they give you?"

"I don't know. A tranquilizer. It makes me sleepy." Her voice changed to a sad plea. "Mom, why don't you come?"

"I want to. I've tried. They won't let me. They say they are restricting your visits until you cooperate."

Emma's voice hardened. "They mean until I tell them what they want to hear."

"Can't you do that, honey? Can't you try?"

"Never mind that," she said curtly and dismissively, the softness gone from her voice. "I'm sorry I brought it up. But maybe you can do something for me."

"Of course. Anything. What?"

"They won't tell me anything. Have you heard anything about Paco? Is he still in jail? Is he okay? Can you find out?"

Jennifer felt a wave of disappointment, but it was mixed strangely with a perverse touch of pride: They hadn't broken her. "I'll try, okay?

And I'll come to see you soon. José said he might be able to legally force them to allow visitors. They can't keep you isolated because they don't believe you. Not without proof."

"Thanks, Mom. But remember to ask José about Paco." She paused and Jennifer could hear some angry women's voices in the background. She could tell that Emma was muffling the sound, but she could hear her shouting back something angry in Spanish. Her voice sounded odd—more strident and aggressive than usual. "I gotta go. Someone needs the phone," Emma said into the receiver and hung up.

Jennifer held the phone to her ear a minute or so more, then slowly put it back in its cradle. She thought fleetingly and sadly that Emma had become in so many ways a stranger to her. She called the front desk to ask for some help with her bags and went downstairs to pay her bill. She noticed a few more reporters hanging out in front of the door, so she asked the doorman to have a taxi waiting when she exited so she could slip into it as quickly as possible.

As she exited the hotel followed by the porter who carried her luggage, she practically bumped into Roberto, who was on his way in. Before she could stop herself, overwhelmed with relief, she ran to him, threw her arms around him, and tried to plant a kiss on his cheek.

"No, senora," he whispered, stiffening and holding her at arm's length. But it was too late. Two cameras clicked as reporters caught the moment.

He ushered her into the waiting cab and helped load her bags, ignoring the reporters' questions. "Any new developments?" "Is Emma still claiming she was attacked?" "Why hasn't her mother visited her?" "Looks like your job description has changed," a reporter from London's *Daily Mail* shouted in English, referring to Jennifer's hug. The others laughed knowingly. Roberto climbed in next to her and the cab sped away. No one followed.

Jennifer was mortified. "I'm so sorry. I didn't think. I was just so relieved to see you. Where have you been? I was so worried."

"I know. I apologize, and I'll explain. But not here. Why are you leaving the hotel?"

She explained what had happened and where they were going. When they arrived, he paid the taxi driver and helped her carry her bags up the two flights of stairs to her new apartment. The rental agency had left a bottle of wine and a corkscrew on the kitchen table in welcome, and Roberto opened it, found two glasses, and carried them into the living room. He sat down on the couch and Jennifer took a chair across from him.

"I found my daughter," he said. The words hung there for only a second, barely giving Jennifer time to exult with him. And then he said, "But I lost her again. Maybe this time forever."

She was stunned. He explained that he had hired several private detectives who had been trying to find his ex-wife and child for years, but they had eluded every method he had employed to find them. It was as if they had simply vanished . . . or died, he said after a pause. While he was driving back to Seville, one of the detectives called him and said he thought he might have located Roberto's ex-wife in Gerona. He'd found a woman in a mental institution, where she had been committed two years ago after being charged with abuse and neglect of her young daughter. The child, who was now thirteen years old, had gone to foster care. Roberto had rushed there, forgetting all else.

"But how did you know it was really her?" Jennifer asked.

"They had taken pictures of my wife and, although she was much changed—her hair was unkempt and completely gray, for example, and she had lost at least thirty pounds from when I'd last seen her—I knew it was her."

"How did you find your daughter?"

"She has a name," he said reproachfully.

"I'm sorry. Of course she does. I don't know it. What is her name?"

"Isabel," he murmured. "It was not hard to find where she was sent. She had been assigned by the court to a family in a small village on the outskirts of Gerona."

He returned to his narration, his voice flat. He related that he couldn't reach the family by phone, so, wildly excited, he drove there without an appointment. His dread grew when he saw the house and mounted even higher when he went inside. It was small, dark, and messy. Dirty dishes filled the sink and empty beer bottles littered the floor and tables. Only one man was at home. He was unemployed and a little drunk, although it was early in the day. Roberto asked him about Isabel, but instead of answering, the man complained bitterly about his poverty, his lack of a job, the indifference of the government.

"He smelled money," Roberto said. "He sickened me, but I handed him fifty euros and asked again about Isabel." He poured himself another glass of wine, staring at it disconsolately before tipping it to his lips.

"Well?" Jennifer said. "What did he say?"

He shrugged helplessly. "He said she was a heroin addict and had run away six months ago. He claimed he hadn't reported it because he didn't want to get her in trouble, but of course the real reason was he wanted to continue getting the government support checks."

Jennifer got up and joined him on the couch. She reached out to touch his hand, but he removed it to take another sip of wine. "Oh, Roberto, I'm so sorry. Did you go to the police?"

"Of course. We searched the known gathering places, the bars, the street corners. We talked to everyone we could. How do you think a thirteen-year-old girl who is a heroin addict supports her habit? She becomes a prostitute, and we went to the street corners where they work. The most recent picture we had was when she first went to foster care two years ago, and no one recognized her. Or no one admitted to it. Of course they are still looking. I've got a good man working on it, and he won't stop. But I don't know if I can find her, and it may already be too late to save her."

Jennifer asked if he had seen his ex-wife.

He said he had. He had gone to the institution. He was filled with rage, but when he saw her he found a defeated, confused woman who was heavily medicated and barely knew him. The doctors said she was schizophrenic, and while the medicine stopped her hallucinations, it also flattened her emotions and blurred her consciousness.

Roberto was filled with self-loathing. He was, he said, supposed to be the best detective around, but he had been unable to find his ex-wife or help his daughter. He didn't know her and now he probably never would. There was no point being angry at his wife, and while others might be angry at God, Roberto was an atheist; his frustration was that he had nowhere to direct his hatred. He felt he would explode.

Jennifer listened in silence. When he finished, she reached again for his hand. "I know how you feel," she said. "It's not the same, but I know, in my own way, what it is to lose a child, even to lose a fantasy of that child."

He didn't answer, and she withdrew her hand. Her mouth felt so dry it was difficult to talk, so she walked to the sink, got a glass of water, drank it down in one long gulp, and returned.

"Lo siento, Jennifer," he said. "I'm sorry. I know you are suffering too. But we will get your daughter back to you. I won't rest until we do."

"I know," she said. "I believe you."

He looked tired and uncharacteristically dispirited, but after an uncomfortable pause, he asked her to tell him what she had discovered about her own case while he was gone. She hesitated, feeling it was wrong to involve him in her problems when his own wound was so recently reopened. He saw her hesitation and assured her that he was ready to work. He claimed that trying to solve the problems of his clients would distract him from his own. He seemed sincere, and in fact his manner was slowly changing, she noticed with surprise. His posture became more erect as he returned to his habitual self-confident professionalism. So she told him about seeing Julia and her plan of going to Triana at midnight to meet someone who might have more information about Paco. He smiled wistfully. "That's good detective work, Jennifer. You are a natural." He stood up. "Muy bien. We will go together."

He walked to the table on which he had left his briefcase and retrieved a notebook, leafing through it for a few pages until he found
what was been looking for. "I have done some detective work myself,"
he said, not looking up from his notes. "This village that I visited, the
one to which he has been sending the money he made from selling
drugs—probably the money he got from Emma as well—I went there,
as you know."

She nodded. He knew she knew. Why the buildup?

"I spoke to everyone I could who might have information—the
mayor, the police chief, the unemployment organizations, the unions,
the foundations." He held up the notebook, full of scrawlings, in which
he had meticulously recorded his questions and their replies. "There is
no record of any person or any group receiving contributions either
from him specifically or from anyone else anonymously."

Jennifer was getting excited. "I knew it," she said triumphantly. "I
just felt it. Call it instinct."

"But there is more," Roberto said. "And this, I must admit, neither
of us guessed."

"Tell me," she said impatiently.

"He is not from that village, Jennifer. He has no family there and
has never had any roots there of any kind. It's a complete invention."

CHAPTER 21

Roberto said he would pick her up at her apartment at 11:00 P.M. She had suggested they go out for dinner first, but he'd said he had too much work to catch up on. She thought he'd seemed a bit cold, as if he regretted the recent intimacy of their conversation and wanted to return to a more professional footing. She didn't mind. She wanted that too. She liked him and respected him and she empathized with his pain, but that wasn't going to help Emma.

She went out to buy some groceries and, after coming home to put them away, realized she didn't feel like cooking and decided to take herself out for dinner. She wandered into a nearby restaurant and ordered some rioja and a light dinner of her favorite tapas: jamón, croquetas, and huevos. She was happy to be alone because she wanted to think things through. She was convinced that Emma's salvation lay in telling the truth about that terrible night. Jennifer didn't know what the truth was, but she accepted by now that Mark was right in at least one respect—that Emma was lying. She was pretty sure the story of the Algerian was an invention, probably thought up by Emma and Paco together. But she also knew, or thought she knew, that whatever had really happened, Emma wasn't guilty. Not *really* guilty, she corrected herself, because guilt, she firmly believed, was relative. She understood that if Emma was conspiring to hide and protect the murderer, that was a form of guilt. But she knew in her heart that Emma's guilt didn't go beyond that. She hadn't—she couldn't have—planned to kill anyone or watched without trying to stop it.

She found herself obsessively going over likely scenarios. Maybe Paco was a violent man with a hair-trigger temper, she thought. Maybe he had snapped when he saw this boy trying to rape Emma.

Jennifer tried to puzzle it out, step by step. Emma loved him, or thought she did, Jennifer figured, and she'd have been grateful that he'd saved her. She was young and foolish, of course—she should never have lied to the police and made up that whole story about the Algerian. After all, if Paco had been trying to save her, maybe he would get off on a plea of self-defense. But Emma had said that Paco had already been in trouble with the police, and she'd implied they would throw the book at him. That forced her to lie to protect him.

That satisfied her for a bit, but then another thought occurred to her. If the police had checked up on him, which by now they must have done, they would know that he didn't come from the place he'd claimed. Had they told Emma that? Had they told José? Didn't they have to share any evidence they had with the defense team? Jennifer's knowledge of police procedures came exclusively from *Law & Order* on American television, and she was pretty sure she remembered that sharing evidence was compulsory. She knew they hadn't shared anything, however, because José and Roberto had had no idea that Paco wasn't from that village until Roberto checked it out himself.

Her head began to throb, so she reached into her bag and took out the bottle of Advil she had taken to carrying for just such moments. She shook out three pills and washed them down with a big swig of wine. Then she paid her bill and walked back to her apartment to wait for Roberto.

He came a few minutes early and rang the bell. Instead of pressing the buzzer to let him in, she took the stairs and met him in front of the building. She was relieved to see that he seemed refreshed, all traces of his recent vulnerability buried. It was a beautiful night, and he suggested that since they were early, they should go on foot, about a fifteen- or twenty-minute walk. She fell into step with him and they discussed their plan. She explained that Julia seemed very wary of Paco's friend, even a little frightened, and very much didn't want anyone to know she had identified him. Roberto quickly agreed to protect her anonymity.

They passed small groups of people on their way to dinner, over-hearing snippets of conversation, a shrill complaint or a burst of raucous laughter echoing down an alleyway. At one point, Jennifer heard the soulful strains of a flamenco guitar even before she saw the musician, an elderly Gypsy with long black hair and deeply lined leathery skin wearing a blue shirt and a beat-up leather vest. He was sitting on a wooden box, a paper cup set in front of him. She stopped to put some money in while Roberto waited. The Gypsy smiled at her, flashing two gold teeth. They kept walking, and as they turned the corner and crossed the street, she could still hear the haunting chords of the guitar, getting softer and softer.

When they reached the bridge and crossed over to the Triana steps, Jennifer spotted Julia right away. She was sitting in the center of a group of four other young women, laughing and talking, a bottle of beer in one hand, a cigarette in the other. When she saw Jennifer, she looked surprised, as though she wasn't expecting her yet, but then caught herself, stubbed out her cigarette, and walked toward her. Jennifer started to introduce her to Roberto, but, uncharacteristically impolite, Julia cut her off.

"He's here," she whispered nervously. "He's behind me, on the top of the staircase, standing alone to the right. He's the guy with the shaved head and a black T-shirt. Please don't go to him right now. Wait till I'm back with my friends so he doesn't know I pointed him out."

"What's his name?" Roberto asked.

"Everyone calls him Raul. I don't know his last name."

Jennifer and Roberto looked up as casually as they could manage and studied him. He looked much older than the others, probably in his midthirties. His forearms were covered with tattoos, the nature of which Jennifer couldn't make out from that distance, but she could see that they were multicolored and seemed to include several geometric designs that looked like symbols. He wore three gold hoops in one ear and a gold necklace. He was talking to a very blond Scandinavian-looking man in jeans and a Real Madrid T-shirt, and after a minute or so, the blond man nodded and walked away.

"He's selling drugs," Roberto said softly. "He just passed a packet to the blond kid."

Jennifer checked Julia's group and saw them getting up and beginning to walk away together toward the line of bars and restaurants at the top of the stairs.

"Stay here," Roberto ordered, and moved toward the man in the black T-shirt. But Jennifer ignored his instruction and walked up to join him. He looked annoyed but said nothing. As soon as Raul noticed two well-dressed adults walking in his direction he bent his head to obscure his face and started to walk away, but Roberto caught up with him, greeted him by name, and said he'd had business with Paco.

"Cómo se llama?" the man asked. "What is your name?"

Roberto told him, placing his hand in a restraining gesture on his arm.

"Are you a cop?" Raul mumbled suspiciously, switching to English as if he were a foreigner and pulling his arm free.

Roberto shook his head. "I am worse than a cop as far as you're concerned, *chulo*," he said in a voice so hard that Jennifer barely recognized it. "I'm a dissatisfied customer."

Raul looked around nervously, but seeing no one else who looked threatening, he jerked his head in the direction of Jennifer. "And her?"

"We're together," Roberto said, reverting to Spanish. "I am doing business with Paco for friends in Madrid. A big order for people *muy importante*, you understand? We were supposed to meet here. But he has not arrived. I need to find his partner in his village. Where is it?"

"What makes you think I know him?" Raul said, turning to go.

Roberto blocked him and moved closer. He talked softly but with great intensity. "I think you won't want to get involved in this any more than you have to, *niño*," he said, continuing in Spanish. "I know you know him. Tell me where he is or my people will come for you instead of him. I don't think you want to cross them."

"Look, I don't know the guy well. I've done business with him from time to time, that's all. But he's been arrested. I heard he was involved in the murder of that rich kid at the university. Don't you read the papers?"

"Where does he come from?"

"I don't know. Some village."

"Where?" Roberto's face looked frightening. He had moved so close to Raul, their faces were practically touching.

"I don't know. I swear."

Roberto pressed on. "The next guy who questions you won't ask so nicely. So I'm going to ask you one more time. Where is he from?"

Raul shrugged and stepped back to create more space between them.

"If I tell you, will that be the end of it?"

"That depends on whether what you say is true." Roberto stepped closer to him again.

"Granada. He's from the outskirts of Granada," Raul mumbled.

"What is his family name? Is it Romero?"

"No, it's Frias. Paco Rodriguez Frias."

Roberto nodded and moved back, making room for Raul to pass. Raul took advantage of it and slithered away as quickly as he could.

Jennifer had understood very little of their conversation, but she'd heard the name. After Raul left, she questioned Roberto. "Did he say Paco Romero? Is that Paco's real name?"

"I don't know if it's his real name, but it's clearly another name he uses," Roberto said. His voice had returned to its familiar smooth timbre.

"You sounded like a different person when you spoke to him."

"Ah, that is because I am speaking Spanish. You're used to my bad English."

"No. Your English is perfect, and I've heard you speak Spanish. It was different. Hard. Ruthless. It frightened me."

He laughed and put his hand under her elbow to steer her back over the bridge toward her apartment. "Well, it seems to have frightened him too—enough to get him to give us some information, so it's useful, no?"

She smiled tentatively. "I guess so."

They agreed during the walk back that Roberto would go to Granada to find out more about Paco and his family. He wanted to learn why he had changed his name and lied about where he came from. He doubted it, but now that he knew where Paco's family was, he wanted to know if he was really giving them and others who were struggling any money.

"We need to prove two things," Roberto said. "I think you only are aware of one of them."

"What are they?" she asked. "I mean, I know we need to prove to Emma that Paco is using her and that she need feel no loyalty to him."

"Yes. That's what we need to prove to Emma. But we also need to prove something to the police," he said. "And also to me," he murmured almost inaudibly.

Jennifer felt a rush of anxiety. "What is it? What are you talking about?"

"We need to prove that Emma never knew or had any relationship with the murdered boy until he threatened her at the door of her apartment that night. We are pretty sure she lied about the Algerian, but we must not let anyone believe she lied about the attempted rape."

Jennifer stopped short and turned to face him. "She wouldn't do that, Roberto," she said earnestly. "Look, I know she's been acting strangely. You never knew her before, so you don't know what she's really like. I wish you did. I have to ask you to trust me and take my word for it about her. She's gotten herself involved in something she doesn't understand, and I know her behavior is haywire. One day she needs me, another she wants to be completely independent, another time she wants to show off how much she's learned and how sophisticated she's become, and yet another she wants to tell me how spoiled and privileged and unworthy I am. She goes from hot to cold to hot again. Sometimes I feel like she's been invaded, like in that film, *The Exorcist*. But not by the devil—by Paco, and the ideas he's filled her head with. It's confusing, and it's been painful to me to see how quickly something like this could happen and reverse twenty years of living with us and sharing our values. But she's my child and I know her. I know her deep down. And she's a good person. She wouldn't accuse a dead boy whose family is grieving of something so terrible if he hadn't done it. Not even to protect Paco. You have to believe me."

Roberto started to walk again and Jennifer caught up with him. "I told you once I believe in evidence," he said, "not in faith." He paused and, seeing her worried face, he added, "But I hope you are right."

CHAPTER 22

Now that she had left the hotel, there was no morning newspaper delivery, so it wasn't until she had showered and dressed and made her way to the closest kiosk that she saw the photograph. As she reached for the *Diario*, her eye was caught by a two-column photo on the front page. She froze. Her heart felt as though it had been detached and was in free fall, plunging down through her body like an elevator car whose cables had snapped. She was looking at a close-up of her and Roberto, taken the day before when she had expressed her relief at his return by an impulsive kiss. She recalled that when she had flung her arms around him, he had turned his head in surprise so that her lips, which had been aimed at his cheek, had grazed his. That was the moment that the camera caught. It was clear that although he had pushed her back and held her at arms' length, it had been too late. The headline, in large bold letters, screamed DE TAL PALO, TAL ASTILLA. She didn't understand it so she looked it up. Roughly translated it meant "Like Mother, Like Daughter."

She was mortified. It wasn't bad enough, she thought, that they were portraying Emma as some sort of femme fatale, a promiscuous predator who engaged in random casual sex, a characterization that was completely false. Now she had stupidly and unwittingly given them more—a mother who appeared to be sexually involved with the man she entrusted with managing her daughter's case. She could imagine what they would do with it, how they would make her look, how they would use it to hurt Emma.

It was too early to call Mark. She knew she'd have to explain the photo to him and ask the public-relations company they had hired to counter the bad publicity it was sure to bring. She wasn't worried about Mark's reaction, because having seen how the local press was vilifying Emma, he would know that it was not to be trusted. She did worry that it would be picked up by the tabloids in the States and that the kids would see it, or hear of it from friends, so she needed to talk to them too. It was so frustrating to wait. They were all still sleeping, having no idea of the new bomb that had fallen out of the sky, sending its deadly shrapnel out in all directions.

She needed to see Emma. She hadn't been allowed in for almost a week, and she also realized that with the close press scrutiny of her, the reporters knew that. But maybe they didn't know how hard she'd been trying and how the prison had restricted Emma's visitors. She wondered if she ought to try to explain that.

She finished her breakfast, gathered the papers, and returned to her apartment. Her first call was to Roberto, but she only reached his voice mail and this time he wasn't picking up. She punched in José's number, but it was still early and he wasn't in the office yet. It was hard to wait, but she sat at her kitchen table and checked the *NYT* to see if it had covered the story. Relieved that there was nothing, she looked through *El País* and didn't find either the story or the picture. Now she could turn to the *Diario* and try to translate the story. She brought out her Spanish dictionary but, although she managed to decipher a few words here and there, her fledgling Spanish was simply not up to the task. Finally, her phone rang.

It was José. Yes, he had seen the picture, he reported in answer to her frantic question. She explained what had happened and he listened quietly, murmuring his regret in a worried tone. He said he had a call in to Roberto and they would try to work out a strategy together to counter the bad publicity. But he also had good news. He had arranged a meeting for Jennifer with Emma. He had complained at a high level about the illegal cessation of her visiting privileges and the officials at the prison had relented and agreed to let her come.

She was so happy at the prospect of seeing Emma again that even this latest blow receded somewhat by comparison. "When can we go?" she asked.

José said he would drive her to the prison and could pick her up in an hour. She was overjoyed and hurried out to buy some presents for Emma. She stopped at the *charcutería* to buy half a kilo of jamón serrano and at the bakery for some fresh bread. She made a trip to the English language bookstore and picked up a few paperbacks that she thought Emma might like. At a nearby bakery, she noticed some chocolate tarts, and knowing how much Emma loved chocolate, she picked up a dozen, thinking that maybe she could share them with people Emma liked. Maybe Jennifer could even give some to the guards to smooth her relationship with them. It wasn't a bribe—it wasn't enough for a bribe. It was more like the way a relative of a hospitalized person sometimes brings candy to the nurses on duty—a friendly gesture that one hopes will predispose them to be extra kind.

When they arrived at the prison, they underwent the usual security procedures. The guards confiscated all the food Jennifer had brought, examined it thoroughly, and then returned it to her. But before they were led to the visiting area, Jennifer and José were told that they had to meet with the director of the facility. Jennifer looked nervously at José, trying to catch his eye, but he simply shrugged and whispered, "Don't worry, we will see," as they walked down the long hallway, past several closed doors, until they reached the comfortable, spacious office of the director. There were two upholstered chairs facing the central desk. The director rose to welcome them but did not engage in pleasantries. Looking straight at Jennifer, she got right to the point.

"There has been some trouble involving your daughter," she began.

Jennifer's face showed her alarm. She leaned forward, her body tense, her heart pounding. "What happened? Is she all right?"

"Yes, yes, she is all right," the director answered. "She is a bit bruised, but she has been to the infirmary and is now back in her room."

"What happened? When can I see her?"

"You can see her as soon as we finish this conversation."

Jennifer could feel the heat rise to the surface of her skin. Her neck and face burned and she felt beads of perspiration on her face although the office was air-conditioned.

"Is that why you finally allowed me to come?" she asked bitterly. "Did Emma's refusal to cooperate finally frustrate someone and did a guard hurt her? Is that what happened?"

José put a restraining hand on her arm. "Cálmate," he murmured. Then, to the director, in a firm but polite voice, he said, "The mother, of course, is upset. Please tell us what has happened."

The director shifted once in her chair, straightened some papers on her desk, and plunged in.

"I'm afraid that one of the other women in your daughter's room made an unwelcome advance on her."

Jennifer stared at her, but she continued before Jennifer could speak, and José once again put his hand on her arm to calm her.

"Apparently, this happened several times, and although your daughter rebuffed these advances, the other woman continued to make them. Eventually, Emma reported this to one of the guards. That was what led to the trouble."

Jennifer could no longer be restrained. "What are you saying? That led to the trouble? Didn't the trouble begin when a woman was allowed to make advances on Emma? I'm sure you knew that this woman had those interests. Why did you put them together? Was this more of your attempt to frighten her into cooperating with you?"

The director looked pained, but continued. "Her roommate is a Gypsy, and she is part of our large *romaní* community. Probably about forty percent of the women here belong to it. When Emma complained and we responded by placing her roommate in a separate room and restricting her privileges, her friends were angry. I'm afraid they cornered Emma the next time they went to the shower and roughed her up a bit."

Jennifer sat stonily staring ahead of her. Part of her didn't believe this was happening. There was a strange disconnect that had been operating for some time. Things were moving too fast and the only direction was down. How had she gone from being the mother of a Princeton junior to being the mother of an accused murderer beaten up by a group of Gypsies after one of them made a sexual pass at her? It was almost more than her mind could take in. But of course, she did take it in, and after a minute's silence she responded.

"'Roughed her up a bit'? What does that mean?"

"She has a black eye, a few bruises on her arms and chest, a cut on her lip. Nothing serious."

"Actually, that sounds serious to me. Maybe you are used to that here, but I am not."

"This is extremely unusual here, Mrs. Lewis. Because of our unique population, most of the prisoners abide by the rules."

Jennifer was beginning to feel angry. "What are the rules? You mean a prisoner has to give in to all advances since you seem unable to protect them from them? Or is it just Americans who don't learn the rules and are not told what they are?"

José tried to placate her again, but she wriggled away from his hand and glared angrily at the director.

The director continued as if she hadn't been interrupted, ignoring Jennifer's outburst. "There is an old woman, a Gypsy, who has been here for many years for murdering her husband and his girlfriend. She sits in the lounge all day—she's been here so long she has special privileges and she is a very easy prisoner. The young Gypsy women respect her and she has become the person to whom they go for advice. She acts as the unofficial head of the clan here, and her word settles disputes, mediates claims, and is usually followed. If Emma had gone to her, the advances would have stopped."

"Did anyone bother to tell Emma that?" Jennifer shot back.

José now joined in as well. "When Emma came to you and complained and you punished her roommate, did you not think it more prudent to tell Emma to pretend she hadn't spoken to you and to go directly to this old woman?"

The director turned her attention to José. "Yes. Of course we thought of it. But once she came to us, we were obligated to write down her visit and the reason for it. Once that was done, there is a protocol that must be followed."

"I don't understand," Jennifer said. "And anyway, it's too late. I want to see my daughter." She turned to José. "I want you to make an official complaint. I want to take this as far as we can. I think and believe it could have been avoided and I'm not at all sure that it wasn't part of some plan to break her."

The director pushed back her chair and rose. "I understand how you feel, senora. But your daughter is in a prison, not a boarding school, and sometimes no matter how hard we try to avoid it, these things happen. It is true that she is not doing all she can to free herself and to bring an easier confinement with the privileges that go with being a cooperative prisoner. But we did not deliberately allow this to happen."

"I just want to see her," Jennifer said, looking pleadingly at the director and speaking softly. "And not through glass. I want to hold her and comfort her and show her that her mother is here with her in her trouble. Please allow this."

José said something in Spanish and the director seemed to consider it for a few seconds. "You are a mother," he continued. "Surely you can feel for this mother's pain."

The director frowned, and spoke as though thinking out loud. "It is true that by now she might have earned a private visit," she began. "She hasn't earned this the easy way, but perhaps I can grant the privilege, given the circumstances. But not today. It takes some administrative work to arrange. I will have to change her status, which is complicated." She turned to Jennifer. "You can see her the usual way today and come back next week for a private visit."

Jennifer started to object, but José interrupted her.

"Gracias," he said. "I'm sure Senora Lewis is very grateful."

He put his hand under Jennifer's elbow and gently led her from the room.

CHAPTER 23

lutching José's arm, Jennifer walked into the visiting room. She took a seat in front of the plexiglass partition and sat erect, leaning forward, straining to see if Emma had already entered. José put his hand on her shoulder, gave her a reassuring squeeze, and departed. There were only a few other visitors and they were busily engaged in conversation with the prisoners they had come to see. An elderly woman in a black dress, her gray hair done up in a bun from which stray strands had escaped, sat talking to a young dark-haired prisoner who might have been her granddaughter. On Jennifer's other side, a man and a boy who looked to be about ten years old were talking to a heavyset dark-skinned woman with jet-black hair and a noticeable dark fuzz over her upper lip. The woman glanced up when Jennifer sat down and then, quickly losing interest, turned back to her visitors. Were these women who had joined in hurting Emma? Jennifer wondered, trying not to stare.

Emma entered from the back of the prisoners' room. She was limping slightly, and when she sat in the designated chair, she eased herself into it as though it hurt to bend her body. One eye was swollen with reddish-purple lines radiating out in a circle like a child's drawing of the sun. Her hair was dirty and clung to her bruised face. She was wearing jeans and a long-sleeved shirt that buttoned in the front, so Jennifer couldn't see if there were bruises on her arms or chest, but what she saw was enough.

"Emma, what have they done to you?" Tears were streaming down her face and her voice was overflowing with love and sympathy.

Emma rolled her eyes and looked around furtively to be sure no one else had heard. "Please, Mom, don't be so overdramatic. It is what it is. Did you see that bitch of a director? Did she tell you this was all my fault?"

Jennifer wiped her eyes and tried hard to stem the flow of tears. She was in a constant push and pull between her natural maternal reactions, the ones that had served her and her children well for twenty years, and the new restraint and distance her daughter seemed to need. It confused her because she didn't know what was expected of her or why, although it seemed that anything natural to her was wrong. She wanted to help Emma and not react selfishly, not give in to the feelings of hurt, rejection, and even anger she'd so often experienced since she'd arrived, but sometimes she just felt bruised.

She lowered her voice and tried to even her tone. "Of course it wasn't your fault. No one thinks it was your fault. Emma, please, I know this has been horrible, the worst possible thing, worse than anything any of us ever imagined would happen in our lives. But you're strong, you'll get through it, and we'll go home, and you'll go back to school and put this behind you."

Emma laughed with her voice but not her eyes. "Go back to Princeton? Right. Not likely."

Jennifer sighed. "You can go wherever you want. You can go to school or stay home, or get a job and move out, if that's what you want, and we'll help you whatever you do. But you have to get out of here first and that still depends on you."

Emma looked up belligerently, ready for a fight, but Jennifer continued.

"I see in your face that you're ready to argue about this. But there's new information you might want to consider first. Roberto has been to Paco's home village, the one he tells everyone he is helping by giving money to sustain all those poor people who are unemployed." She paused to see Emma's reaction, but Emma didn't oblige. She didn't look up, though her mother, who watched her intently, could see her body stiffen and her mouth tighten as she bit her upper lip and waited.

"He doesn't come from that village, Emma. No one has heard of him. No one has gotten any money from him. It's all a complete invention."

Emma looked at her mother with contempt. She spewed out her response in a stream of verbal bile.

"Of course you'd think that. You'd believe that. Did you and Roberto have a good laugh over that? Well, sorry, but you're dead wrong. Did it ever occur to you that he might be using a different name? That he wanted to remain anonymous?"

"Emma, listen. What will it take to convince you? It's a beautiful dream, this wonderful self-sacrificing boyfriend who wants to help the poor and doesn't even want to be thanked for it. He's done a great job convincing you of his virtue. But you are too intelligent to hang on to that, as much as you want to, in the face of the facts. I don't want to believe anything bad of anyone you love, Emma. But I want you to make your decisions based on truth, not fantasy. It's okay to be taken in. You're young and you fell in love. You made a mistake, but you can correct it and you can be free to go on with the rest of your life."

Emma looked down at the shelf running along the edge of the plexiglass as if something very interesting were on it. She didn't respond for a few minutes and Jennifer hoped she was seriously considering what had been said. Finally, she looked up.

"How's Dad, Mom?" Her voice was bitter, hard, insinuating.

Jennifer responded cautiously, not sure where this was headed. "He's fine. He's working very hard on your behalf in the States, dealing with the press, working with the company we've hired to get everyone as much as possible on your side."

"So he hasn't been here for a few days. But I guess you've found other things to keep you busy, right?"

"Emma, I spend all my time trying to find ways to prove your

172 / NINA DARNTON

innocence and get you out of here. What has this got to do with anything?"

"I saw how you spend your time on the front page of the newspaper today, Mom. Maybe Lily and Eric saw it too. Maybe Dad saw it; did you think of that?"

"I want to explain that. I didn't think you would've seen it yet."

"I'm not completely cut off here, you know. We get the papers. There's a computer in the library. Everyone here is laughing about it."

Jennifer stiffened. "That picture and that story implied something completely false, Emma. Roberto was out of town trying to find information that we hoped would help you. He was delayed and didn't get in touch with me. I worried, because I knew we needed him to get you out of here. When he returned, I was so happy to see him, I hugged him. That's all."

Emma smirked with knowing disdain, an expression her mother had not seen since she was fifteen. "You kissed him, actually," she said. "Unless you're saying they doctored the picture."

Jennifer raised her voice in exasperation—too much, apparently, because the few other visitors turned toward her and Emma cringed, but her patience was at an end and she couldn't control herself. "On the cheek, Emma. I tried to kiss him on the cheek." She lowered her voice and leaned forward confidentially. "The picture made it look more intimate than it was." She noticed Emma's look of disbelief and raised her voice again in exasperation. "With your experience here, even after everything they say about you that you deny, do you find it hard to believe that they would distort and lie and do anything to rile people up and sell papers?"

Emma looked around nervously and spoke in a whisper, through her teeth. "Stop, Mom. Calm down. Everyone is looking at you. This doesn't help me."

"It helps me," Jennifer said.

"Yeah. Of course, that's all that matters, isn't it? That's all that's ever mattered."

The anger that had roiled inside Jennifer but that up until then had been mostly stanched, only leaking out from time to time, now threatened to explode. She could feel it in her throat, taste it in her mouth, but she spoke softly, with all the self-control she could muster.

"What's always all that mattered, Emma?"

Emma was not equally in control. "You," she spit out. "It was always about what made you feel good about yourself. About maintaining your perfect, privileged life."

It came then—her self-control collapsed like floodgates battered down by an onrushing torrent. "My privileged life?" Jennifer shouted. "How about yours? You had everything—*everything*. Lessons in anything you wanted, every toy that ever interested you, the best schools, the best camps. And you didn't get all that out of guilt like some mothers do because they're working and not spending enough time with their kids. Because I gave up acting; I gave up my career. I was always there when you came home from school with treats and cupcakes and conversation. We talked all the time." She was trying to control her voice and fight back tears at the same time, but Emma appeared unmoved.

"We talked, but you never really listened," Emma flung back in an angry but low voice, with a calm delivery that made its message even more hurtful. "You never were interested in whether I was happy, only in some new accomplishment I did so you could brag about it to your friends. You gave up your career for me? I don't think so. You did it for you. It was easier to live through us. You pressured us to be 'perfect' so you could see yourself as the perfect mother, in order to justify your own sacrifices and make up for your sense of failure in the world outside our family."

Jennifer was speechless. At some point during Emma's harangue, she had stopped hearing her. Or she had heard her, but stopped being wounded by her words, as though she were a sponge so full of liquid it could no longer absorb the continuing stream. She stared at her. She took a deep, steadying breath. After what felt to both like a very long silence, she spoke.

"Do you know what the police think you did, Emma?"

"What has that got to do with this?"

"They think there was no Algerian. In fact, they think there was no attempted rape. They believe that you were sleeping with this Spanish boy. Maybe you knew him or maybe you picked him up that night at the bar. You'd had a fight with Paco earlier, so you didn't expect him to come home, but he did, and he found you in bed together. He flew into a jealous rage and killed him. Then, to protect Paco, you concocted this absurd story to cover everything up."

She was looking at Emma while she spoke. Her tone was straightforward and she surprised herself by how emotionally removed, even cold, she suddenly felt. It was a relief, but it was not to last.

Now it was Emma's turn to be stunned. "Is that what you think too, Mom?"

"I don't know what I think anymore. I think it's not impossible."

Emma blinked a few times. She opened her mouth wider and then covered it with her right hand. "You are my mother and you believe I could do that?" she said incredulously. She was choked up, hardly able to spit out the words. "I didn't know that Spanish kid. I'd never seen him before. He followed me and tried to rape me. But you, you take this high moral ground while you are fucking the guy who's supposed to clear me. How dare you?"

She turned away and stood up, then turned back slowly. "Go away. Don't come back. I don't want to see you again. I don't want your help or anything else from you ever."

Jennifer's sense of distance evaporated. This was her daughter. How could this be happening? She noticed everyone looking and saw one of the guards approaching and she begged Emma to calm down, to sit again so they could work this out, but Emma had started to weep, sucking in her breath between loud racking sobs. Jennifer wanted to comfort her, wanted to take back everything she'd said, to take her in her arms and hold her, but she couldn't touch her through the yellowed plexiglass. "I'm sorry, Emma; I didn't mean it. I was just striking back. I was wrong. Please sit down. Please forgive me."

But Emma remained standing, her back to her mother. Still sobbing, she collapsed into the arms of the guard who had come to investigate the commotion and who led her away. She didn't look back as she left the room. Jennifer remained at the partition long after Emma had disappeared, frozen with grief and regret.

CHAPTER 24

She called Mark as soon as she got back to her apartment. It was early morning in Philadelphia and he was still groggy but was jolted awake by her urgent tone. She told him, despondently, what had happened and begged him to come right away. She needed him. She had failed Emma, and now Emma wouldn't speak to her. He was their only hope.

He promised to clean up a few things, make some necessary arrangements, and come by the end of the week. He tried to console her, but she didn't think he sounded completely sincere. He wanted to put Lily and Eric on the phone to say hello, but it was clear that she wasn't up to it. Once again, he urged her to come home, at least for a visit, to help their two younger children and to derive some comfort and sustenance from the normalcy of their lives and their eager love for their missing mother. She would, she said, very soon, and she'd call them later when she had regained some equanimity. She was convinced, she said, that although they missed her it was good for them to see that when one of them was in trouble, she was there for her and would retain that commitment no matter what happened for however long it took. They would know that they too would receive that kind of dedication if anything bad happened to them, and in the long run, that would make them feel secure. His voice sounded skeptical—she remembered sadly how in the past her word on child-rearing psychology was taken without question, as if she were the acknowledged expert—but after a small pause, he said he understood. Still, he reminded her again to call them later. There was a slight uncomfortable silence and then, repeating that he would be there in a few days and mechanically urging her to hang on until then, he signed off.

When she hung up, she felt relieved that he was coming, but the churning anxiety didn't abate and even seemed to increase, now augmented by worry and guilt about her other children as well as the awkwardness between her and Mark. His response was dutiful, she acknowledged, but not loving. Mark used to always be able to calm her, she thought. Now she was alone.

She hung up by holding the phone's disconnect button down with her finger, and without pausing long enough to make a decision, she punched in Roberto's cell phone number. He picked up on the first ring and, having seen that the call came from her, started talking in an uncharacteristically exuberant voice before saying hello.

"Jennifer," he said. "I was just going to call you. I have some news for you that I think will help us."

She could hear his excitement and felt a slight smile begin to cross her lips in spite of herself. She took a deep breath and exhaled. "I could use some good news. Can you tell me on the phone?"

He laughed. "How suspicious you are becoming. And yes, I can, but I won't. I think this is something I will show as well as tell. I'm on my way back. I should be there by around nine. Meet me for dinner?"

She agreed, and he said he'd pick her up at her apartment. She took her time getting ready, choosing a dress that she knew flattered her, fixing her hair and her makeup. She told herself she just needed to feel attractive again, to think of herself as an independent person and not just an unhappy mother. But the truth was deeper. Her guilt was turning to anger. She was attracted to Roberto. He was closer to her now than anyone else in her life. But she hadn't acted on it for many reasons—her attachment to Mark, for one thing; her sense of propriety, for another; but especially because it would complicate Emma's case and her ability to help her. But Emma had become so hard, so estranged from her, that when she saw a picture that looked suspicious—that might, if there had been enough goodwill, have caused her simply to ask for an explanation—she leapt immediately to the most damning conclusion. It felt so unfair, so unloving, so opposite of what Jennifer had been trying to do in support of her daughter, which was to reject any evidence that differed from Emma's story, to stick by her at all costs. Part of her thought she might as well have done what Emma had accused her of, since Emma believed it anyway. But that thought, born of anger and hurt, wasn't long lasting. She knew that would be the worst thing she could do right now.

She was waiting downstairs when Roberto arrived, and he noticed immediately the care she had taken with her appearance. He also noticed the slowness of her step as they walked toward the taxi stand, and the sadness in her eyes. He didn't comment until they got to the restaurant, but once they had been ushered to their table and ordered drinks (he a Scotch, she a vodka tonic), he gave her an opportunity to tell him what was wrong.

"I have some good news for you," he said. "But perhaps before I give it to you, you would like to tell me why you are so sad."

She looked down, refusing to meet his eyes. "Maybe not. Maybe it would be better if you told me the good news. Maybe it will cheer me up."

He took a swig of his drink. "Maybe," he said. "I will if you want me to. But I think you would be happier if you told me what has happened."

She so yearned for a sympathetic ear. "It's Emma," she blurted. "I saw her today. I visited her in prison. We had an awful confrontation. I lost my temper and behaved terribly and she left crying. We both left crying, actually." She looked up now and saw that Roberto looked genuinely worried and upset. This kindness, this caring, brought tears again to her eyes.

"I'm sorry," she said, embarrassed, wiping them away with her hand and reaching for the napkin to blot her cheeks. The tears had made thin black lines under her eyes where her mascara had run.

He reached out and put his hand on hers, but she nervously jerked her hand back, looking around to see if anyone had noticed. Once the accusation had been made, every gesture, even innocent ones of friendship or compassion, seemed wrong.

"I'm sorry," she said when she saw his hurt expression.

He nodded sadly. "Did Emma see the photo in the paper today?"

Jennifer told him what had happened, how their conversation had deteriorated, what each had said. He told her that he was sure Emma had many regrets too, that she had spoken in anger and frustration just as Jennifer had, and hadn't said what she really felt, only what she knew would hurt. But Jennifer thought differently. She started to try to explain, but it was hard to talk without breaking down and she didn't know how deep she should go, how personal.

"I think that I realized maybe for the first time that Emma is not just acting strangely because of this situation but that she isn't, maybe never was, what I had thought," she said. She gave a rueful smile. "Of course, I suppose that's obvious, but I mean I think she is damaged in some way, and if that's true, I have to take some of the responsibility for it."

He tried to contradict her, but she couldn't stop. She felt something well up inside her, words and feelings that needed to spill out because there was simply no room for them anymore. He tried again to say something, but she interrupted him and continued to talk, slowly and softly, not looking at him.

"It's very hard to admit, to accept. I mean, you know what they say about facing the fact that you have a deadly disease? They say this back home; I don't know if they say it here. They say it happens in stages. First, there's denial, then anger, and finally acceptance. I think it's meant to be a universal reaction. Well, I've been experiencing the same thing since I got here in my reaction to Emma. Except that in the case of recognizing a serious flaw in your child, something else enters in. Somewhere after anger and before real acceptance, you experience guilt."

Roberto interrupted forcefully. "You have nothing to feel guilty about, Jennifer. Nothing that happened here is your fault."

She kept talking, as if to herself, without acknowledging his interruption. "The thing is, before long, you realize that you're not even just worried about your child. You're worried about yourself."

He looked puzzled. She put her hand on her chest and rubbed it lightly with her fingers as she spoke. "There's this terrible emptiness where your pride used to be. There's this pathetic realization that you failed, that you made some terrible mistake that caused this."

Once again he tried to interrupt but she stopped him. "Please," she said, "I need to say this." He let her continue.

"And then you feel a second wave of guilt, this time because you are turning your child's crisis into a story about yourself." She paused. "Like I'm doing right now," she said with a self-effacing shrug.

He shook his head in disagreement but she ignored it.

"And you worry that maybe that's what you always did and that's why she's so messed up. I mean, I used to think that the love you have for your children is the one pure unselfish love there is. But now I'm not sure. Maybe it's like everything else. Maybe it's also about your own self-image and maybe the anger you feel when you discover how messed up your daughter is comes from the fact that she's ruined your perfect image of yourself. That's what Emma thinks. And I think there's some truth to it. And it's so, so hard to overcome that and go on." She was talking louder now and trying unsuccessfully not to cry.

He got up and moved to the banquette so he could sit next to her.

They both noticed that others in the restaurant were looking at them.

"I'm so sorry," she said. "I am embarrassing both of us."

He assured her it wasn't an embarrassment. "Although perhaps you'd better stop. That muscular man behind us thinks I have hurt you and has been giving me threatening looks." She smiled through her tears, wiped them away yet again, and sniffled. He handed her a white handkerchief from his pocket.

"Thank you," she said, accepting it. "I haven't been given a hankie to wipe my tears since my dad did it when I was a little girl." She returned the handkerchief and he used it to wipe a smudge off her cheek before putting it away.

"Now listen, Jennifer," he began. "I have heard you. I am going to talk now and you are going to give me the same courtesy, de acuerdo?"

"Sí," she said. "De acuerdo."

"You are much too hard on yourself. The situation isn't as black-and-white as you are making it. You can't accept all the responsibility for everything your daughter does or thinks or becomes. Your children can get into trouble without it having anything to do with you. I have seen this many times in my work. It's even overly self-important to think it all comes down to mistakes you made. There are many influences on children, especially after they go off and make friends or take lovers you don't even know."

"But why do they take those lovers?" she began, but now it was his turn to barrel on without letting her interrupt.

"In a minute, okay? I want to say something else about all these accusations you've hurled at yourself. Of course you were proud and of course you feel terrible that the daughter you thought you knew so well has disappointed you in such a major way, but wanting your children to do well in life, to succeed, to excel, doesn't mean you are trying to live through them or are pushing them for your own self-interest. It's what we all want for our children. We'd be poor parents if we didn't want the best for them."

She sighed. She thought about what had happened to his daughter and felt sorry for him and ashamed that she was acting as if her crisis was more important. He hadn't had the chance to even try to be a good parent. Was that worse or better?

"I don't know, Roberto. What in the end is the best for them? Maybe I should have just wanted her to be happy."

He leaned forward, rolling his eyes in an exasperated gesture. "Sí, claro. You wanted her to be successful *because* you wanted her to be happy."

She took a sip of wine. "Yeah. That's what I told myself. It didn't work out that way. You know, I've been thinking about the mothers I know who I had judged to be cold, or neglectful, or overly strict with their children, and you know what? Their children seem to be doing better. Certainly none of them are in jail suspected of being involved in a murder."

"That is an accident of circumstance."

"They even seem to like their mothers more," she mused. Neither spoke for a few seconds. Jennifer finally broke the silence.

"If I'm honest, Roberto, I have to admit that Emma doesn't seem to like me very much."

Once again, he started to object but she cut him off.

"No, it's true. And it's weird. I have lots of friends, you know, and they all seem to like me a lot. That's even true of my kids' friends. I'm their favorite. In fact, I've never even known anyone who didn't like me. I guess acceptance has been important to me and I've always tried to be liked." She uttered a single syllable of self-deprecating laughter. "But here it is; there's no denying it—the cringe when I try to hug her, the complaints about my behavior, the criticism, the coldness, the holding back, the lies, the refusal to share either the facts or her feelings about what is happening to her, the lack of trust of me, her mother, who has loved her so much for so long." Once again her eyes filled with tears. "I'm selfish, I'm pushy, I'm too optimistic, or I'm overly dramatic, or I'm too blind, or I'm naive or I see only what I want to see. . . ." She stopped to catch her breath. "It's not only her. My husband actually doesn't seem to like me very much either, come to think of it." She laughed through her tears at that last statement and wiped her eyes one last time. They were red and puffy, but the flood, finally, had ebbed.

Roberto placed his hands on her shoulders and turned her toward him.

"I like you," he said.

CHAPTER 25

I t was late when they left the restaurant, but the streets were, as usual, crowded with people, and Jennifer could hear their chatter and laughter as they walked past. She noticed too that the outdoor tables still had many patrons around them, although the crowd was thinner than when they had arrived. It was a beautiful night. The heat had subsided, eased by a soft breeze that brought with it that familiar sweet scent of jasmine that soothed Jennifer's raw nerves. It was hard to believe this country, and even more, this beautiful city, was in the throes of a huge economic crisis. She knew it was true—she read about it daily—but looking at the number of people in the restaurants and the seemingly festive atmosphere on the streets, she wondered if it was as deep as had been reported. She mentioned this to Roberto, but he told her she was mistaken. She was in a major tourist center, he said. Many of the people she saw were just there for a few days or weeks. She didn't see the suffering, but he assured her it was there. One day, when all this trouble with Emma was over, he said, he would take her to some of the villages and show her a part of Spain she didn't know. She sighed and said that when all this was over, she wanted to leave and never come back.

He stopped short. "Ah, Jennifer, don't blame Spain for this."

She shook her head. "I don't. It's not that. It's just that I will always associate the place with what happened here. I would rather that you let me show you around Pennsylvania—we could go to New York too. Have you ever been?"

"Yes. But not with you. I would enjoy that."

They continued in silence. She was glad they were walking and that, for now, they weren't talking. She didn't know where they were going, but Roberto seemed to have a destination in mind and she followed him, grateful to leave the decision in his hands.

They passed a bench on which a discarded copy of the day's tabloid caught her eye.

"I do hate the Spanish press," she said. "They have tried their best to destroy Emma's reputation, to treat her as if she were a degenerate and as if that is typical of American students. And now they have begun to attack me as well. Not you, of course. I'm the femme fatale who dared to give you a friendly kiss in public and had to pay for it." She couldn't keep the bitterness out of her voice.

He didn't answer for a while. "Have you seen the American tabloids recently?" he asked softly.

"No. Mark doesn't send them. I think he doesn't want to upset me."

They turned off the street they were on, cut through a cobblestone alleyway, and emerged onto a wider avenue that led them to a car park.

"I have my car here," he said. "Let's take a ride."

She followed him down the ramp to a Honda sedan. She got in, pleased he had not suggested he'd take her home. She didn't want to be alone with her thoughts just yet.

"Well, I've seen some of them," he said as he pulled out of the garage.

"Seen what?"

"Your American tabloids."

"They're not mine, Roberto. What do they say?"

"They defend Emma by attacking Spain, making this a case of national hostility instead of a straightforward crime investigation. They use anything they can find. They are bringing up the Spanish Inquisition, if you can believe it. They imply Emma is being held and punished because of anti-Semitism. They even suggest that you are living in a Jewish ghetto, forgetting to mention that it hasn't been used that way for over five hundred years.

Jennifer laughed, dumbfounded.

"It isn't a joke, Jennifer."

"But it's ridiculous. Surely no one believes it."

"No one sophisticated does. But it creates an atmosphere that is very bad for my country. I think your public-relations company thinks that the best way to defend Emma is to defame us."

This line of conversation was so absurd that Jennifer hadn't been taking it seriously, but now she wondered if what he said was true. She shook her head in disbelief. "I don't think it could be them," she said. "But I will find out, and if it is, I will stop it, I promise. It's dishonest and stupid and it won't help Emma anyway. Maybe it will even hurt her."

"Would you stop it even if you thought it would help Emma?" He asked this very gravely.

"Yes," she said without stopping to consider her answer. "Of course."

She looked out the window. They were on a highway, passing modern apartment blocks and office buildings, leaving the city center. She noticed that many of the apartments were dark. It was 11:00 P.M.

"It looks like a lot of people in Spain go to bed at a normal time after all," she said.

He laughed. "Normal for Americans, you mean? But no. Those apartments are dark because no one lives in them. You are looking at the main reason for the economic crisis in Spain: too much construction. We borrowed money and built and built and now there are not enough people to live in these new apartments and the banks cannot collect the money they lent and the whole system is falling apart."

She considered this. "We did the same thing in the States."

"Yes. But not as much. You are beginning to emerge from it."

She settled back in the seat and looked out the window at the night and the glare of headlights as the cars whizzed by.

"Where are we going?" she asked.

"To my place."

She didn't ask why because she thought she knew and she didn't trust herself to discuss it.

When they arrived, she followed him nervously to the door of his apartment building, watched him punch in a security code, and joined him in the small elevator, which took them to the fourth floor. He opened the door to his apartment and was greeted by a very excited little schnauzer, who danced in circles of joy at his return. He flicked on the lights and led Jennifer into the living room, which was beautifully appointed, as she would have guessed, with handmade rugs and modern but comfortable furniture. He excused himself and she wandered around the room, noticing that he had several collections displayed in glass or in carved wooden boxes. She found a collection of wristwatches in one box and pens in another. The most curious was a glass table with a shelf under it upon which were crowded a dozen old-fashioned beaded evening bags. He came back into the room as she was looking at them and stood next to her. "These were my wife's," he said. "I somehow couldn't bear to get rid of them."

She turned to him. "Did you bring me here to show me the surprise you found?" she asked.

He breathed deeply and walked over to a cabinet, opening it and retrieving an album from the bottom shelf.

"No. I think that can wait one more day. I brought you here for a more selfish reason. I wanted to show you something else." He sat on the couch and patted it for her to sit next to him, which she did. He opened the album, touching the pages gingerly, and came to one of himself, several years younger, pushing a swing for a little girl who looked to be about four years old. Jennifer knew at once who it was, of course.

"Your daughter?" she asked softly.

"Sí," he said a bit crisply. "I wanted you to see her."

She didn't know what to say. "She's beautiful," she murmured, feeling it was a lame response.

"Have you spoken to your other children recently?" he asked.

She shook her head. "I need to call them."

"Why not call now? Just to say hello. To remind them you are thinking about them."

"They know that."

"Call them anyway." He handed her a cordless phone and walked out of the room. She punched in her home number. After three rings, Lily picked up.

"Hi, darling. It's Mom. How are you?"

"Mom? Oh, Mom, I miss you so much. I was waiting for you to call. How is Emma? When are you coming home?"

Jennifer felt a pang of longing for her home and children, a reminder of everything she had forced herself to put aside during her obsession with Emma's case. But she also felt a renewal of her determination to rescue not just Emma but their family, to return it to what it had been.

"I'll come home soon, darling. Please hang on a little longer."

"But when, Mom?" It sounded like a whine. "We need you too."

"I'll come home when I can bring Emma home with me," Jennifer said, cutting off the conversation too late to avoid hearing the hurt in Lily's voice. She forced herself to be strong. "Is Eric there?"

"He's at a playdate. I'll tell him you called. He misses you a lot."

"I miss him too. And I miss you. I love you."

She hung up just as Roberto was coming back to the room. "I think I should get home now," she said, looking up.

"Of course." He headed for the door but turned to face her before he opened it. "You see, Jennifer, you have many things to worry about and many people who need you. Not just Emma. Maybe it would be good to remember that."

"I do remember it," she snapped, then, hearing her own tone, repented. "Thank you for showing me the picture of your Isabel," she said. "I shouldn't be crying on your shoulder when you have so much trouble in your own life."

"It helps me. It reminds me that I'm not the only one who has problems." He stopped and opened the door, then turned back again. "Or remorse, or confusion, or guilt either, for that matter."

She felt her heart swell with gratitude. "You're very kind, Roberto. Thank you."

CHAPTER 26

He hadn't told her his surprise that night. It could wait, he had said. She knew he wanted to give her some time to recover from the emotional blow her conversation with Emma had delivered. She accepted his reasoning, thinking he would divulge his secret the next day. But he phoned in the morning to say that since she had told him that Mark was coming in the next few days, why not wait for him and he could report to them both?

She wasn't happy with this. First of all, as much as she had begged Mark to come, she also resented his intrusion into what she had come to think of as her world. She had been dealing with this pretty much on her own, she thought, and she liked being the go-to person, the one who translated, reported, and analyzed developments to Mark rather than sharing their discovery with him. Even more, she didn't want to share Roberto, and she felt affronted that in spite of their recent closeness, he had reverted to this professional tone, hesitating to give her important information on her own. He had offered her his arm when he walked her to her door last night, and she had taken it. He had kissed her on both cheeks to say good night—a customary gesture of friendship but not one he had ever initiated before. She simply didn't want to give that up or weaken it with Mark's presence. She recognized that this was wrong in every way—off message, essentially, which should have been only about freeing Emma—and even detrimental to repairing the rent in her relationship with Mark. She fought to disguise her real feelings as she told him fine, she would wait for Mark. But she knew her voice sounded cold and she knew he knew why.

When Mark called to tell her his flight information, she called both José and Roberto to set up a meeting. José offered to meet Mark's plane but Jennifer said she would go alone, and at the appointed time, she took a taxi to the airport. She waited for him to retrieve his baggage, and when he emerged, she waved so he would see her and moved to greet him. He nodded in recognition and quickened his step. When he was in front of her, however, both hesitated. The few seconds that passed were barely noticeable yet inescapable. He bent down and gave Jennifer a chaste kiss on the cheek, which she returned. The awkwardness between them was obvious but was soon covered by his need for information, which she was able to provide. They took a taxi to Roberto's office and she filled him in. The bottom line was that she had not spoken to Emma since the scene at the prison and Roberto had some good news he was eager to share with them both.

Roberto greeted them at the door, shook Mark's hand, and ushered them into his inner office. José was already there, seated in one of three chairs facing the desk. Roberto offered them coffee or something stronger, but they refused, Mark asking only for a glass of cold water. He straightened some papers, a gesture Jennifer recognized, and addressed himself directly to Mark.

"Welcome, senor. I am very glad you are here."

Mark was less polite. "I'm glad I'm here too," he said in a slightly belligerent tone. "I hear my daughter has been brutally assaulted in prison and that neither you nor her lawyer"—he looked accusingly at José—"were able either to prevent it or to respond to it adequately by demanding a change in the conditions under which she is held. She hasn't even been officially charged, for God's sake, yet she is held punitively to make her talk and has been put in a dangerous situation."

Jennifer couldn't help noticing the difference in approach between Mark and Roberto and felt embarrassed by it. Mark, the hot-shot American lawyer with his aggressive accusatory tone, jarred her after all this time in Spain, and upset her. Surely, she thought, this attack was both unnecessary and unproductive. But Roberto didn't respond in kind. He nodded sympathetically and continued.

"That was most unfortunate, and I assure you we have made the necessary official complaints." He smiled ruefully. "I'm afraid we are not in a position to make demands. But for the moment, what I have to say is even more important. May I go on?"

Mark started to answer, but Jennifer cut him off. "Yes, of course. Please go on."

Roberto turned to her and shifted his gaze back and forth between them as he continued. "We have reached a crucial juncture. The police are getting ready to formally charge Emma as an accessory to murder. We need to act quickly. If we can convince her to tell the truth, which will, in my opinion, mean incriminating her boyfriend, we may be able to get her released without a trial in exchange for testifying at his. But as you know, this has not been easy to accomplish."

Mark nodded, a worried look on his face. Jennifer glanced at him, saw his concern, and impulsively reached over to put her hand on his thigh. He patted her hand. They shared a look of commiseration.

"Has any new evidence emerged that is detrimental to our case?"

"I will tell you all I know," Roberto said. "As you remember, Emma has claimed that the so-called Algerian savior came in and found the Spanish boy attacking her on the bed. As the Algerian advanced, she claimed the boy jumped off the bed and pulled a knife. They fought and the Algerian tried to wrest the knife away from him. In the scuffle, the Spanish boy, Rodrigo Pérez, was stabbed.

"There has already been ample evidence that this story is flawed; at best, incomplete. For one thing, the victim, Rodrigo Pérez, had multiple stab wounds. Emma claims Rodrigo kept fighting and the knife changed hands several times and each got cuts. She says the Algerian also had stab wounds, which we can't verify since we can't locate him. Given that several of Rodrigo's stab wounds are superficial, this could be true, although unlikely. But we could have argued that point. However, as you know, we found a kitchen knife that when luminol was used, revealed a bloody fingerprint. There was not enough blood toidentify with any certainty either whose blood or whose fingerprint it was, but the wound corresponded, if you remember, exactly to the blade on the knife. Emma claims she cut herself a day earlier while preparing dinner. Even if that explains the blood, it doesn't explain the shape of the blade and its correspondence to the wound."

Mark fidgeted in his chair. Jennifer sat stone-still. "We know most of this," Mark said impatiently. "What is the new evidence?"

Roberto sighed. "I will review everything with you and I ask for your patience. Much of this you already know, but in order to understand the pattern of the prosecution's case, you must see it all together."

Mark nodded and waited.

"So, as you know, they applied luminol to the floors throughout the apartment, which was not difficult since it was quite small. What they found was that there was a good deal of blood in the kitchen and traces of blood from the kitchen to the floor near the bed, where the body was found by the police. This indicated that the boy was stabbed in the kitchen and his body was later dragged to the bedroom. The police believe that the murderer knew where the knives were kept, ran to the kitchen to get one, and that the victim followed him. He was killed there, not with his own knife, which everyone who knows him claims he didn't own, but with the kitchen knife that matches his wound. They claim that Paco was the murderer and that Emma was his accomplice."

"I still don't see how they think they can prove that, or what motive they think they have uncovered," Jennifer said, her anger and frustration obvious.

Roberto leaned forward and spoke in a very quiet voice. "There is more, senora."

"What? What more?" she snapped. "Please don't play cat and mouse with us."

José and Roberto looked at each other. Roberto nodded at José, offering him the floor, which José, seemingly reluctantly, took.

"They think that Paco and Emma knew Rodrigo and knew he was carrying a lot of money that night. They claim the whole thing was a scam aimed at robbing him. Emma lured him to her apartment promising sex and, as planned, Paco burst in and started a fight. They assumed Paco would easily win and in the scuffle, Emma would empty his pockets. But he fought back, and Paco killed him. Then he and Emma made up the story they would tell the police and Paco, fearful the police wouldn't believe him, left her to handle it."

Mark spoke first. "That's crazy. That assumes a level of depravity that there is no evidence Emma has sunk to. She is an American college girl with no blemish on her record and excellent grades and recommendations everywhere she went. There is no history to support such behavior on her part. She was an innocent. I doubt she had ever even slept with anyone before Paco, let alone been capable of seducing someone for profit. And I heard that there is nothing to indicate that she ever knew or saw the victim before he attacked her the night of the murder, am I right?"

"Yes," Roberto said. "And I too have investigated it in every way I can. No student ever saw them together. None of Rodrigo's friends ever heard mention of either Emma or Paco. The prosecution, at least so far, will not be able to prove that they knew each other or even met that night. It is pure conjecture. But there is something else you should be aware of."

Roberto once again ceded the floor to José, who looked apologetically at Jennifer as he spoke.

"Her first months here were not as devoted to study as you may have imagined. She apparently did a great deal of sexual . . ." He hesitated, as if searching for the right word. "Experimentation," he finally said. "She had as many as five documented lovers in three months, all before she met Paco. This adds credence to the idea that she might be capable of seducing someone sexually without compunction."

"Why?" Jennifer burst out. "What does one have to do with the other?"

Mark stood up. He was clearly angry but very controlled. "Look, José, I don't know how your legal system works, but I find it hard to believe that any of that would be admissible evidence in a court of law. Her past sexual history would be irrelevant, and this wild leap of prosecutorial imagination is absurd and not supported by evidence."

Roberto intervened. "Of course, senor, this cannot be used. My colleague reports it only to tell you the kind of psychological pressure the prosecution is exerting. We assume you want to know what is going on."

Jennifer was trying to process this new information about Emma. She had known that the media had accused her repeatedly of being a promiscuous American, putting down both her and her country in one phrase, but she had thought it all media hype. Now she was shocked to discover at least some of it was true—another blow to what she thought she knew about her daughter. She looked at Roberto, hoping he would say something to contradict this, but he looked on without comment and her gaze shifted to Mark. Maybe he would think of something.

Mark wasn't concerned about Emma's promiscuity for the time being. He was centered on her legal defense. He paced up and down as he spoke. "The evidence that they do have is subject to other interpretations," he said. "It's our job to come up with one that supports Emma."

"Sí," Roberto said. "And we have. But we need Emma's cooperation to advance it."

Jennifer's body slumped. She shook her head despondently. "Emma won't cooperate. I don't know how to convince her."

"What is your interpretation?" Mark asked.

"Something more straightforward. Rodrigo followed her. He tried to rape her. Paco came in by accident. He flew into an uncontrollable rage. They fought and Rodrigo was killed by Paco, who in fact did go to the kitchen to get the knife. Emma was distraught. She had been begging Paco to stop, but once the boy was dead Paco told her he would be sent to jail for the rest of his life if she refused to help him. She loved him, she believed his stories claiming that he was an altruist and a defender of the poor who was persecuted by the police. She agreed to the elaborate deceit he planned, and she watched helplessly as he dragged the body to the bedroom. There is no proof that she helped him do it, and I think this is close to what actually happened. I don't know what happened to the money—let us assume Paco took it. But Emma will need to corroborate this for us if we are to have a chance of getting the charges against her dropped in exchange for her testimony."

Mark sat down and reached for Jennifer's hand. His voice was grim, determined. "I'll go to her. I'll convince her."

Jennifer was still slumped in her chair. She gently withdrew her hand and looked at him. She spoke softly, despondent. "It's impossible, Mark. You don't know her. She loves him, and she believes he loves her. Nothing you say will convince her."

Roberto stood up. He smiled for a second, which struck them all as inappropriate. "I think I know someone who will convince her," he said, walking to the door of his office. "It's time for my surprise."

He opened the door and said something they couldn't hear. Then he held the door as a woman entered. She was about thirty-five, pretty, with long dark hair, olive skin, and arresting black eyes. She gave a timid smile to the group, and Jennifer noticed that she had a space between her two front teeth. She also had a raised mole above her lip, which didn't diminish her attractiveness. She looked tired and slightly ragged, with clothes that had been washed many times and dirty white cloth espadrilles on her feet. She was carrying a baby wrapped in a sling around her neck and shoulder. Everyone in the room looked puzzled. Even José looked questioningly at Roberto.

"I'd like to introduce Consuela Sanchez and her daughter, Imaculada Sanchez Frias," he said quietly. "Paco's wife and child."

CHAPTER 27

There were many questions to be asked and answered, but the essential facts were clear. Roberto revealed them to the stunned assemblage as Consuela sat down and asked for a glass of water, which he provided and which she drank in a few thirsty gulps. Paco was married and had a child, Roberto explained, as she sat mutely looking around the office, seeming intimidated by its luxurious appointments and not understanding the English conversation. She stared at a silver-handled letter opener on Roberto's desk, picked it up, and fingered it gingerly as he spoke.

Paco was neither divorced nor legally separated, Roberto continued. His wife believed he was working in a hotel in Seville. He came to see her and their daughter once in a while when he had a few days off. He had sent them some money from time to time, mostly when she threatened to report him to the police for nonsupport. But he sent piddling amounts, nothing like the money she had just learned he had been making from his drug sales. In fact, she pointed out bitterly, when he'd leave after his short visits, he'd as often take some of the money she had managed to save from her housecleaning jobs as leave any for her.

Jennifer interrupted to ask if she could ask Consuela a few questions; Roberto said he would be happy to translate. Uncomfortable with the language barrier and the nature of the conversation, Jennifer addressed herself directly to Roberto.

"Would you please ask her if she knew that her husband was living with Emma in Sevilla?"

Roberto translated. Consuela shrugged, a tired look on her worn face, and answered Roberto without looking at Jennifer.

"She says that she stopped worrying about who he was living with or sleeping with years ago," Roberto reported. "There was always a new one. She didn't care as long as he kept working and sending even the little money he gave her."

The baby started to cry, and Consuela unwrapped the sling in which she was carrying her, opened her shirt, and put her to her breast. Imaculada continued to fuss for a while, pulling at the breast but seeming unsatisfied. Finally she settled down and suckled contentedly.

Jennifer asked if she would be willing to tell Emma everything she had told them. Roberto translated, and she answered in an angry, aggrieved tone.

"She says she will tell anyone, including the police. She says that Paco's consistent lies and neglect have resulted in his meaning nothing to her."

Consuela stopped talking and a thoughtful look crossed her face. When she spoke again, she directed herself to Jennifer and Mark, even though they couldn't understand her. Roberto continued to translate.

"She says she will talk to your daughter, but she is worried. She says your daughter may go free, but Paco will probably go to jail and she will have no extra money for her and her daughter."

He stopped translating and addressed himself to Mark. "She wants you to pay her, senor. She asks for five hundred euros."

Mark considered this. "I don't mind the expense, but if she is to be a witness, I cannot pay for her testimony."

"No, senor," Roberto said quickly. "She will not need to testify. She knows nothing of this case. She will simply tell your daughter that her boyfriend has lied to her and isn't what she thinks he is. I believe this is worth five hundred euros."

Consuela broke into the conversation, shifting her daughter from one breast to the other. Roberto listened and said something. Consuela laughed—a bitter, cynical sound. "No puede ser," she said, before launching into a longer reply that Jennifer couldn't understand. She spoke for what felt like a long time. José nodded knowingly, encouraging her to go on. Jennifer and Mark looked questioningly at Roberto. When Consuela finished talking, he got up and walked to the bar. He refreshed his drink and asked if anyone else wanted anything. Mark and Jennifer shook their heads impatiently. What they wanted, Mark said, was to understand what she had said.

Roberto nodded. "And the five hundred euros? You agree?"

"Sí, de acuerdo," Jennifer said quickly. Surprised, Mark looked at her briefly before turning back expectantly to Roberto.

"I explained to her that Paco had told everyone he was an activist for the country's poor and that he collected money for a fund to support the unemployed in what he called his home village. You already know that I checked that out separately and he had no connection to that village. I explained that Emma, an American with an allowance from her parents, contributed money to this fund."

"What did she say to that?" Mark asked.

"That is when she laughed," Roberto said simply. "She said, 'It cannot be.'"

"How can she be sure?" Mark asked.

Roberto reported that she had said she'd been married to Paco for ten years, that his parents, both of whom were upper-middle-class Spanish doctors from Marbella, had tried to help him but finally disowned him after he repeatedly stole money from them to buy drugs. He had been thrown out of three different private schools and dropped out of university, where he had only taken courses, not having been accepted for a degree program. He had been enrolled in two different drug rehab programs and left both of them before he was released. He had spent time in jail in France, she said, though she claimed she wasn't sure why, but she knew he had a fake passport and was using a different name. Roberto explained that when he had first told her about the amounts of money Paco had conned people out of or made through selling drugs, she had become furious—not that he did it, she had admitted, because nothing he did surprised her, but that she hadn't seen any of the profits.

Consuela interrupted him to ask for a beer. As he walked to the minibar to get it, she said something else, her voice hard and sad at the same time. He delivered the beer and sat down again, turning back to the others.

"She says he has stolen from and betrayed and double-crossed everyone who ever knew him," he said. "And the one thing she swears he has never done was give a shit about anyone but himself."

No one spoke. Finally Mark broke the silence. "Who should tell Emma?" he asked Roberto.

It was decided pretty quickly that it shouldn't be Jennifer. Mark volunteered to speak to her himself, but Jennifer and even José vetoed that proposal, remembering their last interaction. That left José and Roberto. Roberto said he thought he should talk to her, but Jennifer rejected that proposal so vigorously that both José and Mark looked at her with curiosity.

"No. Emma hardly knows Roberto. The person she trusts is her lawyer."

Roberto, of course, understood.

Jennifer turned to José. "You should do it," she said.

He nodded gravely, accepting the assignment. "She may not believe me," he said.

"She will believe Consuela," Jennifer insisted. "We will bring her as well. I think she will be the most convincing."

CHAPTER 28

After Consuela left, the air practically vibrated with optimism and excitement. Jennifer was certain that although Emma would obviously be upset by this new information, she would also be released from Paco's spell and perhaps even a bit relieved. In any case, she would see that she no longer needed, or even wanted, to protect him. Hopefully, she would be angry—that would be the healthiest response—but even if she felt ashamed and embarrassed, she would no longer feel he deserved her loyalty at the expense of her own freedom. But she worried about Consuela. Would she change her mind? Would she simply disappear? She didn't have a cell phone. How would they reach her?

Roberto tried to assuage her fears and dampen her enthusiasm at the same time. He too hoped that Emma would react positively to this news, but he wasn't sure—and even if she did, he pointed out, it wasn't clear what Paco would say and what the prosecutor would believe. But he was relatively confident about Consuela. He had installed her in a small rooming house, and she had been promised the money she demanded. She wouldn't risk losing that.

Several separate conversations competed in the room—Jennifer and Roberto, José and Mark, Mark and Jennifer, everyone talking about a different aspect of the case at the same time, creating a chaotic buzz that Roberto finally put to an end by calling everyone to order. They faced him expectantly.

"So, we have had some good news and we are all hopeful. But now we must act," he said. He turned to José. "How long before we can get Consuela in to see Emma?"

José considered before answering. "No está claro," he said to Roberto. Then, in English, "She is not family, so she does not automatically have visiting rights. Emma must request her. Then she will be able to enter with me."

This caused some consternation.

"How will that work?" Jennifer asked disconsolately. "We can't ask her to request a visit from Paco's wife."

"No, of course not." Mark's voice sounded annoyed. "José, can you tell her you need to bring someone, a consultant or something, who you believe will help in her defense and ask her to request her by name?"

"You mean lie?" Jennifer asked.

"Do you have a better idea?"

She thought about it. "No," she finally murmured.

José said he was willing to try. As her lawyer, he could see her on a few hours' notice. He would go that very day, he said, and try to arrange a meeting with Consuela the day after. Everyone agreed on that course and the meeting ended.

As they gathered their belongings and started to leave, Jennifer had the unsettling but undeniable feeling that she belonged right where she was. She wanted to have some private time with Roberto and tried to think of some excuse that would delay her departure. She tried to catch his eye, but he didn't look in her direction. Instead, he thanked everyone for coming and excused himself, saying that he expected another client and had a great deal of work to do to prepare. Jennifer felt offended, even jealous. It always came as a slight shock to her when he mentioned other clients—as if she thought she should be his only one. Of course, she knew that was absurd, and she felt embarrassed and a bit ashamed. Something about her relationship with Roberto sometimes made her feel like a schoolgirl with a crush on her teacher—hopeless and inappropriate.

Mark watched her hesitation and walked to the door, holding it open for her. "Jennifer? Are you coming?"

"Yes, yes, of course."

She left without looking back. They walked onto the street in silence.

"Well, things are looking up," Mark said a few minutes later.

"Yes. I hope so."

They continued walking, without a destination. After a few blocks, Jennifer broke the silence. "Where should we go? Would you like to see the sights of Seville?"

"No. Not now. I think we need to talk. Let's stop at a café."

She had known this moment was coming, but she dreaded it. They walked several more blocks without speaking, both distracted by their own uneasy thoughts, until they passed a restaurant with several out-door tables shaded from the sun with red umbrellas.

"This one looks okay," she said.

When they were seated and had ordered drinks, Mark reached over and took Jennifer's hand. He seemed to do it deliberately, almost clinically. They knew each other so well—too well, in a way, Jennifer thought—that she knew he was not acting on an impulse of true rec-onciliation. She stiffened and pulled her hand away.

"Jennifer, it's me. Remember? I know things are tense, but damn it, Jen, a bomb fell into the middle of our lives. This . . . this trouble between us, it's the fallout, the radiation. We can make it go away."

She sighed and looked in his direction, but not at him, not ready to meet his eyes. "Can we? I mean, I really felt last time like you were blaming me for this in a way."

He pulled back, trying to control his frustration. "I never said any-thing like that. I don't feel that. I'm afraid you think that, but it's not true; it's not even remotely true. You have been a wonderful mother, Jennifer, and this whole thing, *it isn't about you*. How can I make you understand that?"

She shrugged. "I guess you can't. Because in a way it *is* about me. I'm her mother. What happens to her happens to me."

"Okay. It happens to you. But it happens to me too. And to Lily and Eric. Even to your parents, who are living in our house, giving up their own lives to take care of our children. We're a family. But it didn't happen *because* of you. There's a difference."

"I know."

He reached for her hand again, and this time, though she didn't look at him, she didn't pull away.

"I said a few things that I believe are true, but I shouldn't have said in anger, not during this time when you are feeling so fragile. But they're things for us to work on together, to change, to improve, not things to tear us apart."

She wanted whatever it was that was keeping her from looking at him to melt and disappear, but it didn't.

"Mark, did you ever have an affair?"

"What?"

"Since we've been married, have you slept with anyone else?"

He let go of her hand. "Why do you ask that? Why now?"

"Just answer, Mark—yes or no?"

He got up and put some money on the table. "This is getting us nowhere. Let's go back to the apartment."

"I'll take that as a yes," she said. She got up and fell into step beside him. "I ask it now because when you said we have to work on things, I wanted to know if you thought it was only me who needed to change."

He didn't answer. He hailed a cab and they both got in and each looked fixedly out the window and didn't say a word until they arrived, climbed the stairs, and settled in the living room. Still silent, she put on some water for tea.

"Want some?" she asked.

"No, thanks."

He put his head in his hands. She waited for the water to boil, poured her tea, and sat down across from him. She realized they were positioned exactly as she and Roberto had been when he told her about finding and then losing his daughter. She thought about what Roberto had just done—how he had ignored her obvious desire to catch his eye.

He was making it clear that anything more between them was not appropriate and wasn't going to happen. The same way he had told her what to say to the police, what not to say to the press, what to do to help Emma in each situation, he was also showing her how to behave with him. She didn't doubt his affection for her, so she knew he was protecting her from her own impulses. And he was right, of course. Her own emotions were so strained and volatile right now. She was confused about her feelings for Roberto—admiration, certainly; dependence; friendship; and, yes, attraction, maybe even love. But she had loved Mark for twenty-three years. They had raised three children together and emerged with their sexual life remarkably intact and their affection deeper. They had weathered frustration and boredom and sleeplessness and the stress of babies and young children. They had obviously even weathered his attraction to and probably his affair with someone else. And with a little more effort, they would ultimately weather this. They were hopefully coming to the end of this nightmare with Emma, and there would clearly be a long road ahead to get her home and get her help. It would be mad to push any revelations and confrontations that would cause a breach right now, or to make any decision that would hurt their marriage.

Mark looked up and was about to speak.

"Never mind," she said. "I'm sorry I asked. I don't even really want to know."

He looked perplexed but relieved. "Maybe someday, when this is all over, we will talk about everything, Jennifer. Maybe that's what we need."

"Maybe."

She got up and moved next to him on the couch. She put her hand on his knee and spoke softly. "I'm sorry, Mark. This has been hard on both of us, and I've only thought of myself. And Emma, of course; it's hardest on her—but you're right, it has hurt all the kids and my parents too. And you—you've had to try to work to earn the money to pay for all the help she's getting and deal with all the problems at home. And I don't think I ever really thought about how hard it must be for you to not be here, to have to hear about it all secondhand."

He looked at her gratefully and shook his head to minimize his sacrifices in comparison to hers.

"Of course, it's hard for me too, trying to cope with a crazy and dangerous situation in a strange country in a language I don't understand," she said. "I know you get that. So I think that nothing we say or do during this time should be held against either of us, okay? We get a free pass."

He looked skeptical. Maybe he'd noticed that look she had tried to share with Roberto. "Well, not completely free."

She laughed. "No, not completely. But I love you. I'm sorry if I haven't been acting that way."

He smiled and put his arm around her in the old way. "I love you too," he said.

Now she could look at him, and she did, full in the eyes, before he bent to kiss her. Then, for the first time since Emma woke them with her middle-of-the-night phone call, they made love. She felt better after, and it was clear he did too. One thing bothered her, but she pushed it aside. They had fallen immediately into the sensual, comforting, familiar pattern of their lovemaking. But there were times when, her eyes closed, and against her will, she fantasized that she was with Roberto.

CHAPTER 29

José called early the next morning. He had fixed the meeting with Emma for 11:00 A.M. Did they want to come?

They met him at his office and set out from there. Jennifer sat in the back, her body taut, her lips clenched, looking out the window. Consuela sat next to her, nursing her baby. Mark sat in front. Occasionally Jennifer commented on something she saw—a series of half-finished buildings abandoned, like so many throughout the country, because of the economic crisis; the abrupt shift from a cityscape to the dry, rust-red desert earth. Mark and José tried to respond in kind and make small talk to ease the tension. But it was clear Mark was feeling it too. When his phone rang, he quickly pulled it out, glanced at it apprehensively, and then, with obvious relief, turned it to vibrate.

"It's not Emma," was all he said and all Jennifer wanted to know.

The baby finished nursing and started to cry. The sound was loud, grating. Jennifer had never been able to hear a child cry without responding. When her children were little and she would hear other mothers say they could always pick out their own child's cry from any others, she wondered how they did it. She thought any child crying was her own, and hearing a cry at the playground, she would startle, look around anxiously, and not relax until she saw her own smiling child in the carriage, or in the sandbox or on the swings. Now she turned to Consuela sympathetically. She asked José what the problem was—the baby had just eaten; why was she crying? Did she need to be changed? He translated and passed on her reply.

"No, just gas. And she is tired and needs a nap."

Jennifer rooted around in her bag and found a set of keys, which she dangled in front of the crying child. Imaculada paused and reached for them, shaking them like a rattle and then putting them straight into her mouth. Her mother grabbed them roughly away and handed them to Jennifer, setting off another loud bout of wailing. "Sucio," Consuela said, "Dirty."

When they arrived and had gone through all the by now familiar security procedures, José said he wanted a few words with them before he saw Emma. He told them that he had secured a private visiting room for this meeting and had gotten leave to spend as much time as was necessary talking to Emma. If everything went as they hoped, Jennifer and Mark could join them later.

"Good luck," Mark said. "We're counting on you."

Realizing it was time to go, Consuela abruptly handed Imaculada, who had finally settled down and fallen asleep in her sling, to Jennifer. The movement woke her up and she started howling again. Consuela stuck a pacifier in her mouth, which seemed to quiet her, and followed José through the heavy metal door separating the prisoners from everyone else. Jennifer tried to distract her, but the baby would have none of it and screamed frantically again as her mother moved away, leaning after her and wriggling so hard Jennifer nearly dropped her. Nothing calmed her until Jennifer took out the keys again and jiggled them. At that, Imaculada, who by now was sweaty, her hair plastered around her face and her nose running, stopped crying and reached for them. When she grabbed them and put them in her mouth, Jennifer didn't take them back, though she bent to rescue the pacifier, which had fallen on the floor.

"It won't hurt her," she said to Mark, who gave her a questioning look.

She took a tissue from her bag and wiped Imaculada's nose and face. A half hour passed. Then an hour. Imaculada, having tired of the keys and regained her pacifier, had fallen asleep on Jennifer's lap, and fearful of waking her and unleashing another torrent of screaming, neither Mark nor Jennifer said a word. Finally, just as Imaculada was beginning to stir, José and Consuela appeared through the doorway. They couldn't decipher the meaning of Consuela's expression; it was grim, but she broke into a smile as she saw her baby, who, now wide-awake, stretched both her little arms out toward her. Consuela lowered Imaculada into her sling. The baby settled in, sucking contentedly on her pacifier. Mark and Jennifer looked eagerly at José and saw that he had a reassuring smile on his face.

"She has asked to see the prosecutor and is ready to make a statement."

Jennifer had risen to hand over the baby when José appeared, but now, overcome with relief, she sat down again.

"Is there a deal?" Mark asked.

"None of that is worked out yet. First she must tell her story. Then they must find it credible. Then Paco will tell his. But if all goes well, there will be a deal. I will ask them to release her in exchange for her testimony. They want Paco, and she appears ready to deliver him. She wants to see you before she speaks to the prosecutor."

"Both of us?" Jennifer asked timidly.

"Yes, senora. Of course."

Emma was standing in the middle of the room. When she saw her parents she didn't run to them. She could barely look at them. Her eyes stared at the floor. They stood in the doorway awkwardly. Jennifer spoke first.

"Emma, I'm so sorry."

At this, Emma's eyes brimmed with tears. "I'm so ashamed," she said.

Jennifer walked into the room and wrapped her arms around her. Emma allowed herself to sink into her mother's embrace. She hugged her back. They held each other for a long moment.

"You have nothing to be ashamed of," Jennifer murmured softly into her ear. "He lied to you. He manipulated you. Nothing in your life prepared you for someone this cunning. This isn't your fault."

She remembered with a twinge of pain Emma at fourteen thinking about growing up and falling in love and getting married. "But Mom," she had said, "how will I know? What if I make a mistake? Will you tell me? Will you promise to tell me?" And Jennifer, touched at her trust and innocence, had said, "Of course, honey. I'll tell you." But that wasn't what she should have said, she thought now. She should have said, *You'll* know. You'll know because you are smart and intuitive and by then you'll be mature enough to know those things on your own. Maybe that would have given her more confidence. Maybe if she'd had more confidence in herself and less need to prove she didn't need her mother, this wouldn't have happened. Maybe.

Woulda, coulda, shoulda, she thought. It's too late now. "If it's anyone's fault other than his, it's mine," Jennifer said.

Mark joined them, standing on Emma's other side and holding out his arms. "How about a hug for me, honey?"

She let go of Jennifer slowly and then threw herself into them, laying her head on his chest, the way she had as a young child when he'd carry her in sleeping from the car.

"Oh, Daddy, I don't know how you can ever forgive me."

He just squeezed her tighter and caressed her hair. When he released her, she turned to Jennifer again.

"I said such awful things, Mom. I didn't mean them. Please believe me. I just said what I thought would hurt you. I was so angry, and I didn't know what to do with it."

"I said some terrible things too," Jennifer replied. "That's what people do when they lose control. I didn't mean most of what I said either, and some of what we both said was probably true. It doesn't matter. We'll have a long time to talk about it, but not now and not here. Let's talk about what we all have to do to get you home."

"I know what I have to do. I should have done it all along. I'll tell the police what really happened. You know, Paco lied to me in almost everything he ever told me. I have to live with that and what I did to go along with him and how foolish and pathetic I was. I am. But the truth is, he didn't purposely kill Rodrigo. They had a fight, and I think Rodrigo might have killed him if Paco didn't stop him first." She sat down, shaking her head in anger at herself. "I wanted to tell them that at the beginning. I begged him to go straight to the police. But he said they'd put him in jail and throw away the key. He said they hated him because of his activism for the poor." She closed her eyes and threw back her head momentarily. Then she took a very deep breath and let the air out slowly through pursed lips. "I feel like such an idiot. Such a dupe. He must have laughed at me with his friends—if he had any friends. I never really saw any. Anyway, I thought the decent thing to do was to protect him, considering all the sacrifices he was making. What was my little life worth next to his?" She laughed, and there was a shadow of that harder Emma Jennifer had seen during the past few weeks. But it softened again when she turned to José.

"Please ask the prosecutor if he will speak to me now," she said. "I'm ready to tell him anything he wants to know."

Jennifer and Mark were eager for her to get started, but José asked them to sit down first. His voice sounded more somber than they expected under the circumstances and Jennifer felt a stab of anxiety.

When they were seated around the table in the center of the room, he pulled over another chair and sat facing Emma.

"Emma, the story you told me may not satisfy them," he said.

Emma looked puzzled. Jennifer took a deep breath and Mark stiffened. "Why not?" he asked in a sharp tone.

José sighed. "She is barely changing her story. She admits there is no Algerian, but everyone already knew that. She claims that Rodrigo Pérez tried to rape her and Paco fought him to save her and killed him in self-defense. The police, as you know, believe the story is more complicated. They think they planned to rob him and they will want to know what happened to the money Rodrigo was carrying."

He looked at Emma. "Did Paco take it? Did he know it was in Rodrigo's pocket?"

"I don't know," she said.

"It wasn't there when the police came, Emma. Someone took it. Was it Paco?"

Emma didn't answer and José continued.

"Another thing: Emma is still claiming that Rodrigo was killed on the floor near the bed, but the police know that he was killed in the kitchen and dragged to the side of the bed. He was a big man and Paco probably would have had trouble moving him alone. They believe Emma helped him. In that scenario, Paco is the murderer and Emma is his accomplice."

Mark glanced at Emma and then got up and paced as he spoke. "But in order to have known he had money in time to make this plan, Emma would have had to know him. Roberto confirmed that there is no evidence, in spite of everyone trying to find it, of Emma ever having seen that boy before the night of the murder."

"Paco had to know him. Possibly Emma didn't."

Mark looked incredulous. "But you say they think she seduced him. How did she do that if she'd never seen him before?"

José nodded. "I am not saying I believe their accusations, senor; I am only reporting them. But perhaps they will argue that she met him that night."

"But the police, and also Roberto, have spoken to everyone they could find from the bar Emma was at and also from Rodrigo's *caseta*, and no one ever saw them together," Jennifer said.

Mark looked approvingly at Jennifer. "Yes, exactly," he said.

"I think the police might recognize that not being able to prove that Emma knew Rodrigo or even met him that night will hurt their case against her. Because of that, I do think they will be ready to make a deal—Paco is who they want. They don't care about Emma and would be glad to see her go back to the States and take the media with her. But she will have to give them more than she has offered so far."

212 / NINA DARNTON

Mark and Jennifer looked at Emma. "Well, Emma?" Mark asked. "Remember what you learned today. He used you. He lied about who he was, what he wanted money for, and what he felt about you. He made a fool of you. Do you still want to protect him?"

Emma had been sitting with her shoulders caved in, not daring to look at anyone directly. Now she drew herself up and stood.

"Let me speak to Fernando," she said. "I will tell him everything."

CHAPTER 30

It wasn't until the next day that Fernando came to the prison to get Emma's statement, and he brought a stenographer with him. He entered the room briskly, his face composed and his manner cordial but distinctly unfriendly. Emma appeared very nervous and she requested that José and her parents be allowed to stay. Fernando agreed.

"I am told you have a statement to make," he said coldly. "I await it and regret only that it took so long for you to come to this decision."

Emma was contrite. "I know. You have every right to be angry. I'm so sorry."

"I think that Rodrigo's parents, who will suffer from this for the rest of their lives, would like to hear that you are sorry and would appreciate knowing, finally, the truth about what happened to their son."

Emma looked down sorrowfully and started to say something, but her voice broke and she seemed too shaken to speak. Mark suggested she sit down and when she did, he sat next to her. Jennifer sat on her other side and took her hand. Emma looked at her gratefully, then at Mark, and finally, timidly, at Fernando.

"I feel terrible . . . terrible for his parents. And I don't know. I'm confused now hearing what everyone says about Rodrigo; maybe he didn't try to rape me. Maybe he didn't see it that way. But it felt like that. He followed me." She turned to her father. "I don't know what the lab tests showed and I don't even know how good their labs are or how long they waited to do the tests, but I can tell you that he smelled of alcohol and he acted drunk."

Fernando bristled. "Our labs are state of the art," he said. "As good as or better than any in the States. And the tests showed that he had some alcohol in his system. It's questionable whether that is enough to explain what sounds like a complete break in his usual behavior."

Emma was about to answer, but Mark cut in. "But it was established that he rarely drank. Maybe that little bit of alcohol was enough since he wasn't used to drinking."

Fernando paused, then nodded. "That's possible," he said. He turned to Emma. "Let's get back to the night of his death. What happened next?"

Emma resumed. "He came up behind me as I was entering my apartment and he pushed me inside."

"You said he held a knife to you to force you inside," Fernando said.

"Yes, I know I did. I thought he had a knife. Maybe it was just his keys in my back; maybe he was pretending to have a knife." Mark thought about their discussion in José's office when he had suggested that interpretation and was glad she had remembered it.

"I had never seen him before," she continued. "He said he'd heard about me. That I was a 'famous American.' I knew he meant promiscuous because I'd heard the gossip"—she looked at her mother—"the unfair, untrue gossip about me, just because I'm American and did and said things a little differently, maybe a little freer, than them. Maybe I talked wilder than I was. It was stupid, I know. I told him what he heard was wrong and he should go, but he grabbed me and tried to kiss me. I fought him, but he got me to the bed. He ripped off my blouse. I screamed, and he put his hand over my mouth. He kept acting like it was no big deal, like I was just playing and really wanted him. I couldn't believe it. I managed to squirm away and I ran into the kitchen. I picked up the kitchen knife from the counter and held it in front of me to scare him away. But he just laughed and grabbed it from me. I screamed again and then I heard the door open and I knew that Paco had come home. He burst into the kitchen. He saw what was happening and he advanced on Rodrigo and they started to fight. Rodrigo still had the knife and as they were fighting Paco got cut a few times, nothing serious, just little nicks, on the arm and one hand. But when Rodrigo saw the blood, he got scared and he threw the knife down so they were both just fighting with their fists. But Rodrigo was stronger and he was winning and Paco finally saw the knife on the ground and picked it up."

"And you?" Fernando asked. "Why didn't you call the police during this fight?"

"I wanted to, but Paco kept saying, no, don't call anyone, I'll take care of this."

"Did you see Paco stab Rodrigo?"

Emma was becoming more and more agitated as she remembered and recounted the scene. She bit her lip and covered her face with her hands as her voice shook. It was hard to decipher the words, so Mark very gently reached over and moved her hands away. She gripped the edge of the table and continued.

"I don't know, exactly. They were fighting and Paco kept sticking him with the knife, cutting him hard, purposely, like he was playing with him, tormenting him, trying to scare him and show him what he could do." She stopped talking and they waited for her to go on.

Finally Fernando spoke softly, encouraging her. "Yes, Emma. What happened next?"

She covered her eyes again and then put her hands down on the table. She had started to cry. "I was screaming at Paco to stop, that he was really hurting him, that he should put the knife down, and then suddenly Rodrigo swung at Paco and went for the knife and Paco cursed and lunged forward, and the next thing I knew Rodrigo was on the ground and there was blood all over and Paco was standing over him. I was huddled in the corner crying and begging them to stop. I ran over to see how Rodrigo was, but he didn't move and his eyes looked like glass and I think he was already dead."

"But you didn't think you should call an ambulance to try to save him."

"Paco said he was dead. He said if the police came they would never believe he killed him in self-defense, no matter what I said. He said the only way to save him was to say someone else did it and for him to disappear until the cuts on his arm and hand healed. He made me help him move the body to the bedroom and we made up the story about the Algerian. I wish I hadn't listened to him. I wish I had told the truth from the beginning." She was crying.

Fernando paused. He cracked his knuckles—first his right hand and then his left. He got up and circled Emma's chair, leaning over, closer than seemed comfortable, to look directly into Emma's eyes. "He made you help him move the body? How did he do that? With a knife? A gun?"

She winced, looked down again, and closed her eyes. "No. I just did what he said. I was used to doing whatever he said."

Fernando approached her other side and leaned in again. "And the money, Emma?"

She paused and swallowed and looked away, leaning her body away from his, trying to regain some personal space, but he continued to lean toward her, his face close to hers.

"We didn't know him. He went through his pockets to find his identification to see who he was. He found the money and he took it. He said he would give it to his movement but I shouldn't tell the police. I knew that was wrong, but I was so afraid, so I listened to him."

"This is the truth, Emma?" Fernando said softly. "No more lies? Not even a little one?"

She looked at her mother and father for help, but there was nothing they could do. Jennifer squeezed her hand. She forced herself to look straight at Fernando.

"No more lies," Emma asserted. "This is the truth. Paco did it, but I don't think he meant to. He was trying to protect me. It was self-defense."

Fernando looked at the stenographer to be sure she had gotten it all. He moved away, increasing the space between them, and Emma took a deep breath of relief. He spoke formally, in a professional tone, telling her the statement would be typed properly and then brought to her for her signature.

As Fernando reached the door, he turned to José. "Self-defense? I'm not sure. It may have appeared so to her. But killing an unarmed boy because he is stronger than you and is beating you in a fight is not self-defense. Especially when you add the robbery."

"That is for his lawyer to discuss with you," José said. "Will you accept my client's statement, as we agreed, in exchange for her freedom?"

"Perhaps," Fernando said. "Let us see what Paco says when he hears this statement."

When he left, Emma's body seemed to collapse. She hunched over and no one said anything for a little while, trying to give her some space to collect herself. Jennifer assumed Emma was feeling relief, and she was elated. Even Mark, usually more temperate in his reactions, seemed to feel optimistic. For the first time it looked as if this nightmare might end and they could bring Emma home. Finally, Jennifer spoke.

"Well, honey, that was hard and very brave. I'm proud of you."

But Emma didn't seem relieved. Her eyes looked wide and scared and she was staring ahead of her at the wall, almost talking to herself.

"They are going to talk to Paco," she said so softly they could barely hear her. "What if he tells them something different?"

"What do you mean?" Jennifer asked, her sense of danger suddenly aroused. "Are you afraid of him? He can't hurt you anymore."

Emma looked at her. Her voice was louder now, and they could hear every word easily. She spoke slowly, as if talking to someone who had trouble understanding her language.

"I mean, what if he's mad that I spoke to them and told them? I promised him I wouldn't. What if he wants to get back at me and tells them a different story?"

Mark looked up and so did José.

"What different story?"

"I don't know—I'm not saying he will; I'm just saying he could do anything if he's mad. He could say I was more involved than I was. Consuela said he's a pathological liar. I know that's true from everything that has happened, and she said he is vengeful and she's seen him lie to hurt people, to get even, not just to get what he wants."

Mark and Jennifer shared a look of worry and sadness. Jennifer thought that this was more proof, as if any was needed, of how abused her daughter had been by this man. She had always thought abused women started out weak and damaged and that's why they let the abuse happen, but Emma had seemed so strong and self-confident before. This could happen to anyone, she realized. Emma thought he had power over everything because he had such power over her. She was about to tell her daughter this, but José spoke first.

"If the prosecutor believes your story—and it is not yet certain he will—then Paco will be charged at the most with assault with excessive force during a fight and robbery. If he saves them the cost of a trial and pleads guilty to this, even with his background, he will probably end up with maybe five years in prison. If he doesn't, and if he implicates you, as you seem to fear, they may go back to their first interpretation of the events. This would mean, if you are convicted, long jail sentences for both of you. I am sure his lawyer will tell him this. If he doesn't go along with you, he will be putting his desire to hurt you above his desire to save himself. He may do that—you know that better than I—but it would not be wise."

This speech seemed to calm Emma a bit. But she was still worried. "He is not wise. He is passionate. He acts on impulse."

"But he is passionate in the service of himself," Mark said. "I think José is right."

Jennifer turned to José. "When will we know something?"

There was a knock at the door. José opened it and a guard informed him that the visiting time was over and Emma had to return to her room. He thanked him and reported that it was time for them to leave.

As they were hugging Emma and saying good-bye and promising her that everything would be all right and she had done the right thing, José gathered his papers and walked to the door, waiting for them.

"I think we will have an answer, at least provisionally, by later today or tomorrow. They will speak to Paco and his lawyer. If he agrees to a plea, he will remain in custody and Emma will be released. It could happen as early as tomorrow or the day after."

"Would I have to stay here until the trial?"

"No. If he pleads guilty to that lesser charge, there won't be a trial. You will be free to go home. But let's not think too far ahead. We have to wait. It depends on him."

Mark walked to the door. "This is ridiculous. You are saying her whole future depends on the decision of a psychopath."

José shrugged helplessly. "I think that's been true since she met him."

"No," Mark shot back, his voice sharp and angry. "Her future always depended on her own decisions. I hope she sees that now."

Jennifer whirled around, shocked and furious. "Mark!"

"It's okay, Mom," Emma said. "He's right."

There was another knock at the door and an impatient voice told them in Spanish that the visit was over. Mark hugged Emma one last time and walked out. Jennifer hugged her too and smoothed her hair. "You've made the right decision now, Emma," she said into her ear. "That's what counts."

"I hope so," Emma murmured, as Jennifer followed Mark and José into the corridor.

CHAPTER 31

The decision didn't come the next day or the day after or even the day after that. Jennifer called Roberto and José every day, asking when they would hear, what was happening, why was it so slow, and each reassured her that these things take time, that they would call her the moment they heard anything and that the delay was actually a good sign. The wheels were turning, they maintained. If they had been stuck in the mud, they would have heard.

Mark managed to arrange his schedule so he didn't have to leave during what they hoped would be the final tense time. Jennifer had mixed feelings about this. She was grateful, of course, and understood he needed to be here as much as she did. But his presence also meant she saw less of Roberto. In fact, she couldn't come up with a reason to see him at all, and he didn't call or try to see her. But not seeing him didn't mean not thinking about him, and she had to force herself to be present when she was with Mark and not allow her mind to wander to something Roberto had said, or to the comfort and occasional relief he had provided. She found it helped if she tried to share at least some of her relationship with Roberto with Mark, and she told him about Roberto's own personal tragedy. Mark was sympathetic—he was a good man—but he had no attachment to Roberto, whose problems were peripheral to his own concerns. Still, she talked of Roberto's lost daughter and mad wife so often and so intensely, Mark would sometimes look at her curiously while she spoke and then gently change the subject.

Who's not seeing what he doesn't want to see now? Jennifer thought. But she said nothing about it and took it as a warning to hold back.

She and Mark took a cab to see Emma the first day it was permitted, two days after she had made her statement. José was too busy to take them and Jennifer didn't want to ask Roberto—it was too difficult to be with him and Mark at the same time. The taxi driver spoke a little English and he and Mark engaged in conversation about Spain's economic problems and the harsh cutback and privations Germany was imposing on the people in exchange for forgiving some of the debt. Trying to explain the cultural differences between Germany and Spain and how what worked for one wouldn't work for another, the cab driver said emphatically, "Aquí es aquí y allí es allí!" She was able to translate this for Mark. It meant simply "Here is here and there is there." But for Jennifer it struck deeper. It spoke directly to her quandary about Roberto and Mark. It was all about "here" or "there," she thought. And she would be spending her life "there." She wanted but couldn't have both. She had to find a way to live with that.

Jennifer had been nervous and Mark had been edgy, but both were nothing compared to Emma, who had bitten her nails to the quick and was unable even to sit down during their entire visit. She paced and sighed and scratched her leg or her arm. She was so agitated that if she hadn't been in prison, Jennifer might have thought she was on amphetamines. But it was all adrenaline, self-produced and unavoidable under these circumstances. They did their best to calm her down. Mark was decidedly better at it than Jennifer. Her own anxiety was so high, and Emma was so plugged into her, that no matter how hard she tried or how careful she was in what she said, she only seemed capable of augmenting rather than ameliorating Emma's anxiety. So she hung back and said little. Emma seemed to understand and even to sympathize with her mother. When it was time to go, she put both arms around her and hugged her and whispered into her ear, "It's okay, Mama. I'm going to be fine, whatever happens. Please don't worry so much. I love you."

"I love you too," she answered automatically. But she didn't believe for a second that any of them would be fine, "whatever happens."

Three more days passed. Jennifer called José to see if he had spoken to Paco's lawyer and learned anything that way, but José said he still knew nothing, though he expected a decision very soon. He advised her and Mark to take a trip to Granada for a few days. The idea seemed preposterous to her. She couldn't think of anything but Emma's fate, rolling around different scenarios in her mind by day and in the middle of the night. Mark wanted her to see a therapist and get some antianxiety medication, but she bristled at the idea. She feared a therapist would feed her the usual bromides: "Disentangle yourself; separate yourself; you can't fix this for her; she has to do it herself." "If need be, she has to serve her time." "You have to concentrate on the rest of your life and your other children and stop obsessing over Emma."

She didn't want to hear them. It wouldn't help. When did an obsession ever stop because it was the sensible thing to do? The only thing that would help would be to take Emma home. Then they could work on fixing everything—Emma, her, even her relationship with Mark.

She hung around the apartment, trying to read or find English-language movies on television. Mark urged her to go out, take a walk, do *something*, but she feared the reporters who continued to hound them and refused. There was one thing she did want to do, however. She remembered Roberto saying that the tabloid press back home was defending Emma by attacking Spain—in particular, implying that the beautiful former Jewish section of Seville somehow represented current anti-Semitism. This was so absurd that at first she had thought it didn't merit intervention, that Roberto must have simply misunderstood. But it had bothered him, so she decided to see if he was right. She called Suzie, who was managing the public-relations company. Suzie's reaction was defensive.

"Well, maybe there was a little implication that one of the reasons they were suspicious of Emma and attacking her as promiscuous was both anti-Americanism and residual anti-Semitism. It's probably true."

"It's not true at all, Suze. It's completely out of line and even a little crazy."

"Well, so what? Whatever gets people here riled up is good. It exerts pressure."

Jennifer was feeling too upset and tired to enter into a prolonged argument with her best friend. She spoke curtly. "It's not good and it does matter, and on top of that it doesn't help. It can only hurt. Please tell them to stop any of that immediately and to recant it if asked. I think we have a chance to end this, Suzie. Let's not fuck it up."

Suzie heard the tone and got the message. She agreed to take care of it right away.

Otherwise, one day followed the next without much change until, a full eight days after Emma gave her statement, the long-awaited phone call came through.

It was José. He said they had a decision. Would she and Mark join him in his office at 1:00 P.M.?

Jennifer's heart was pounding. Mark stood by and gripped her hand. "We'll be there, José. But we can't wait until then. What is the decision? Mark is here. Tell us now."

"They have accepted her statement," he said, not hiding the satisfaction in his voice. "She will be going home. We have only the bureaucratic details to work out. Congratulations."

He was still talking—something about wanting to tell them in person and celebrate with champagne, but she had dropped the phone. She took several deep breaths, and then threw herself into Mark's arms. "She's coming home, Mark. It's over. Oh, God, thank you, thank you."

They were hugging and laughing and finally noticed the phone still hanging off the hook. Mark picked it up and spoke into it, calling José's name, but he had already hung up.

"That's okay. We'll meet him at his office at one o'clock to go over the details," Jennifer said.

She reached for the phone even before Mark had placed it back in its cradle.

"Who are you calling?"

"Roberto. I have to tell him."

Mark looked confused. "Surely he knows, Jennifer. We need to call Lily and Eric and your parents and Suzie, not Roberto."

She felt chastened. "Yes, of course. You're right. It's just that he's helped so much in this. This wouldn't have happened if he hadn't found Consuela. But it's true, he probably already knows. Maybe he'll be there at one. We should all celebrate together."

Mark had pulled out his cell phone to call home, but Jennifer stopped him, reminding him of the time difference. "It's the middle of the night there," she said, laughing. "And to tell the truth, I'm glad. I still can't really believe it. I'd rather call after we meet with José."

Mark slowly put the phone down. They stared at each other, happy but still uneasy.

"What do we do now?" Jennifer asked. "How do we survive until one o'clock?"

He smiled affectionately at her and put both hands on her shoulders. "We get dressed. We eat a big breakfast at our favorite café. We take a walk and smell the flowers and enjoy the sunshine. We make plans about going home and what is the first thing we'll do as a family when we arrive. We talk about how happy and lucky we are that it ended as it did."

She put her arms around him and hugged hard. "So, so lucky," she said. "That's a great plan."

But it didn't work out that way.

As they exited the building they were surprised by a bevy of news reporters, both print and television, and who knew how many others— bloggers, tweeters, "citizen journalists," or just nosy passersby with iPhones. Cameras clicked, microphones were shoved toward them, questions shouted out. "Have you heard the news?" "How do you feel?" "Does Emma know yet?" "What was the deal she made?" "Did she get away with murder?" And those were just the ones they could understand. There were hostile-sounding questions in Spanish too. They backed up, fled upstairs, and bolted themselves inside the apartment.

Mark was not as accustomed to this as Jennifer had become. He looked at her questioningly.

"What I do when this happens," she said, "is call Roberto." As usual, the recording sounded.

"Roberto. If you're there, please pick up."

There was a brief pause.

"Diga."

It was bittersweet to hear his voice.

"It's me."

"I know."

"Have you heard about Emma?"

"Sí, por supuesto. I am delighted. Congratulations."

"It would never have happened without you."

"Or without you."

A pause.

"Roberto, the media is surrounding our apartment. We are supposed to meet José at one p.m. Will you be there?"

"I can be."

"Will you help us get there?"

"Sí. I will come with a taxi. I'll call when I am in front. I'll escort you both to the cab. Say nothing to any of them until she is free and at your side."

"Okay . . . Roberto . . ."

"Sí?"

"Thank you."

"I'll see you later."

He hung up and she held the phone for a few seconds. After she put it down, she noticed Mark standing in the doorway staring at her. She took a deep breath and turned to him, trying to make her voice as buoyant as possible.

"Well, that' a relief. He says he'll bring a taxi and pick us up for our meeting with José. And you were right. Of course he knew about Emma. He is delighted."

Mark nodded but didn't answer.

Jennifer got up and walked to the kitchen. "But I'm afraid our breakfast and celebratory walk will have to wait. Luckily we have a full fridge. I'll make us a big American breakfast, okay? Fried eggs, toast, and bacon sound good?"

"Sure," Mark said. "It sounds great."

He sat at the kitchen table, and she took out the frying pan and put two pieces of bread into the toaster. Then she walked back to the table, bent over, and kissed him on the top of his head. He smiled at her.

"We did it," she said. "We can take her home."

"Yes," he answered. "Now the real work begins."

CHAPTER 32

Emma's initial euphoria about her upcoming release was short-lived. In spite of everything she now knew about Paco, she worried obsessively about what would become of him. Her parents had little patience with her concern.

"What difference does it make?" Jennifer asked.

"Do you think he spent much time worrying about what would become of you when you were questioned and arrested and he skipped town?" Mark asked.

They were visiting Emma for what they hoped was the last time in the prison. They had been given one of the private visiting rooms, leaving José alone in the waiting area. Emma, seeming very tense, said she needed to speak to him. Mark left to ask the guard if Emma's lawyer could be called in and returned with him after a few minutes. José entered, probably expecting a tearful Emma to thank him for his help in securing her release. Instead, he found her pale and worried, brushing aside his congratulations with a request that he sit down so she could talk to him.

Mark and Jennifer stood awkwardly in the doorway, not sure whether to go or stay as José pulled out a chair and sat at the table in the visiting room, waiting for her to explain herself. She didn't ask her parents to leave, so they remained standing, leaning against the wall, worried that something dangerous and unexpected would be revealed. Emma sat next to José and leaned forward, speaking softly, her breath shallow and her eyes wide.

"He'll be very angry," she said.

Jennifer was puzzled, but José understood immediately.

"Yes. And so?" he answered.

She looked bewildered. "I don't understand."

"I mean, so what if he's angry? Why does it matter? He can't hurt you."

He paused and patted Emma's hand, continuing in a fatherly tone, "I worry that you are still . . ." He hesitated, looking for the right English expression. "How do you say it? Under his thumb."

"You don't understand," she insisted, breathing in and exhaling in a thin stream. "He *can* hurt me. If he doesn't like this deal, he can still stop mine."

José shook his head to disagree, understanding her drift.

"Not anymore, Emma. He has made his deal. If he hadn't, yours wouldn't have gone through and he might have been charged with premeditated murder. He knows that. He has admitted to all that you set forth in your statement in exchange for a sentence of five years. It's over. You can relax."

She nodded, biting her upper lip. "Okay. Thank you. I hope you're right."

After that, the delight in the outcome was followed by bureaucratic confusion. Looking back on it later, from the safety of their home in Philadelphia, none of them could really remember the exact sequence of events after they got the news that Emma would be free. It all blurred into a single sharp sense of relief mixed with eagerness to be done with the formalities and board the plane home. There had been that first, congratulatory visit to the prison followed by the frustration of having to leave without her when they were so close to seeing her walk free. There was a flurry of activity—meetings with the warden and other prison officials, a closed-door session with José and the magistrate in charge of Emma's case, and finally, a brief appearance in court, where the charges were officially dropped and Emma was released. The session was closed to the media, but Jennifer and Mark were there, seated, holding hands in the front row. Mark squeezed her hand so tightly that her wedding ring dug into her fingers. She caught a glimpse of Paco in court, a disheveled-looking, stocky man with a thick black beard and bushy black eyebrows. He kept his head down until he saw Emma enter, and then he turned to look at her, his angry regard so intense it seemed to scorch the air. Jennifer turned quickly to see Emma's reaction and noticed Emma's resolute stare straight in front of her, as though she had determined not even to look in his direction.

Then there was the family's appearance outside the courthouse, surrounded by a horde of journalists. Jennifer remembered Emma blinking into the camera lights, pale and frightened as questions were fired at all of them. Roberto had told them to make no comment and they obeyed. In response to the questions, both congratulatory from the Americans and hostile from the Spaniards, Roberto spoke for the family, making a short, predictable statement thanking the Spanish judicial system for its fair handling of the case and expressing the family's eagerness to return home. Then he ushered them into a waiting car. And at last, bags packed, fees paid, they took their final trip to the airport, escorted by José and Roberto.

Through it all, Jennifer and Roberto hadn't had any time together. She longed to talk to him but didn't know how to get him alone. He mostly behaved in a controlled, businesslike manner, but once, as they got into the car after Emma's release, he caught her eye and smiled. It was a crooked smile, half-affectionate, half-rueful, and she took it as an intimate gesture, the best he could do under the circumstances. She smiled back.

At the airport, after their bags had been checked and just before they were about to enter the security zone for passengers, they said their good-byes. Mark thanked José and Roberto effusively, crediting them with brilliant engineering of the favorable outcome. He shook each man's hand. Then it was Jennifer's turn. She turned first to José and thanked him, saying, for Mark's benefit as well as his, that he had helped in so many ways that she could never adequately express her

230 / NINA DARNTON

gratitude. He demurred graciously, saying he was just doing his job and was, happily, well paid for his efforts. Then she turned to Roberto. She realized that her heartbeat seemed too fast and too loud, and she feared they would all hear it. Not knowing what was appropriate, she thrust out her hand to shake his. He raised his eyebrows and smiled, as he took her hand. Hers was sweating and clammy to the touch, but his was cool and dry and comforting. She couldn't bear to look at him, so she thanked him awkwardly, her eyes focused somewhere to his right. As he started to leave, her body tensed and she took a deep breath before turning to Mark and starting to walk away with him. Mark stopped her, bent down, and whispered something in her ear, and she looked up, surprised. She squeezed his hand in thanks and ran after Roberto, shouting his name to get his attention as he was about to disappear around a corner. He turned and she ran to him.

"What are you doing?" he asked sharply.

"No, Roberto. It's okay. Mark asked me if I would like to have a few private words with you to say good-bye. That's all. I think we deserve that."

He nodded solemnly. "It doesn't make it easier, but it is perhaps better."

She was nervous and spoke quickly, running the sentences together. "I don't even know what to say. I just wanted somehow to tell you how grateful I am—not only for your help with Emma, but for your friendship. I hope we might correspond from time to time. Remember when I offered to show you around New York? That still stands."

He smiled. "No, cariño," he said. "I am not that strong. You must go back to your life and I to mine. But I thank you too, for everything."

She glanced over her shoulder and saw Mark and Emma in the distance, waiting. Emma was shifting from foot to foot. Mark stood firm. He lifted his hand to acknowledge he'd seen her.

"Will you at least promise to tell me if you find your daughter?" she asked, turning abruptly back to Roberto.

"Yes, I will. I'll let you know if anything important happens."

"You promise?"

His mouth wrinkled into another crooked half-smile. "Sí. Te prometo."

Unable to say all the things she wanted to, not even sure what they were, she repeated a simple but insufficient "Thank you," and hoped he understood.

She walked back slowly to rejoin her family. Mark studied her face for a few seconds, then hugged her, pulling her close. She picked up her carry-on bag, and the three of them passed through security.

She didn't look back.

CHAPTER 33

At first it seemed like every day at home was a holiday. Lily and Eric, of course, were happy to have Emma home and thrilled to have their mother back, at first vying for time with her like three-year-olds, and then plunging back into their everyday concerns of friends and activities as though nothing had ever happened. Jennifer's parents wanted to hear everything, were delighted that it had all worked out and, she was sure, very relieved to be able to return to their own lives. And of course there were their friends. Jennifer and Mark were invited to many dinner parties, which were clearly built around them and their recent crisis, their dubious star power adding some vicarious drama to the otherwise predictable suburban scene.

And Emma? Emma was treated like a conquering hero. The *New York Times*, *The New Yorker*, *Charlie Rose*, the *Today* show, all asked for and were granted interviews, arranged and managed through the public-relations company that had been working for them all along. The company continued to position Emma as an innocent American, bullied and victimized by the Spanish legal system, which was deeply disturbing to Jennifer because she knew that wasn't the case. She read Emma's interviews and watched her on television with a troubled heart. Emma was beautiful, articulate, and likable. She spoke movingly of the random violence that had touched her life, the pain and fear during her imprisonment, and the love and support of her family, "without which I couldn't have survived," she said. The stories sent a chill into the hearts of junior-

year-abroad applicants and their parents everywhere and made her a
sought after talk show guest. But the fanfare left a bad taste in Jennifer's
mouth. Worse, she thought it was bad for Emma. There were many
references by both Emma and her interviewers to the trauma she had
endured—a stranger forcing her into her apartment and trying to rape
her and then being stabbed to death in front of her—and of course Jennifer had long suffered whenever she imagined how devastating that must
have been for her daughter. But everyone glossed over the fact that Emma
had been living with, loving, and protecting a criminal and that together
they were responsible for the death of a young man, no matter how repre-
hensible that young man was. She was eager for Emma to start therapy, to
try to understand why she had allowed herself to be so dominated by Paco
that she could abandon the values she had grown up with and embraced
all her life. But, she realized, it was hard for Emma to realize the serious-
ness of her problems when she was being turned into a celebrity.

Emma was almost always on the phone, speaking, texting, or
tweeting, but Jennifer had hoped that they could sit together this morning and discuss a way forward that included getting Emma to start
therapy. Emma had managed to avoid any discussions with her mother
since she'd come home, kissing her breezily on the cheek before going
out and coming home so late Jennifer was already in bed. Whenever
Jennifer tried to corral her, asking her a question or suggesting they
have a family dinner together, Emma found a way to wriggle out of it.
Jennifer knew that Emma had arranged to return to Princeton in the
fall, but they had never discussed it.

One evening Jennifer called Emma to dinner and she shouted
back curtly that she wasn't hungry. Jennifer looked at Mark and shook
her head, trying to get him to share her exasperation, but he urged her
to back off, saying the time in jail had forced Emma to grow up faster
and that she was simply exercising her independence.

"The last time she exercised her independence she ended up in jail,
Mark. Don't you think she needs to see someone, to work this out? She
can't just go on as though she doesn't need help."

Mark agreed but said he thought she needed more space for a while. They ate together in silence until he gave her a peck on the cheek and, picking up his book, walked into the living room, and settled into his favorite chair.

Lily and Eric had gone off to summer camp—Lily was a junior counselor this year. Both were eager to reconnect with the friends they had made the summer before. Jennifer marveled at how well her parents had taken care of the preparations—the name tags on their clothes, the permission slips and doctor's reports, everything. In fact, there wasn't much for her to do. So it should have been easy to fit back into her previous pattern. In the past, Jennifer would have filled her days with community projects as well as finding worthwhile activities for the children when they returned from camp and planning in delicious detail the wonderful, two-week family vacation they always took together at the end of the summer. But she couldn't seem to work up the energy for it. On most days, Mark was at work, Emma was at a part-time job with an international justice foundation she had gotten as a result of her interviews, and Jennifer spent most of her time reading magazines and watching repeat episodes of *Law & Order* on television. Friends called and she occasionally met one for lunch, but she neglected to shop or make dinner as she once had, and Mark often came home to find her in their bedroom, the shades drawn and the only light coming from the television set. He begged her to get some help—even told her to forget the couples counselor and just go into therapy herself—and she promised she would, wanted to, but didn't seem to be able to arrange it. But when he reminded her that Eric and Lily were expected home, she forced herself to swing into action to welcome them, buying the treats each preferred and planning their favorite meals.

A week later Eric and Lily arrived. Jennifer marveled at how quickly they fell back into their old routine. She tried too, but something was missing. When Lily showed her the eleventh-grade summer reading list and asked her to help her choose which book to write her essay on, she glanced at it, commented on how interesting it seemed, and suggested that Lily choose it herself. When, annoyed at what she took as a brush-off, Lily asked for help writing the essay, Jennifer said she hadn't read the book and thought it would be best if her teacher saw Lily's unedited work to better help her progress. Lily looked confused, then angry. "You don't care about anyone but Emma," she said as she stalked off to her room.

"That's not true, Lily," she called after her.

Eric spent his days skateboarding, catching balls from his pitch-back in the yard, and playing video games, and Jennifer found that it wouldn't actually destroy his chances for success if she allowed him a few more hours of downtime doing what he liked instead of ferrying him around to lessons to keep him busy. She even let go her restrictions on his use of video games, allowing him much more playing time than she ever would have in the past. She backed off and found that nothing fell apart.

She called Suzie and asked her to visit. The two women spent many hours together walking through the nature reserve and talking. When Suzie left a week later, Jennifer was up and the television was off. For the first time in years, she asked herself what she needed, and she knew the answer immediately. She needed a job.

It took time and thought and lots of conversations with Mark, her friends, and even a career counselor before she settled on what had been obvious to everyone but her from the start: the theater. She didn't think she wanted to try acting again, but she had heard of a local private school that needed a teacher of English in the upper school who would also run the theater department and direct school plays. She had applied and, given her excellent education and professional experience, thought she had a shot, even though she'd been out of the job market for a long time. She checked the mail every day, awaiting a reply.

One sunny morning two weeks later, Jennifer was alone in the house with Emma. Lily had spent the night before at a friend's home and Eric had finished breakfast and was shooting hoops in the backyard. It was getting late and, as usual, Jennifer knocked on Emma's door to see if she wanted breakfast.

"Thanks, Mom," Emma said. "You don't have to make me break-fast." She smiled sweetly at her mother on the way to the shower. "But I'm glad you do that for me."

Jennifer was delighted at her daughter's kind words and she re-turned to the kitchen to prepare the food and wait for the mail. Emma was in a good mood. Maybe this would be the right time for them to talk, she thought.

She felt a surge of optimism. She mused that as terrible as this Spanish experience had been, some good had come from it. After all, Emma was going to be fine. She would be back at school in the fall and all this publicity would calm down and everyone's life would resume in a normal way. Even the distance between them would be bridged, she thought. They would become close in a new way, like two adults in-stead of a mother and dependent child. And she recognized the part she had played in creating Emma's need to submit to a controlling man who manipulated her into thinking he had all the answers. She wouldn't make the same mistakes with Lily and Eric.

She poured herself a bowl of granola, adding skim milk and trying to concentrate on the *Times* as she ate. But the paper couldn't hold her attention. Her mind shifted to Mark. She knew her relationship with him had suffered a big blow and needed to be repaired. But she felt op-timistic that they would work it out. Hadn't they always managed? She would find a couples counselor, she resolved, as Mark had suggested, and she would start paying more attention to him and his needs. She felt that she had dodged a bullet and she took a deep, cleansing breath.

The mail arrived, and still Emma hadn't appeared. Jennifer sifted through it quickly to see if the letter from the school, the one she hoped would tell her she was hired, had arrived. A lot of mail had been deliv-ered that day—magazines, catalogs, bills—and she sorted it into piles, as was her habit. There was no letter from the school, but before she could register disappointment, her eyes fell on another letter, addressed by hand in a fountain pen and with a Spanish postmark. She glanced at the upper left-hand corner for a return address but found none. Her heart lurched and sped up, and for a few seconds she felt afraid, but then stopped herself with the realization that they were home and Emma had been released and no one could harm them. But she didn't calm down, because now her fear was replaced by excitement, a suspicion that she knew whom the letter was from and the hope that she was right.

She deliberately didn't open it right away. She poured herself another cup of coffee, took it to her bedroom, and closed and locked the door. Then she sat on her bed and carefully opened the letter.

She pulled out a single piece of folded stationery. When she opened it, a photograph dropped out. Even before looking at it, she checked the signature on the letter and saw, as she had hoped, that it was from Roberto. Then she picked up the photograph. In it, Emma, Paco, and another boy are all dancing together. Or maybe not dancing, maybe just hugging, their arms around each other. They are laughing. Emma's hair is wild and partially covering her face. Paco doesn't have the beard he had in court, but his dark bushy eyebrows dominate his craggy face. The third boy has light brown hair and an open, handsome face. He is on the other side of Emma. The shot has caught him as he is leaning on her, the side of his face resting against her shoulder. There is something strange about their expressions. Their eyes look glazed. They are probably drunk or stoned, Jennifer thought.

She put the photograph down and picked up the letter, refusing to allow herself to imagine what it meant or why Roberto had sent it, though her heart was pounding and her mouth was dry.

Dear Jennifer,

I thought very long and hard about sending this to you. I hope I have made the right decision. I am guilty of having kept it a secret for a long time, since before Emma was released—you will understand why. But I believe it is a secret that needs to be revealed, if only to you.

Perhaps you don't recognize the third person in this photograph. You never met him. Neither did I. We believed that Emma never met him either until, as she has repeatedly avowed, his attempt to rape her resulted in his death. He is Rodrigo Pérez. It appears the photo was taken in the apartment Emma shared with Paco. Notice, if you will, the poster on the far wall and you will perhaps remember having seen it there when you visited Emma's bedroom.

The camera that took this picture had a time setting. The date is on the bottom in the right-hand corner. Look at it.

This is the only copy of this photograph. I have destroyed the negative, which also came into my possession, for a fee.

I do not send this to bring you grief, but in hopes your knowledge will help you to prevent more pain to yourself and others.

                    I remain your devoted friend,

It was signed simply, without a flourish, with his name: Roberto.

She picked up the photo again and found the time stamp. February 2012, two months before the murder.

She sat frozen on her bed. There was no copy. Roberto was telling her she could destroy the photo and be completely safe. She stared at it for a while, especially at the drunken face of the dead boy. She remembered his parents and their television interview swearing that he would never have tried to rape anyone. She started to tear it up, but stopped herself. Instead, she put the photo back in the envelope with the letter and opened the bottom drawer of her dresser. She placed the envelope in a zippered makeup pouch and put that under a pile of her nightclothes. She climbed back into bed and pulled the covers up over her head.

"Mom," she heard Emma shout. "Where are you? I thought you said you were making breakfast."

Jennifer got up slowly and went to the bathroom to wash her face. Then she walked into the kitchen. Emma was sitting at the kitchen table drinking orange juice. Jennifer stared at her, her mind spinning but tossing out bits of remembered information that when pieced together with this latest revelation created a likely narrative. The Spanish cops had been right. Emma had known Rodrigo Pérez. She and Paco had set him up. He hadn't tried to rape her; she had seduced him. Paco had come in, and they had robbed him. Maybe they had planned it. Maybe Emma even helped kill him. Her fingerprints were on the knife. Maybe she handed it to him when it dropped.

Jennifer didn't know what to do. She didn't even know if she should tell Mark. The person she wanted to talk to, to go to for counsel and comfort, was Roberto, but she knew she couldn't do that. What did he think she should do, she wondered. Why had he sent it to her? Why couldn't he have just left it alone?

Emma needed professional help; she had known that for a long time. But now she wondered if it would even do any good. She needed time to think. She needed advice, needed professional help herself. She stared again at Emma. Who was she? Did she feel any remorse at all? Was it possible something like this could happen again and by doing nothing to stop her now, she, Jennifer, would be responsible? But what could she do? What could she do?

"Mom, you're freaking me out. Why are you staring like that?"

Jennifer turned away and busied herself at the stove.

"What do you want for breakfast?" she asked.

ACKNOWLEDGMENTS

I would like to thank several people in Seville, Spain, who gave so generously of their time to help an American author in need of background on the Spanish legal system. I used the factual information they supplied, drawing on it when appropriate. I hope they will forgive any fictional license I have taken. Any inaccuracies are entirely my own.

For their hospitality and for helping me create a world that has, hopefully, the aura of truth, I am grateful to Leticia Pérez Desena, my translator and guide; José Manuel de Paul Velasco, presiding magistrate of the Seville Court of Criminal Justice; José Luis Lledo González, another magistrate of the Provincial Court of Criminal Justice; Fernando Martinez Pérez, a prosecuting magistrate; Rafael Salvador Moreno, former chief of the Judicial Police Detectives; and José Manuel Sánchez del Águila Ballabriga, an attorney who graciously provided background material as well as access to his esteemed colleagues.

I also want to thank my dear friends Ana Westley and José Antonio Martínez Soler, who accompanied my husband and me to Seville, introduced us to the people named above, and made all of our time in Spain—both earlier, when we lived there and on this trip—so memorable. To my great friends Teresa Maravall and her husband, the late Juan Badosa, I send my eternal gratitude for teaching me to love their beautiful country.

In addition, I'd like to thank my friend, in-law, and editorial adviser, the incomparable Phyllis Grann; my dear friend and agent, Kathy Robbins; my publisher, Clare Ferraro, who inspired me to write this book over a delicious, lengthy lunch; my editor at Plume, Denise Roy; her assistant, Matthew Daddona, and my copy editor, Kym Surridge.

As always, in all my endeavors, I am deeply grateful for the love and support of my husband of forty-eight years, my hero, mentor, and muse, John Darnton, and for our family, Kyra, David, Liza, Jamie, Blythe, Zachary, Ella, Asher, and Adara, who fill my life with so much light and joy. I am blessed.

Also by Nina Darnton

AN AFRICAN AFFAIR

a novel

NINA DARNTON

"You feel the heat, taste the frustration and smell the fear.... A thrilling read."—ROBIN COOK

978-0-452-29802-6

Available wherever books are sold

PLUME

WHEN AN AMERICAN EXCHANGE STUDENT IS ACCUSED OF MURDER, HER MOTHER WILL STOP AT NOTHING TO SAVE HER.

A midnight phone call shatters Jennifer Lewis's carefully orchestrated life. Her daughter, Emma, who's studying abroad in Spain, has been arrested after the brutal murder of another student. Jennifer rushes to her side, certain the arrest is a terrible mistake and determined to do whatever is necessary to bring Emma home. But as she begins to investigate the crime, she starts to wonder whether she ever really knew her daughter. The police charge Emma, and the press leaps on the story, exaggerating every sordid detail. One by one, Emma's defense team, her father, and finally even Jennifer begin to have doubts.

A novel of harrowing emotional suspense, *The Perfect Mother* probes the dark side of parenthood and the complicated bond between mothers and daughters.

PRAISE FOR NINA DARNTON'S *AN AFRICAN AFFAIR*

"A vivid portrait of a troubled country." —*THE NEW YORK TIMES*

"A thrilling read." —ROBIN COOK

www.penguin.com
Cover design: Samantha Russo
Cover photograph: Joseph Squillante/The Image Bank/Getty Images

A Plume Book
Fiction

U.S. $16.00
CAN. $18.00

ISBN 978-0-14-219673-1

51600

EAN 9 780142 196731